The Great and the Good

by Michel Déon

Michel Déon is a member of the Académie Française and the author of more than fifty works of fiction and non-fiction. He lives in Ireland with his wife and has many horses.

Julian Evans is a writer and translator from French and German. He has previously translated Michel Déon's *The Foundling Boy* and *The Foundling's War*.

Praise for Michel Déon

'Remarkable ... deserves a place alongside Flaubert's *Sentimental Education* and *Le Grand Meaulnes*' *New Statesman*

'A big-hearted coming-of-age shaggy-dog story ... [Déon's] novel leaves you feeling better about life' *Spectator*

'It is shamefully parochial of us that this eminent writer has been so ignored by the anglophone world' *Sunday Times*

'Quiet, wryly funny prose ... a delight' *Independent on Sunday*

'Michel Déon is a storyteller par excellence' *Irish Times*

'As witty as its English forebear [Tom Jones] but with French savoir-faire, *The Foundling Boy* may win new readers for books translated from French' *New York Times*

'I loved this book for the way, in its particularities and its casual narration, it admitted me to a world I knew nothing about and the many ways it made me care. It is not just a glimpse into the past, but the study of the heart of a man and his times' Paul Theroux

'This is a book to devour, savouring every last mouthful' Pierre Moustiers

The Great and the Good

by Michel Déon

translated from the French
by Julian Evans

Gallic Books
London

This book is supported by the Institut français du Royaume-Uni as part of the Burgess programme.
www.frenchbooknews.com

A Gallic Book

First published in France as *La Cour des grands* by Éditions Gallimard, 1996
Copyright © Éditions Gallimard, Paris, 1996

English translation copyright © Julian Evans, 2017

First published in Great Britain in 2017 by Gallic Books,
59 Ebury Street, London SW1W 0NZ

A CIP record for this book is available from the British Library
ISBN 978-1-910477-28-1
Typeset in Fournier MT by Gallic Books

Printed and bound by CPI Group (UK) Ltd, Croydon, CR0 4YY
2 4 6 8 10 9 7 5 3 1

Per Augusta ad angusta

'You're going to Switzerland? You should go and see Augusta. She—'

The lights turn green, unleashing a flood of cars that drowns out Getulio's voice but fails to interrupt him.

'… recognise her immediately. Quite unchanged, in spite of—'

A cement mixer, its drum revolving as it chews gravel, slows in front of them.

'… still awfully attractive … you know, I … her grace … her number …'

He pulls a dog-eared visiting card from his coat pocket and reads out a Lugano phone number. Arthur tries to memorise it, unsure if he will remember it an hour from now.

'Excuse me, must dash,' Getulio says, raising an odd tweed hat perched on his sugarloaf-shaped skull.

The lights change again, and in three strides he is on the far side of Rue des Saints-Pères. From the opposite pavement he waves a white handkerchief over his head, as if a train was already bearing Arthur away to Switzerland and Ticino. A bus drives between them. When it has passed, the Brazilian has gone, leaving Arthur alone with a phone number that has been so long coming, he isn't sure he actually wants it any more. Especially not from Getulio.

*

As Arthur walks up Rue des Saints-Pères towards Boulevard Saint-Germain, his mind elsewhere (though not without looking back, half hoping Getulio will reappear behind him and carry on talking about Augusta), the phone number etches itself on his memory and he feels his chest gripped with anxiety. But why? To whom can he say, 'It's too late, too much time has passed. There's no use reopening old wounds'? Not the hurrying Left Bank pedestrians, or the medical students queuing outside a pâtisserie who force him to step off the pavement, which he does, without looking out for traffic. A car brushes past him and its driver yells a volley of insults that make the students giggle. To get himself run over and killed . . . that would be bitterly ironic, wouldn't it, twenty years later, when he would have done much better to have died back then, so that he didn't have to drag around the burden of a failure that still haunts him as an adult, even now.

He makes his way into the restaurant where two signatories from a German bank are expecting him. He likes business: it has taught him how to lie and dissimulate. Bit by bit, a sort of double has been born inside him, a made-up character who serves him remarkably well in his negotiations: a man of few words and a dry manner, who affects a careless inattentiveness while not missing a word of what's being said, a sober figure, a non-smoker who, in the American style, takes his jacket off to talk in his shirtsleeves, always has a cup of coffee to hand, and switches to first-name terms the moment the deal looks done. 'That's not me. It's not me!' he says to himself, if he happens to catch sight of himself in a mirror behind the table where he's sitting. But that 'me', his real self, is fading by the day. Does it still exist? If it does, it lies years behind him, a heap of fragments mixed up with the love

8

affairs and illusions of his twenties. And if, very occasionally, in the heat of telling himself yet another lie, that self happens to rise from the ashes, it still carries the scent of Augusta.

Twenty years earlier, in the autumn of 1955, the *Queen Mary* had been making ready to leave Cherbourg for New York. The crossing normally took no more than four days but on this occasion would take six, the liner calling first at Portsmouth, then at Cork to take on more passengers. The prospect delighted Arthur. At twenty-two, everything was brand new to him, including the touching surprise his mother had prepared for him. Without telling him, she had exchanged his tourist-class cabin (which he would have been perfectly happy with) for a first-class stateroom. He dreaded to think what it must have cost her, she who was so careful, always going without ever since his father had died, so that she could keep up appearances and give Arthur every possible opportunity to be the bearer of her maternal ambitions. His recent award, after a remarkably unchallenging competitive exam, of a scholarship to an American university that specialised in commercial law had made her nurse even more extreme hopes for his future. The first-class cabin had been her reward for his success, but it was way beyond her means, sheer madness really.

There had been another such occasion, when he had been invited to the home of one of his classmates who lived in a big house in Neuilly, and his mother had sold a Japanese fan she had inherited from a distant aunt so that she could buy him a made-to-measure suit. She had silenced his protests, telling him sharply, 'From now on you're going to be with the great and the good, so you'd better know how to behave.' When the day came he had been horrified to discover that the other birthday guests – all fifteen- and sixteen-year-old boys and girls – had come in jeans and sweaters. In his blue pinstriped suit, tie and starched collar, a stranger to the way people lived in the city's smart neighbourhoods, Arthur had died a thousand deaths.

This humiliating memory returned when, at the purser's office, they handed him to a steward who swept him and his suitcases away to the upper decks while the neighbouring desk was besieged by a ruckus of shouting and swearing emigrants who elbowed their way forwards, stamping on each other's feet: young Hasidim in frock coats and black felt hats, their faces hidden beneath reddish beards, ringlets in disarray; Italians, much noisier and more cheerful than everyone else; and refugees from central Europe with grey faces, eyes wide with worry, and saying little, mainly concerned to put an ocean between themselves and the hell they had left behind.

How his mother afforded his first-class ticket he never found out, despite repeating the question in almost every letter he wrote her, at least for the first few months. When he insisted, furiously underlining the question, she just wrote back, 'All I care about is that from now on, you're among the great and the good.'

As soon as he had unpacked – the liner was still in port, with a six-hour delay that would extend its crossing time by as long – Arthur went in search of the bar. It was deserted. The barman told him he would not be serving drinks till the ship sailed, and Arthur was about to return to his stateroom to escape from the noise in the passageways when a tall American in his fifties with

11

white hair, beetling inky-black eyebrows, and cheeks traced with broken veins sat on the stool next to his. He was wearing a rumpled tan silk suit. He ordered a dry martini.

'The bar doesn't open till the ship sails,' the barman repeated.

'Paddy, I can tell from your accent that you're Irish. My father was from Dublin. My name's Concannon. So get me a dry martini and perhaps one for this gentleman next to me whom you're terrorising, which is only natural, given that all Irishmen are terrorists.'

Resting his elbows on the bar and turning to Arthur, he introduced himself.

'Seamus Concannon. Teaching modern history to a bunch of ignoramuses – who won't retain a word of what I tell them – at Beresford. And yourself?'

'Arthur Morgan. Student. On a Fulbright scholarship to study commercial law at Beresford.'

'You'll have me for two hours a week.'

The barman placed two dry martinis in front of them.

'Thank you, Paddy.'

'The name's not Paddy, Mr Concannon. It's John.'

'Let's go with John then, or Sean, which is even better.'

He raised his martini glass and emptied it in a single gulp.

'Make me another, my good Paddy, and one for Mr Morgan too. I'm going to wash my hands, and that's not a euphemism.'

A few minutes later he was back, his jacket splashed with dark spots and holding a paper towel with which he meticulously dried each of his fingers in turn.

'As soon as you open a faucet on these damn English boats you get deluged, every time.'

He touched nothing without immediately wiping his hands with a paper tissue, a large supply of which bulged under the breast pocket of his jacket. When the tissues ran out, he darted to the toilet and washed his hands with a bar of antiseptic soap that he carried in a tortoiseshell box. Rubbed raw by washing, the translucent skin of his hands was peeling like puff pastry. It had a violet sheen that was stained with nicotine at his fingertips, and if he made a fist it looked as if the skin would split and reveal, like a motor whose casing has been removed, the disturbing mechanism of joints and network of veins, arteries and tendons that held together the fragile structure thanks to which *Australopithecus* had evolved into *Homo sapiens*, whose use of his opposable thumbs had delivered him from his ape-like state. Or a part of his ape-like state. Concannon used his hands only when it was impossible not to. He pushed swing doors open with his elbows and put gloves on as soon as he came into contact with the open air and sometimes even at table, which led to a heavily powdered American passenger in her sixties, who had served as a nurse during the war in the Pacific, saying, 'I know what's up with him. We had so many cases of scabies among the marines in the war. Sometimes you just can't do anything for it. Professor Concannon must have been a marine. Don't worry: after ten years it's not contagious any more.'

But Concannon had not been a marine, and apart from his bactericidal fixation he was the most delightful of men, a professor of modern history with an independence of mind rare in American academic circles and a considerable dose of imagination, which, he said, he could exercise freely in the knowledge that not one of the fifty students who attended his classes would ever remember anything he had said. He was the first American friend Arthur made, and although there were plenty of others who came after him Concannon was inseparable from his earliest discovery of the United States.

Had it not been he who was responsible for Arthur meeting Getulio, Elizabeth and Augusta? When the *Queen Mary* dropped anchor the following morning in a murky green sea, with a thick haze obscuring both the Hampshire coast and the entrance to Portsmouth harbour, the passengers gathered on the promenade deck to watch a chain of lighters pop out of the yellowish murk one after the other like jumping beetles, laden with new passengers and baggage balanced on decks that gleamed with rain. On board ship, passengers reclined on deckchairs as busy stewards kept them swaddled in rugs bearing the Cunard crest and passed around trays of hot soup, tea and coffee.

A tall young man in a Prince of Wales-check Inverness cape, apparently unmoved by the general curiosity about the new arrivals, was striding up and down the first-class deck, arm in arm with two young women who were as alike as chalk and cheese. One, Elizabeth, was pounding the deck with the marching steps of a soldier, while the other, Augusta, tiptoeing like a dancer beside the man in the Inverness cape, seemed almost not to touch the ground. Elizabeth, wearing faded jeans and a sailor's cap, her hands buried in the pockets of a canvas reefer jacket and her cheeks pink from the damp air, was talking twenty to the dozen in a way that clearly enchanted Getulio but left Augusta unimpressed, as if she was either lost in a dream or preoccupied with not catching cold, wrapped in a coypu coat and a cloche hat crammed down over her forehead and eyebrows and looking so fragile she might buckle at the first strong gust of wind.

'They're different from everyone else,' Arthur said.

'You'll need to get used to them, old sport. They're the

14

new generation our continent has made, young, good-looking and rich. No one asks them where they came from any more, or whether their ancestors arrived on the *Mayflower*. Elizabeth Murphy, the blonde, is fourth-generation Irish American. Her ancestors landed on the Eastern seaboard starving and vermin-ridden. We put them to work building railroads in the Far West, where we treated them no better than coolies and they dropped like flies from disease, but the kids of the ones who survived went to school, and when the boys grew up they joined the cavalry and cut the Indians to ribbons. The third generation went into banking, or politics, and pretty soon they were part of the new American aristocracy. Read Henry James and F. Scott Fitzgerald, they'll tell you everything you want to know about their snobbery and their money, though I dare say Elizabeth Murphy, despite creaking under the weight of her fortune, won't ever strike you as a snob. She attended my classes for three months last year. Among the descendants of the Irish who arrived during the great hunger, there's always a few hotheads ready to burn the place down wherever they go. Elizabeth's a tornado, and although she might dress like a docker and cut her hair like a boy, nobody's fooled: she's a princess. You'll soon learn: with us, money is holy ... It's never rude to discuss it, to say how much your house cost or your car, or the jewellery your wife's wearing. The holy of holies ... Well ... maybe not always, but where the Irish are concerned, very often. Not the Italians. You want to meet them? You will anyhow, at college. Getulio will be in your year. Brazilian, born in Rio, educated in Europe and the States, in New York he's American, in Paris French. I don't think I ever met anyone so gifted and so unwilling to do a stroke of work. At a given moment, something always stops him seeing through whatever idea he's dreamed up. To be perfectly honest, I find him a touch satanic, and at the same time incredibly naive. He claims that because he and his sister have been so lucky they're both destined to screw up everything they do. Augusta has one career path in her sights, which is to be the wife of some very rich guy. The day it happens, I shall throw myself in the Charles River. I guess you should take that declaration of love with a pinch of salt: I only saw her maybe twenty times in my life, when I ran a class on American civilisation. But she can say a dozen words to you, and they can be something like "Pass me the salt and pepper" and they'll still be unforgettable. Can you explain to me the mystery of the instant attraction that's doomed – oh, believe me – to go nowhere? Augusta's not really what you'd call beautiful, she's got that prognathous chin, a little bit, that a lot of South American girls have, and those giveaway lips with their dose of Indian blood. In twenty years' time, if she doesn't look after herself she'll be a big-hipped mama with coal-black hair like the Incas – she must have something from them too – and mysteriously blue eyes. She looks like she was put together from lots of bits of different races. When she comes to Beresford to see her brother, all the boys want to take her to the pool, but they're out of luck because she hates water; in fact she loathes anything to do with the beach and is always scouring maps to find nice places to live a long, long way from the ocean. There was some drama in their childhood, some dreadful thing they can't get out of their heads and that she still has nightmares about sometimes. Without her brother I think she'd burn up, real life would overwhelm her. If a fellow ever succeeds in making her fall for him, she'll make him pay dearly for it, the first chance she gets.'

*

Concannon arranged matters. At lunchtime, as the *Queen Mary* put to sea again, Arthur found himself at the same table as Getulio and the two young women.

Augusta spoke to him in French. 'For a Frenchman, you're lucky; your name won't be hideously deformed. Ar-*ture* as Ar-*thur* with an English *th* won't make you feel too alienated. Morgan will get feminised into the good fairy Morg*ann*. You'll find it very interesting, and you won't suffer nearly as much as Getulio, who instantly turns into "Get ... weelo" or poor me, who gets called everything under the sun because of that "u" in the middle that's never pronounced the same in any Latin language. As for our surname, I'll leave you to imagine what kind of mess Mendosa turns into as soon as the English language gets hold of it. Are you at all interested in onomastics, Mr Morgan?'

Noticing Elizabeth's amused expression, Arthur realised he was on the brink of having his leg seriously pulled. Professor Concannon, who did not speak French well enough to follow, was methodically wiping his cutlery with a square of disinfectant gauze.

'Not only does it interest me passionately, I also happen to be the leading French expert in this relatively new area of knowledge, which has already collected its fair share of martyrs. A transatlantic crossing won't be nearly long enough to do the subject justice. We'd need a round-the-world voyage.'

'Oh ... well, if we can't do it justice, let's stop there, shall we? Because I ought to tell you that I'm a perfectionist.'

Elizabeth burst out laughing. Faces at neighbouring tables turned in their direction, to see where the laughter was coming from. Envy was mixed with disapproval in their expressions. In a voice loud enough to be overheard, one woman stated that the youth of today possessed no self-restraint and their fathers lacked all authority. Concannon swung in her direction and stared daggers at her. She studied her plate.

'Oh what a shame, another lady in need of a good fuck!' Elizabeth drawled, in unmistakable English this time.

The waiter, who was in the process of respectfully setting down a truly wafer-thin slice of foie gras on Getulio's plate, almost choked. He caught his tray just in time. Normally the dining room was a place where passengers hardly dared speak above a whisper, for fear of offending its neo-Victorian majesty and that of its bewhiskered head waiters, but Elizabeth's laughter and shocking language shook them out of their stuffy gloom. It started with a low murmur, like the first cracking sounds of a thaw. By the time the cheese course had been reached it had turned, with some help from the port decanter, into a Babel-like uproar.

'Miss Murphy's laugh is the perfect painless antidote to boredom,' Concannon said. 'Look at all these people: bankers, businessmen, wealthy lawyers with their pasty wives dripping with jewellery, real and fake. At home, in their offices, they're kings; everyone bows down in front of them, while here, where nobody knows them, they're so shy and reverential they can hardly move their facial muscles. It's as if they feel out of place, despite having paid for their staterooms with those handsome greenbacks they earned from the sweat off the workers' backs.'

Arthur remarked that if anyone should feel ill at ease among all these strangers, it was him, because he would have been back in steerage with the other migrants but for his mother's surprise gift of a first-class ticket.

'How interesting!' Augusta said. 'But you shouldn't have accepted. You're depriving yourself of one of life's essential experiences. My brother and I have decided that next time we go across we're going to share a cabin with a very poor family of emigrants. It'll be so exciting, won't it, Getulio *meu*?'

'Fascinating, I'm sure.'

'I'm coming too,' Elizabeth said.

The dining room was emptying. Professor Concannon, having drunk two or three dry martinis before lunch, a bottle of Château Margaux on his own, and several cognacs with his coffee, got to his feet, staggered a little, and regained his balance by grabbing the back of a chair.

'Take my arm, Professor,' Elizabeth said. 'I'll feel more comfortable among these idiots.'

'What about you, Monsieur Morgan, how are you feeling?' Augusta said.

'Captivated.'

'At last! Someone saying something nice. Makes a change from our usual backbiting and nastiness. Are you a sensitive soul?'

'I'm afraid I am.'

'You must harden yourself.'

'Will you help me?'

'Don't count on me. I think it's a very good thing for men to shed tears. A man who cries is touching. A woman who cries is ridiculous.'

'You've never shed a tear.'

'How would you know?'

They walked out to the promenade deck. The Cunarder was making twenty knots out into the Atlantic. Out of a yellow and grey sky the afternoon sunlight brushed the white cottages of

19

the Scilly Isles as it would soon, with its last rays, the Fastnet lighthouse. A trawler struggled against the swell, followed by a cloud of seagulls that twisted and whirled above its nets.

'The sea is completely stupid,' Augusta said. 'I hate it, don't you?'

'I don't really have an opinion. But why don't you go by plane?'

'No thank you! Not when one in two disappears somewhere over the ocean.'

'If that was true, we'd have heard about it.'

'They never find anyone, which is why they never talk about it. But it's boring that you don't have an opinion about the sea. You're not really very interesting.'

'I suppose you mean I don't try to make myself interesting. Well, that's true.'

Elizabeth came back alone.

'I put Concannon to bed and I left Getulio playing poker with three Americans. You don't play cards, Monsieur Morgan.'

She could have said, 'Do you play cards?', which would have required either an affirmative or negative response, or she could have given her sentence an interrogative emphasis, but said like that, her 'You don't play cards' became a simple observation, no more or less than if she had casually mentioned that Arthur had blue or green or brown eyes or a nose that was straight or squashed or turned-up. Perhaps he didn't play cards because he hadn't had the opportunity, or because, absorbed in his studies, he had put off till later an activity that didn't greatly attract him. The error – which he fortunately did not make – would have been to answer Elizabeth, to explain or even to invent, because neither Elizabeth nor Augusta was expecting him to say anything. Elizabeth's 'You don't play cards' had the simple merit of being clear, of situating the Frenchman in a different milieu from Getulio's, without the slightest condescension, one might add, and even with some obvious sympathy for a young man who came from a different country and class from those they inhabited.

Yet Elizabeth had no hesitation in describing a woman three times her age as 'in need of a good fuck' or walking through doorways ahead of elderly passengers who were unsteady on their feet or squeezed into unsuitable baby-pink or lavender-blue dresses, and her contempt for other Americans was boundless. As for Augusta, when she discovered that the wife of a Brazilian ambassador in Europe was on board, she repeatedly made sure that the woman was seated as far away from her as possible. Her stratagems surprised Arthur. His own upbringing had revolved around the family circle and arranged introductions and, being the son of an officer killed in the last war, he had always had the French presented to him as the most heroic and socially acceptable people on earth. Yet what many people take for granted is not enough for some sceptical souls, and Arthur already had his suspicions. The crossing from Cherbourg to New York was reinforcing them.

'It's icy out here,' Augusta said. 'I'm going in, before I die of cold. Arthur? As you're dining with us ...'

This was news to Arthur.

'... I must ask you at once not to wear a tuxedo. Getulio never wears one and he will feel awkward if he sees you turn up in a black tie. Professor Concannon will be at another table. If he makes it to dinner. Every crossing is an ordeal for him. All this water makes him so thirsty. But you'll see ... on dry land ... What I mean is that before, during and after his classes, he's a man of extraordinary intellect and originality ... when he isn't under the table. Elizabeth, don't forget to tell me when we get to

Cork, even if it's dark.'

'It will be dark.'

'I want to see all those hundreds of little priests coming aboard.'

'Not every Irish person is a priest.'

'These are! I have my sources! The purser is ... he pouts awfully, I know, but anyway, he's an *"adorable, absolument adorable"* man, as you French say. And he explained to me that the country around Cork regularly sends parcels of little priests to America, which has a shortage, whereas Ireland, which is blessed by the gods, mass-produces them. Apparently it's very good for regulating the balance of trade.'

Was Augusta really suffering from the cold, or was it all a pretence that she was some kind of poetical creature, doomed to hide indoors, sheltered from every storm, or cough consumptively like Marguerite Gautier? One day a man would expose her to cold reality, loving her with enough lucidity to detect what was real about her character and be just sufficiently intoxicated by the part she had invented about herself so charmingly and cleverly. From the way she muffled herself up, wrapping her arms tight across her chest and hunching her neck and chin deep down into her fur collar, she really made it seem as though the promenade deck was being buffeted by glacial winds, despite being sealed at both ends by sliding doors.

'Anybody home?' she said to Arthur. 'You're miles away.'

'I was thinking about you.'

'In that case you may carry on.'

She kissed Elizabeth.

'I'm leaving him with you. He's a tiny bit odd. You'd better tell me what happens. And please behave: don't get up to anything naughty. It's very bad for your blood pressure in the afternoon.'

She was gone by the time Elizabeth shook her head resignedly.

'What does she know?' she said to Arthur in French. 'Nothing, I'll bet. The man who manages to tie her down will never be bored. Unless, like a caged bird, she suddenly stops singing.'

'Yes, I was thinking the same thing.'

Elizabeth took his arm.

'Come on. We'll go and sit at the bar. There won't be anyone there. You can tell me what you've been thinking about ... we might as well call each other "*tu*", it's so much simpler. Do you think you're already in love with Augusta, like every other man?'

'I wouldn't exactly put it like that. And anyhow it's too soon. I mean, what I'm trying to say is, it's not too soon because we've only known each other since this morning, just too soon in life, too soon because I don't really know what love is, or what you're supposed to do with it. I'm putting it badly, and I expect you think I'm an idiot or a sissy, but you understand French so well I'm sure I don't need to spell it out.'

Elizabeth stopped abruptly, tugging at his arm.

'Yes, I do speak good French, and I like speaking it. My father and mother died in a plane crash. From what I remember of them, they were completely foolish. Though not totally, actually, because they gave me a French governess ... Madeleine ... I'll tell you about Madeleine one day. She's the person I go and see every year, at Saint-Laurent-sur-Loire: my real mother. She taught me to read very young, she made me go to the cinema and the theatre very young too. One day she said to me, "Now you know everything I know ... now is the moment for you to fly away on your own, with a motto: believe nothing and everything."'

23

'Ha! The ghastliness of the happy medium.'

'Oh you sweet boy, we shall make something of you! Now, I've had enough of pacing up and down in front of these mummies bundled up in their rugs. Not to mention the old women glaring at me and thinking that if I'm wearing jeans I must have horrible legs and I shouldn't be wearing a man's cap and it's about time I put on some make-up … They give me the willies. I must know half of them, and they know damn well that I'm a Murphy, but they're so plastered in make-up I find it impossible to work out who's lurking behind which face.'

They walked to the bar past the smoking room. Getulio, sitting with three other players, winked as they went past. He collected the cards, shuffled, and dealt them again. Arthur had seen enough card games to know that the Brazilian did not have the dexterity that marks out the great players. As he dealt, he even dropped a card. One of the other players mocked him.

'Come on! We're putting him off.'

In the bar Professor Concannon was teetering dangerously on a stool in front of the barman who was obstinately refusing to answer to the name of Paddy, his face pink with suppressed anger. Concannon kept insisting: 'It would be so much easier for all concerned, not just on board the *Queen Mary* but on all the ships in the British merchant fleet.'

Elizabeth did not want to wait for the barman to lose his temper.

'After five minutes it stops being funny,' she said to Arthur. 'Now, a ship is a village. Suppose that, not knowing what else to do with ourselves, and notwithstanding Augusta's explicit instructions, I go with you to your cabin or you go with me to mine: in five minutes the whole ship will know, and no one will talk about anything else at dinner. Better avoided.'

'Won't not spending the afternoon together make them gossip just as much? They'll just start whispering that I'm queer or you're a lesbian.'

'Frankly I don't much care, but I rather feel like watching a film this afternoon.'

They were showing, for the hundredth time, *An American in Paris*. Gene Kelly danced exuberantly. Leslie Caron's legs were very shapely, if a bit short. Arthur dropped off to sleep for a spell, as doubtless did Elizabeth. The lights went up. The *Queen Mary* was rolling heavily in the swell outside Cork as it took on what Augusta had referred to as 'the little Irish priests'. Little, however, they were not, but tall and blond or red-haired, their faces made pink by the wind and rain. Without their dog collars they looked more like members of a sports team, and many were in fact laden with tennis racquets, golf clubs or hockey sticks, clumsily tied to their cardboard suitcases with leather straps or string.

Augusta had appeared from her cabin and posted herself at the top of the great staircase and was watching their arrival with a sparkling gleam of mischief in her eyes.

'Couldn't you just eat them up?' she said to Elizabeth. 'Do you think they really intend to resist the sins of the flesh for the rest of their lives? If I were you, I'd try to corrupt at least one of them this very night.'

'Why don't you try?'

'Me? I wouldn't know what to do. Nor him, I expect. Look at him, licking his finger …'

Arthur was startled by her expression: he had never seen anyone look so innocent.

'Why are you making that face, Arturo? What were you thinking about?'

'Nothing. As usual. I'm just listening, and by the way, it looks to me as if that young priest's wetting his finger rather greedily …'

'Mmm. So he can find the bit in his instruction manual about unexpected meetings. You know they all have a little guide to love, to tell them what happens in case the Devil leads them into sin. Whereas you, Elizabeth, would be able to teach them everything without having to open a book. Such a practical girl!'

The *Queen Mary* weighed anchor during dinner. A conspicuous number of passengers had succumbed to the Atlantic swell, and the dining room was no more than half full.

'If I'd known,' Augusta said, 'I wouldn't have bothered changing. My rose gets very discouraged when it's not admired.'

At the point of the V of her white silk blouse, cut lavishly low, she had pinned a rose of the same crimson as her lips. Its petals lay soft against the amber-coloured skin at the dip between her breasts, which were visibly unconstrained. When she spoke, she held her hand up to the flower, dropping it again when someone spoke to her.

'What's going on?' Elizabeth said to Arthur. 'You're wearing a tuxedo.'

Arthur took some pleasure in her surprise. He smiled at Getulio, who was wearing a blue velvet jacket with black silk lapels, far louder than his own altered black barathea jacket, which had been his father's and was too short in the sleeves and too tight at the shoulders.

'I rather thought Getulio would dress for dinner.'

Getulio disputed this. He had merely forgotten what they had decided. He would never have dreamt of making his dear friend Arturo feel awkward, and besides, hadn't everything turned out perfectly, since even Elizabeth, usually so unconventionally dressed, had come to the dining room in a Dior suit? Augusta frowned suddenly.

'Are my ears deceiving me? Arturo and Elizabeth are calling each other "*tu*".'

'What's so extraordinary about that?'

'Nothing, except that you must have decided to pass the time by sleeping together this afternoon.'

'Unfortunately not, I'm afraid,' Arthur said with a deep sigh of regret.

'Don't treat me like a goose. I can tell; it's as plain as the nose on your face.'

Elizabeth threw down her napkin and stood up, pale with annoyance.

'That's enough, Augusta. You're going too far. Say it again and I'll go and eat at a different table.'

'With your lover?'

'All right, stop it!' Arthur said. 'Your suspicion is flattering … but sadly bears no relation to reality. Augusta, I swear on your rose that we did not do that naughty thing you mentioned after lunch.'

'In that case, how bored you must have been! Darling, calm

27

down … I take back my base thoughts.'

Elizabeth sat down, picked up her napkin, and called the waiter. Getulio was oddly silent, his gaze distracted. Augusta revealed the reason.

'He lost rather badly this afternoon. We don't even know if we're going to be able to carry on to New York. Perhaps they'll throw us overboard before we get there.'

'Can you swim?'

'No. If the captain has any feelings at all, he'll have to lend us a lifeboat. Getulio can row, he loves that.'

'I hate rowing. I'd prefer to sink like a stone. With you, obviously.'

Elizabeth spoke to the waiter. 'Mr Mendosa is having a breakdown, or a tantrum, or perhaps both. Even the sight of the menu is likely to bring on a fatal allergic reaction. Would you be very kind and deliver our four dinners to some emigrants of your choice? Preferably some who have only ship's biscuits and salt water to last them for the crossing.'

'I didn't know you were a communist,' Augusta said.

'You don't know everything … The only cure for Mr Mendosa's bad temper is caviar, several tons of it. Mr Mendosa will choose the champagne himself, if your sommelier will be good enough to bring him the list; I'm sure he will, because I can see him from here, yawning, with nothing to do but nurse his contempt for all the passengers who are drinking Coca-Cola with their oysters and scalding themselves with the hot chocolate they've ordered to go with their roast beef and Yorkshire pudding. We have a Frenchman with us, and he is beside himself with rage … You can put everything on my account, obviously. Cabin 210.'

*

When he left them Arthur made his way to the upper deck, where the lifeboats and life rafts were. Its superstructure flooded with light, the liner steamed blindly on into the ink-black night, maintaining its course through the long Atlantic swell. Shorter waves crashed against its bow, sending up spurts of iridescent spray that fell on the foredeck in soaking gusts. Leaning on the rail, Arthur contemplated the uneven line of foam as it curled away from the ship and disappeared into the depths of the night. At the end, the very end of the journey, the skyline of New York was waiting, still hidden. Oh, he certainly wasn't on his way to conquer the New World, as so many passengers on the *Queen Mary* were, and nor had he ever had any ambition to settle there, but something else drew him, an intuition that there he would find the constituent parts of a future denied to a Europe exhausted by its five-year-long civil war.

A hand was laid gently on his shoulder.

'You're not thinking of ending it all, are you?'

Elizabeth had put her reefer jacket on over her suit. As she leant forward to gaze at the ship's wake that was fascinating Arthur, the wind plucked her sailor's cap off her head. They watched it skim away for a second across the breaking crest of a wave before it vanished from sight.

'*Adios!*' she said. 'I liked that cap. Not my favourite, luckily. So when's your suicide scheduled for?'

'I'm not really very tempted. I read, I can't remember where, that every would-be suicide, even the most determined, leaves themselves a chink of hope that they won't succeed. Maybe no more than a chance in a hundred, but at least one, in the not entirely vain hope that some immanent intervention will erase everything – the cause or causes of their suicide – and grant them resurrection in a world purged of despair. If I were to throw myself into the ocean, those one in a hundred odds would become one in a million, particularly at night. No, I have absolutely no desire to commit suicide. What about you?'

'Let's go in, I'm freezing. The wind's very boring. And I've drunk too much champagne. Yes, once or twice I've toyed with the idea. Last year. Not for a very edifying reason. A casual fuck, as you French put it so elegantly. I phoned Madeleine from New York and she burst out laughing when I told her, which made me laugh too. We never talked about it again … My cabin's at the far end. I'm not going to ask you in, though I'd quite like to. But one shouldn't do such things unthinkingly. I'm being honest. However, that doesn't mean I'm ready to go all the way with you, particularly since you've already fallen hook, line and sinker for Augusta's charms.'

She brushed Arthur's cheek with a quick kiss and headed down the passageway, her arms held wide to balance herself against the rolling of the ship. In front of her door she turned round and, before disappearing, gave him a little wave. Arthur's own stateroom had no porthole, and the ventilation shaft carried with it, as if from some monstrous beast, the dull panting of machinery and, at irregular intervals, the shudders of the ship's enormous steel hull whenever a wave made it pause in its rhythm. Sleep refused to come, or rather Arthur surrendered to a half-sleep visited by images and ripples of laughter and lulled by the sound of a falsely innocent voice that left him simultaneously clear-headed and on the brink of a dreamlike delirium. For no apparent reason he saw Getulio at the tiller of a lifeboat, counting out the rhythm ('One, two, three, four') to twenty or so octogenarian oarswomen dressed for a garden party and wearing panama hats decorated with flowers. Exhausted, they died one by one, and then Augusta appeared, standing tall at the prow, unfastened her sari, and let the wind fill it, speeding the lifeboat all the way to the port of New York where a fleet of hearses awaited the desiccated corpses of the old ladies, still clinging to their oars.

The *Queen Mary*'s hull shook at the impact of another concrete-like wave, the sort that had once snapped in two her timber predecessors with their cargoes of gold ingots and china from the East India Company. Arthur switched on his bedside lamp and Augusta disappeared. She was unaware that she had this gift, but those who found her haunting their dreams or their waking reveries all marvelled at how she could be so present and so absent at the same time. Arthur put the blame on the champagne and the confusion Elizabeth had sown in his mind. In a less rational world he ought to have dived overboard to retrieve her cap before the liner's wake carried it away; she would have run to the captain; the *Queen Mary* would have gone full speed astern; he would have been fished out of the boundless ocean, a block and tackle lifting him back aboard; Elizabeth would have comically replaced her cap on her head, water dripping down her face and neck; he would have been a hero. He got out of bed, drank tepid water from the tap, and tried to read a history of the United States that bored him so much he switched the light off again and let himself drowse in a half-sleep, rocked by the liner's steady progress. After the last concrete wave, the *Queen Mary* seemed to be continuing on its course as if over a sea of oil. The crimson rose pinned to Augusta's décolletage now irradiated the cabin's darkness, haloed by a pale trembling light like that viscous ectoplasm supposed to emanate from the bodies of mediums during a trance. Arthur stretched out an arm and clutched at nothing, just as a puff of Augusta's perfume exploded and vanished in the cabin. Or it might have been Elizabeth's perfume. He didn't know any more …

Professor Concannon was rowing energetically, not because the ship's turbines had broken down, he explained, but to detoxify himself from the excesses of the previous day. His face beetroot red, forehead streaming with sweat that pearled into glistening drops in his black eyebrows, a towel around his neck, wearing enormous leather gloves and disappearing inside a voluminous grey wool tracksuit top with 'Yankees' written on the back, he shot furiously backwards and forwards on the gym's rowing machine. Pausing, he mopped his face with the towel and smiled at Arthur, who was pedalling gently on an exercise bicycle.

'The great malaise of the civilised members of our species is that they are imbeciles and snobs in their avoidance of every opportunity to work up a sweat. Little by little they build up blood levels of arsenic, mercury, quinine and urea which eventually poison them. The first thing to be done is to clear the openings of the ducts from the sudoriparous glands. Always use an exfoliating glove, there's nothing better. The day, dear Mr Morgan, you understand that sudoral excretion is an essential requirement for your physical, moral and intellectual health, your life will change completely.'

Apart from themselves, at this early-morning hour, there was only a short, thickset and muscle-bound man in long leggings who was lifting weights with astonishing ease. Concannon winked at Arthur.

'I'll tell you about him later.'

They had breakfast together at the buffet. It was all extremely tempting.

'Here,' Concannon said, 'is where we must show fortitude. These cakes and pastries are unworthy of a man. America has hardly suffered at all from the war, unlike Europe, which had to go on a diet lasting five years. In twenty years' time we'll be a nation of fatties.'

'... and alcoholics!' Arthur blurted out.

'Might you be saying that for my benefit?'

'For no one, or for all of us.'

Concannon could have taken this badly. He slapped Arthur on the back.

'You're right! The consequences would be tragic if I didn't eliminate the toxins regularly. Then a cold shower, to free the mind. I thought about you this morning. What an idea, to study business law in the United States! You'll lose your European intuition and you'll never acquire an American one. By the time you realise that all our virtues are learned, and in no way originate from some mystic and absolute source, it'll be too late. In other words, those virtues – precisely because they're codified – are rigid, and therefore easily circumvented. Consider our anti-colonialism: entirely manufactured to serve a political purpose. On that weighty matter, our so-called "sensitivity" is cause for a wry smile. Perhaps one American in a thousand is descended from somebody who fought in the War of Independence. The other nine hundred and ninety-nine are new blood. But just listen to them ... they "drove the British out", as your Joan of Arc put it, and the French into the bargain, because everyone's so fabulously ignorant. What a wonderful opportunity to preach morality to everyone else! Give up your colonies that make you as powerful as us, the New Nation, Saviour of the modern world.

Go home, leave Africa, leave Asia, take no notice of the vacuum left behind after your ignominious departure: never fear, we Americans are on our way, hands on hearts, with our crates of peaceful consumer goods. You'll be hornswoggled, and it's you who'll be accused of being dishonest.'

Concannon was in his element. The dining room was filling up, and a queue was forming in front of the buffet where two chefs in white hats were cooking eggs and bacon or pancakes and waffles with maple syrup.

'Hornswoggled? Who by?' Arthur asked sceptically.

'Aren't you one of those for whom personal experience, however dearly bought, is preferable to the experience of others?'

'I haven't decided yet.'

Concannon placed his hands flat on the tablecloth. They were transparent, their skin glazed and dotted with bruises and red patches.

'I guess you know the air we breathe is saturated with practically undetectable bugs, ready to attack us the moment we show the slightest sign of weakness. Open your mouth, and they'll swarm into your body in their millions. Touch anything, and they'll climb up your arms and legs, get into your debilitated organism, and block up your pores. Terrifying, don't you think?'

Arthur agreed that by comparison the two atomic bombs dropped on Hiroshima and Nagasaki were pinpricks. He was starting to like this lunatic.

'Yet however terrifying it is,' Concannon went on, holding his hands in front of him as if he was working a pair of puppets, 'it's nothing compared to the machinations that await men of your age and the traps they fall into, yelling – too late – that they won't be fooled again.'

Arthur listened attentively, but could not help being distracted by the latecomers arriving, some still pale from the pitching and tossing they had suffered since leaving Cork the day before, others eyeing the buffet with a sparkling, greedy stare. Neither Augusta, Elizabeth nor Getulio deigned to appear.

'They won't come,' the professor said, well aware of Arthur's waning interest in him. 'The entitled, brought up to a life of entitlement, they'll be having breakfast served in their cabins. Such treatment is granted to very few. On the subject of Getulio …'

Concannon paused, drank his coffee, and lit a cigarette.

'I shouldn't smoke, because of my throat … yes … my throat is extremely sensitive, but the first cigarette of the day is so good …'

After the third puff he stubbed it out in the butter dish.

'I'm listening,' Arthur said.

'What was I saying?'

The crafty devil. He knew perfectly well.

'You said, "On the subject of Getulio …"'

'Oh yes, on the subject of Getulio … but really it's nothing to do with me.'

A horrified waiter cleared away the butter dish.

Arthur said, 'But if it was to save me from some kind of bad experience?'

'Oh … nothing … It's just a thought, you know. If I were you, I wouldn't play cards with him.'

'He lost heavily last night.'

'He always loses at the start of the crossing. This is the third time we've taken the same boat. Suddenly there's a moment when his luck changes. The day before we hit New York he'll make it all back, and plenty more …'

Arthur regretted having his eyes opened so soon: he had

35

thought Getulio above such financial duplicity.

'Oh, he is! At least I believe him to be, but maybe he also has some bad patches when his schemes don't work out, or possibly he's just amusing himself by testing his powers of attraction. Do you recognise that little fellow with the tanned face and the glistening pate?'

In a bottle-green suit and pink shirt, the short man who had been hoisting enormous barbells in the gym with such ease was making his way towards the buffet, poked and shoved by a bony woman who was a head taller than he and wearing an Italian straw hat.

'She treats him like hell,' Concannon said. 'Which is funny, when you realise the influence he has over President Eisenhower. He's the President's *éminence grise* in security matters and the entire White House quakes at his footsteps, but to his dear wife he's a useless dummy who can't even manage to sneak to the front and get the best sausages. Never get married, Mr Morgan. Not even as a joke.'

'I haven't been tempted in that direction yet.'

Arthur became convinced during the course of the morning that an Atlantic crossing on a liner like the *Queen Mary* would be unconscionably boring if you didn't have the good luck to come across some eccentric personality like Professor Concannon or some delicious princesses like Elizabeth and Augusta. The passengers' lives appeared to be ruled and dominated by the next tea or coffee service, the next bell announcing the opening of the dining room. Concannon, locked in his cabin, worked on his opening lecture and, knowing himself all too well, lived on mineral water and sandwiches until dinner. Arthur was looking forward to seeing the two young women and the Brazilian at lunch and was deeply disappointed when the maître d'hôtel stopped him at the entrance to the dining room with the words, 'You are Monsieur Morgan, are you not?'

'Yes. Why?'

'Mr Allan Dwight Porter invites you to join him.'

'There must be a mistake, I don't know anyone of that name.'

'Mr Porter says he knows you.'

'I prefer to lunch with my friend Senhor Mendosa—'

'Senhor Mendosa's table is full … Albert, please show Monsieur Morgan to Mr Porter's table. He is expecting him.'

The waiter led Arthur to the table of the short man with the sunburnt face and the shining bald head, who stood up and held out his hand.

'I very much wanted to meet you, Monsieur Morgan. Allow me to introduce you to my wife, Minerva.'

From lunchtime onwards Minerva Porter had recourse, it seemed, to sacks of kohl to emphasise the shape of her eyes, darken her eyelids, thicken her eyelashes and apply a thick line across the place where her plucked eyebrows had once been. The light-hearted straw hat she had worn at breakfast had given way to a turban of Indian silk held in place by a large pin with a head of imitation pearl.

'Sit on my husband's left side,' she told Arthur. 'That's his good ear. Within a year he'll be completely deaf, and will have to wear one of those ghastly little devices that start whistling most inappropriately when you're at a concert, a wedding, a funeral. Take no notice of me, by the way. I'm used to being ignored as soon as my husband starts talking.'

'But, my dear, no one is ignoring you.'

'A miracle! He heard me. I hope you don't smoke, Mr Whateveryournameis. I hate it when people smoke between courses and with their coffee. There are smoking rooms set aside for that purpose. Let me also say at once that the smell of fish disgusts me. I have asked for us to be spared today's turbot. In any case, one always eats too much.'

'That's a pity, I love turbot,' Arthur said, surprising himself by his nerve in the face of this shrewish woman, who paid no further attention to him, having turned away to summon the maître d'hôtel and demand her table be served first.

Mr Porter, like his wife, had changed for lunch. His bottle-green suit and pink shirt were breakfast attire. At lunchtime President Eisenhower's special adviser dressed sportily: flapping golfing trousers over Argyle socks, a tweed jacket the colour of faded heather, a striped shirt, and a tartan tie. He would have looked clown-like but for his face, which regularly broke into bursts of unrestrained laughter, and the twinkle in his eye that revealed his appetite for life's pleasures: wine, good food, and even attractive women, whom he studied openly whenever Mrs Porter was not watching. Initially disconcerted by the man's self-assurance, Arthur was rapidly charmed and intrigued.

'I had them look for you in tourist class, where you ought to be travelling,' Mr Porter said, in excellent French, 'and you finally turned up in first, which I'm obviously delighted about for your sake. The restaurant is very good. The chef's French. No one has ever seen – yet – an Englishman who knows how to cook. The gym where we saw each other briefly this morning is the best Cunard has. And this ship has plenty of space, which is good for someone like me, who needs to walk in order to think. Two and a half thousand years ago I would have been a peripatetic … One's always behind in something. That old broad who just sat down opposite my better half is the wife of the mayor of Boston.

They're as mean as each other, and more snobbish than chamber pots – as you say in French – a comparison that always charms me.'

'Excuse me,' Arthur said, 'but I can't quite see why you particularly requested to have me at your table.'

'I noticed,' Porter said, ignoring the question, 'that you very quickly made friends with Professor Concannon. Great mind. A little crazy ... You know what it is: the drop of Irish blood that often makes the cup spill over. You'll have him for two hours a week in your first year. Some original views on modern history, not very politically correct it has to be said, but interesting for their ability to stir up controversy. His coverage of the Nuremberg trials is his most polished performance. He describes the trials, then puts Stalin, Molotov and Beria in the dock alongside the other accused. To start with the three Russians are a little standoffish towards the Germans, but soon get pally with them. Beria and Himmler argue good-naturedly about which of them has killed the largest number of gypsies, Jews and Christians in their camps; Ribbentrop and Molotov, old acquaintances from the days when they signed risible treaties together, break open the sparkling wine that the German used to export before the war; Stalin and Göring exchange stories about broads. You'll definitely have that class: it comes complete with his analysis of the indictments, dissection of the defence speeches, legality of the verdicts. It's wacky, but as sharp as you like. One day I had it recorded, without Concannon's knowledge, and the President thoroughly enjoyed it. He played it back three times. That said, Concannon's not without his enemies in the university administration. Young Americans, who hardly know who Hitler was, have complained about his highly liberal interpretation of history. It all happened so far away from them already, in space and time too! Ten years! But as a native of the old, sick Europe, Arthur, I promise you, you won't be bored. I'll call you Arthur, okay? I know your file so well, I feel we're like old friends.'

Apart from his duties in Washington, DC, Allan Porter chaired the foundation that granted three-year scholarships to foreign students. To his considerable surprise, although other European nations had submitted large numbers of candidates, France had put forward only one: Arthur Morgan. This single candidature had appeared suspect, coming as it did from a country whose parliament contained so many Communists. Was Arthur Morgan some sort of propagandist, perhaps one of those spies the KGB ran under the guise of an intellectual rebelling against the injustices that were everywhere in the capitalist world? The inquiry carried out by their Paris embassy had reassured him.

'I can even tell you your mother's maiden name, the date of her marriage, the day your father was killed in action in Germany, your grades in your baccalauréat, your 800-metre time, the eye colour of the girl you went out with during your first year of law and the name of the man she married, to your considerable relief, the agency that employed you for two summers in a row, taking American tourists on guided tours around Paris and to Versailles. We appreciate such qualities, my dear Arthur. The world lacks men who are capable of lending a hand, when the day comes, to save a civilisation that's sinking into horror and lies.'

Arthur, who was instinctively wary, said guardedly, 'Oh, I'm not at all a leader of men.'

Mrs Porter interrupted them, tapping her crystal glass with her knife.

'Mr Morgan, on your left you have a small plate on which your bread should be placed, bread which you have left on the tablecloth, disregarding all hygiene.'

'There are many things you'll have to teach me, Mrs Porter,' Arthur said mirthlessly. 'I'm relying on you. Bread on the tablecloth is an old French tradition which I realise must be left behind at the border, but I do have two excuses, one being that it's French bread, and the other that we're in the middle of the ocean, where borders are notoriously difficult to define.'

'What did she say?' Porter asked.

His wife leant over and shouted in his ear, 'The young man put his bread on the tablecloth.'

'What the hell does that matter?' Porter shouted back just as loudly, twisting his head left and right to make sure the neighbouring tables had heard, and were more amused than appalled.

Disconcerted, Minerva hung her head, her facial muscles tensing and relaxing several times, as if slowly swallowing her husband's rudeness and steeling herself for a deadly last word to end their disagreement.

Porter, with an impassivity that was not entirely feigned, put his hand on Arthur's forearm.

'Do you know why the best Bordeaux are drunk on board Her Majesty's ships?'

'No I don't.'

'After two or three years of crossing the Atlantic, gently cradled in their racks, they have acquired, without losing their youth, a sort of suppleness and grace to which no wine aged in a cellar can ever aspire.'

Three tables away, Augusta's laughter was making heads turn. Arthur could see the back of her head, and Elizabeth and Getulio in profile. Opposite her was a young man with black curly hair that tumbled in waves over his left ear and eyes of a magnificent blue. The discreet cross pinned to the lapel of his black jacket identified him as one of the young priests who had embarked at Cork and vanished into the liner's second-class quarters. Arthur decided that Elizabeth would have no difficulty in seducing him, if she decided to put her bet to the test. Augusta too was in her element, dressed to kill: her piled-up hair, held in place by a comb, uncovered a disarmingly slender neck that was emphasised by the movement of her hand to adjust the comb each time she laughed. The priest looked unsettled by the conversation of his three lunch companions, who were very likely his age but had a profoundly different way of looking at the world. To conquer his timidity, and the embarrassment that swept over him at each outburst of giggling from Elizabeth and Augusta, he drank too quickly from the glass that Getulio kept continuously filled and, with his face blazing, laughed automatically at jokes he could only have half understood.

'Your two girlfriends are entirely charming,' Porter said.

'"Girlfriend" is slightly premature, as I've only known them since we left Cherbourg.'

'It won't be long before you get to know them better. If you intend to win the heart of one of them, I advise you to provoke a quarrel between them. They're partners, and if you don't divide them you'll be caught between the frying pan and the fire, and find yourself cooked like that fellow, who looks as if he's about to explode any minute.'

'That's one of the Irish priests who came on board at Cork.'

'In which case his goose is certainly cooked. When they drop him, he won't bounce back.'

Minerva Porter was pretending not to be interested in her husband's conversation but was listening with half an ear, looking for an opening that would let her go for his throat.

'A priest, that pretty boy with the curls? I hardly think so. Where's his white collar? It's what I've been saying for years: the real fifth column isn't the Communists, it's the papists. If we don't look out, America will be Catholic within a generation: we'll have ourselves a Catholic president, a Catholic administration and Catholic representatives. I know what I'm talking about.'

'Minerva's always been very pessimistic,' Porter said. 'She's a Seventh Day Adventist. You get my drift.'

Arthur did not get his drift. All he got was that Mrs Porter was an appalling bigot and that he had been right to loathe her at first sight.

'You'll see. In a few short years, if we don't make sure we defend ourselves, the Pope's secret legions will have us under their thumb.'

Porter settled for a heavy sigh: he had heard his wife's speech a hundred times before and no longer even bothered to contradict it. Observing an ironic gleam in Arthur's eyes, he lowered his voice.

'Don't take offence. Minerva's a nut. The ability to let storms blow over is a great sign of wisdom in life. We'll meet at Beresford, where I come from time to time to give a lecture on what's happening in the world of diplomacy. I'd be happy to talk to you again. Young Europeans of your age need to understand the United States' policies.'

'And the United States needs to understand European policies.'

'That's more difficult when one's in a superior position. But let's not forget we're all Europeans somewhere along the line.'

'Not all of us.'

'Yet another problem! We'll talk about it, but not in front of Mrs Porter, whose mind is rather too closed on that particular subject. I hope you like desserts. That's my innocent side coming out. There has to be one; I can't just be the guy they say does all the President's dirty work. Waiter! The dessert trolley, please.'

*

Arthur was never to forget Porter's lustful indulgence when he had a plate overflowing with profiteroles put in front of him. Minerva's derisive comments about her husband's disregard of his diet were lost in the general clamour.

That afternoon, when lunch with Porter was over, Arthur glimpsed Getulio in the smoking room with some bridge players, then discovered in his cabin that he could telephone Augusta, who, if she was there, would be alone.

'Oh! It's you!' she said, feigning surprise.

'Who else would it be?'

'You have the same voice as Father Griffith.'

'Aren't you and Elizabeth ashamed of corrupting a man of God who has never come across the Devil's children before?'

'But that's exactly the point! He has to be initiated before he sets foot on American soil, where his virtue will face the gravest tests.'

What an actress she was! Yet, faced with an audience of more than three people, she closed up like a sensitive plant and her usually so expressive face, always on the verge of laughter or tears, lost its animation to the point where those who didn't know her felt sorry for Getulio having a sister infinitely less brilliant than he was. By contrast, at the other end of a telephone, staring into someone's eyes across a table, accompanying Arthur on the promenade deck (leaning so heavily on his arm that she almost let herself be carried) she deployed with rare vivacity such an arsenal of seductive wiles that even a man of considerable experience, or one who was merely blasé, rapidly found himself unable to resist her. Arthur did not yet know – and would only understand much later – that the attraction exerted by Augusta was the attraction of danger, a sensation that even a woman as attractive and intelligent as Elizabeth could never offer.

'Arturo, are you there? Who are you dreaming about?'

'You.'

'In broad daylight! Wait … I need to pull the curtains.'

'There aren't any curtains.'

'How do you know?'

'I have the same cabin as you do. We live in a submarine.'

She let out a long sigh, followed by a silence.

'Is there something wrong?'

'I don't think you're serious. What were you doing up on deck with Elizabeth at midnight? Her cap blew off and you didn't even offer to dive in and get it for her.'

'I hesitated for a couple of seconds, then it was too late.'

'I have to go. Getulio's coming back and he'll be furious that I'm talking to you while he's not here.'

'Getulio's playing bridge with three Americans in the smoking room.'

'Not again! Oh my God, he's going to ruin us!'

Was she in the dark, or his accomplice? Uncertainty hovered over the relations between brother and sister (without the least ambiguity being imaginable), yet if, when no external force threatened them, their attitude to each other slid towards indifference, as soon as any sort of peril materialised they displayed the most brazen solidarity.

'The worst thing is, he won't be able to afford a rose for you to wear at dinner every night.'

'I thought of that. Before we left I paid for five roses in advance. And I did the right thing. Do you know, last night I put my rose in water in my toothglass, and first thing this morning it had disappeared. Isn't that extraordinary?'

Her allusion to her rose revived Arthur's confused memory of

45

the previous night and the image returned of the flower pinned to Augusta's blouse that had floated across the darkness of his cabin in a halo and vanished through the partition. Arthur had never believed in dreams and even less in apparitions, yet now these two stories, of the cap and the rose, had opened a void in front of him. Instinct urged him to step back, not to try to understand, to erase everything and put Augusta's visions down to coincidence. Or to fear her the way he had learnt to fear, during the war, a friend of his mother's called Émilie whose visits always preceded the news of someone else dying.

'Arturo, you're not listening to me!'

'Yes, I am.'

'Something's changed in your voice.'

'My throat's hurting.'

'Liar!'

'I've made an important resolution.'

'Tell me.'

'Not over the phone, there might be spies listening in to us. Meet me in the salon. In any case, I hate using the phone. It gives me a sore throat.'

Augusta laughed quietly.

'You don't often say funny things like that. You'd be much better if you were less serious. Arturo-my-love, we can't see each other now. I always sleep for two hours in the afternoon. I'm in bed. In my nightgown.'

'I'm on my way!'

'Getulio will kill you if he finds you. No. Wait for tonight. I'll be at the bar with Elizabeth at six o'clock. Then we'll have dinner. Now hang up and don't call again. I need to sleep.'

*

46

An ocean liner is a prison with imperious timetables, many prohibitions, drip-fed pleasures, a fixed population that goes round and round in circles in the cramped exercise yards, monitored by the stewards, and nowhere to be on your own apart from your cell-like cabin, assuming you are lucky enough not to share it with a stranger of either sex whose particular smell you are unlikely to like. News from the outside world – but does that world still exist beyond the horizon's perfect circle? You very quickly start to doubt it, as soon as you're out of sight of land and the despairing beams of the last lighthouse – is filtered through the on-board newspaper. The captain and his officers make sure that the four pages with their *Queen Mary* masthead mention no shipwrecks and restrict themselves to the mundane ('We have the honour of having on board with us the Count of Thingamajig who is taking up his post at Washington') and the social, some party or a recital by some diva singing for her supper, or in this case her first-class ticket.

The captain is the ship's spiritual leader. At dinner he gathers around him a list of guests who wait to be invited, not as a privilege but as a right, to his table. He is generally of a sportive disposition and over his career as a navigator he has perfected a number of anecdotes to entertain a new audience at each crossing. Unluckily – and fairly frequently – just as the roast is served, a midshipman appears with a whispered message. God's representative at sea frowns, puts down his napkin, and asks his guests to excuse him: he is needed on the bridge. It's nothing serious, but he's not a man to leave important matters to anyone else. He disappears from the dining room, followed by the midshipman, who glances right and left to see if he can spot any good-looking women. The diners left behind experience a mild anxiety. The empty cover is whisked away by the maître d'hôtel himself, who simultaneously asks the guests to move up and fill the gap. No one says the word '*Titanic*' which is in all their minds. There is always some well-informed idiot ready to tell his fellow diners that after a particularly hot summer the Arctic thaw has produced a steep increase in the number of icebergs in the North Atlantic. The rest of the dining room haven't noticed the captain's swift exit and go on talking loudly, suppressing their giggles, calling over each other's heads, but at the top table an oppressive silence falls. The privileged scramble to finish their roast, to say no to cheese and dessert and the glass of champagne – from the captain's own reserve – and disperse to their cabins, taking care not to show any hastiness that might provoke a sudden panic in which they would no longer be the first to save themselves. One man stuffs his pockets with jewellery; his wife dithers, unable to decide between her mink, her cashmere sweaters, and a sable-lined raincoat, finally grabs one at random and hurries out behind her husband to the upper deck, where the silent row of lifeboats sits, lashed under tarpaulins. It's a superb evening. The *Queen Mary* is a picture as she steams ahead in the moonlight, and one can easily imagine her captain – having perfected his exit for whenever his guests are too dreary for words – relaxing in his cabin with the purser, sipping a brandy and water and smoking a Cuban cigar while he listens to something by Bing Crosby on the gramophone.

Arthur was discovering that the liner was really a very big toy for grown-ups. He explored its secrets, stumbling across a companionway that took him down to the deck where he should have been, then climbing back up via B deck, where the Irish priests were reading their newspapers and smoking their pipes. This stratified world was a picture of order, health and peace. From his bridge the captain reigned like an unseen god over a happy subject populace whose only complaint was the quality of the coffee, which was truly ghastly. Modern societies would do well to follow its example, but nobody dares say so.

Walking past the smoking room, Arthur glimpsed Getulio slumped in his chair, his legs extended under the bridge table, alone, the trolley at his side scattered with empty glasses, his face unpleasantly sullen. His fine hands played distractedly with the cards, shuffling, fanning them out, picking them up with the speed of an illusionist, then cutting the deck into two halves that he peeled back and released, pattering together, to shuffle them again. Arthur remembered Getulio's pretended clumsiness with the three other bridge players the night before. The Brazilian's dexterity when he thought no one was watching confirmed Professor Concannon's warning. He was reeling in the dupes. But who could blame him? He was only cheating those who, seeing his feigned amateurishness, were aiming to cheat him. However skilled he was, the risk was no less great. As with all real players, the cards were his drug, and he needed his fix. Arthur put his hand on his shoulder.

'You look more than annoyed.'

'I don't know anything more tedious than playing with idiots who take you for an idiot.'

'You'll get your own back before we get to New York.'

'I damn well hope so! I've lost more than I'd like. And it's madness staying shut up all afternoon with those creeps! I loathe these crossings.'

'You'll get another chance tomorrow.'

'No, really, the whole thing's just ridiculous.'

'Your luck will change.'

'When it doesn't change, it's like a pit in front of you. Don't mention anything to Augusta.'

'Come and stretch your legs on the promenade deck.'

Getulio put on the Inverness cape that made him look so elegant and walked with Arthur to the upper deck, which was deserted at the end of the afternoon. They paced up and down for a good fifteen minutes without speaking. Getulio became breathless. A burning red scar yawned at the horizon. Behind the *Queen Mary* the ocean poured into a chasm of darkness under a long slab of clouds that trapped in their folds the last lingering gleams of daylight.

'Perhaps we'll see the green ray,' Getulio said. 'That would suit me. I've got a wish to make.'

'Do you believe all that?'

'There are things a thousand times more incredible on this earth. Why are we here, at this moment in our lives, you and I, talking to each other like old friends, when two days ago we didn't know each other, we had no reason to have ever met, and we have very few reasons to see each other again after we finish studying at Beresford?'

Arthur was easily hurt. He clenched his teeth, remained silent for at least a minute, allowing Getulio to savour his unfriendly remark, and then, in the most detached tone he could muster, looking out at the horizon, said, 'I feel the same. Our meeting's completely unnatural. Just imagine: one day, someone fingers you as a professional gambler who works the transatlantic liners and you're banned from the tables of every shipping line around the world. Down you go, all the way to hell. You drop out of your studies, while I leave with a degree that helps me get a job in an investment bank. Our paths no longer have any reason to cross at all. Under various assumed names you eke out an existence in Europe's second- and third-rate casinos; I travel in a private jet. Obviously I have you arrested as soon as your overdraft goes over three dollars …'

'You should write novels.'

'What for? We can pay people to do that.'

Getulio gripped him by the shoulders and shook him.

'Fifteen all,' he said. 'I can see why Elizabeth's keen on you. She's ready to eat you up, or for you to eat her up.'

Arthur laughed out loud. By steering him in Elizabeth's direction, Getulio thought he would divert him from his sister.

'The feeling's mutual. She's terrifically attractive, despite the fact that she's not my type.'

'You're hard to please. She's a beauty.'

Arthur decided to keep his thoughts about Elizabeth's beauty to himself. He would never have said that she was beautiful or (if he was feeling worldly) charming. Only one adjective suited her. She was pretty, very pretty, with a sort of prettiness that since the advent of the talkies American cinema had popularised to the point of making it insipid: a profile you couldn't fault in any way, which retained something of the purity of childhood; blond hair that wasn't entirely natural; a slim, warm figure.

'Blast, blast! The sun's set. No green ray for us tonight.'

'You can't win at cards without the green ray?'

'It wasn't cards I had in mind.'

Arthur knew perfectly well, but Augusta's name was not to be mentioned. It was like a sacrament that imposed on the observer a duty to withdraw into the deepest part of himself, to deflect all questioning from outside. Scattered like little seeds, Augusta's voice, the flecks in her eyes, the mischief in her fine features took possession of a man's thoughts and would not let him go. Getulio's arm, which he had left resting on Arthur's shoulders, tempted him to speak but, stiffening, he refrained. On this territory he foresaw that Getulio would for ever be his enemy. If he got too close to Augusta, the brother with the illusionist's fingers would declare war.

'So what did you have in mind?'

Getulio let his arm drop and gripped Arthur's wrist with sudden force.

'What on earth is it you've all got with her?'

'It seems to me that you're not talking about Elizabeth any more,' Arthur said coldly, without attempting to free himself from the Brazilian's grip.

At the liner's bow a grey shadow merged with the ocean and raced at dizzying speed towards the sunset, extinguishing its final blaze. Night still hesitated, confused by the sudden eclipse, not daring to banish the glimmers that lingered to the south and north. The Atlantic's blue-green turned to a grey of molten lead and white crests whipped across the top of the majestic swell, parted with crushing indifference by the impassive *Queen Mary*.

'Don't you think it's an extraordinary invention?'

'The *Queen Mary*? Are you serious? It's like being in Frankenstein's castle. All that gilding, all those chandeliers make me feel sick. It's so common!'

'I'm not talking about the ship, I'm talking about human beings and their 1400 grams of brain who have taken over the world and will one day perhaps take over the solar system too. Don't you feel intoxicated to be one of those conquerors?'

'I must have crossed the Atlantic at least twenty times. I don't enjoy it in the slightest any more. In fact, I couldn't find it more boring. If flying didn't frighten Augusta to death, we'd be there already instead of killing time in this tub, wallowing across this appallingly tedious ocean. No, to answer your question, I'm not a conqueror like you, or like my ancestors. I'm hardly even a survivor. Who's this clown?'

A short, stocky man, made fatter by a canary-yellow tracksuit and wearing a baseball cap, was jogging towards them, breathing noisily, his elbows tucked in. As he passed he greeted them with a 'Hello Arthur!', changed direction and jogged back the way he had come.

'You keep interesting company! Useful, I suppose. The ship's cook?'

Arthur kept him waiting for a second or two, savouring the suspense and his answer.

'No, he's not the cook.'

Getulio spotted the trap.

'I didn't mean to annoy you.'

He had, but he had missed his mark.

'I'll admit it's not quite the done thing to jog around the deck dressed as a canary. Does he wear that tracksuit when he has breakfast with Eisenhower? I wonder.'

'You win. Unless you're having me on.'

'Not in the slightest! That was Allan Dwight Porter. I had lunch with him and his wife Minerva earlier.'

Getulio gripped the handrail and shook it violently.

'I nearly made the gaffe of a lifetime. I was about to ask him who let the canary out of its cage. How do you know him?'

'He knew me before I knew him.'

'Arthur, it seems to me that we've never talked properly. I need to hear what you have to say, and I'm freezing out here. The night is dark, and the bar is ours.'

They arrived at almost the same time as Elizabeth and Augusta, who demanded, 'Where have you *been*, Getulio? I've been looking for you for two hours. I even asked the captain to search the ship, all the way from the bridge to the coal bunkers.'

'It's been some time since transatlantic liners used coal. In any case, I have a right to a bit of freedom while you're having your siesta. There's no secret. I was with my friend Arthur and we

53

were talking about the fabulous powers of human intelligence, were we not, Arthur?'

'Almost exactly.'

For the rest of the voyage, until the *Queen Mary* berthed in New York, the four of them were hardly ever apart. Concannon joined them at the bar, where he stayed while dinner was served, along with the barman, by now resigned to being called Paddy. One morning, seeing Arthur and Porter coming out of the gym together, Getulio managed to get himself introduced. Draped in a lavender-blue dressing gown, Porter, barely civil, said only, 'I knew your father,' and led Arthur away.

'My dear young man, Providence, with its poor sense of justice and almost complete absence of discernment, has nevertheless granted to men a gift whose richness often goes unsuspected by them: friendship. If, sad to relate, they sacrifice that gift on the altar of social or professional ambition, or to vague passing interests or even – more foolishly still – to love, they're cutting themselves off from the best of themselves or, more precisely, from what could make them better men than they are. Criminals know this: their friendships are more important to them than life and death itself, as they like to have tattooed on their chests. These beings, whom you would think abject specimens ready for all manner of depravity, keep hidden in the deepest recesses of their soul – yes, everyone has a soul – an inextinguishable flame, a rushlight that defies time, misfortune, all the vicissitudes of existence. Legend has not raised up Butch Cassidy and the Sundance Kid because they robbed banks under the police's nose, but because their friendship placed them way above your ordinary highwayman. Experience teaches us that the friendship between two men is a lifeline, on condition of course that both possess the same moral outlook ... or lack of moral outlook. Wait ...

let me finish … I'm not talking about just anyone … I did know Getulio Mendosa's father, just after the war. He was Minister for Finance and Economy in Rio, a wonderful job if you wanted to get rich. I brought him a message from President Truman. He had immense charm. He also had no difficulty in accepting the message in question. Was he corrupt? You may well ask. In the Americas everything's a question of degree. Allow me to maintain a little discretion. I prefer to remember his elegance, his lively political intelligence. What then happened probably went unnoticed in Europe: Europeans are weary of South America's revolutions and assassinations; but a very few days after my visit His Excellency Senhor Mendosa was coming out of his splendid house in Ipanema and about to get into his armoured official car to drive to the ministry when "they" opened fire. I say "they" because it's too complicated to be sure which shadowy faction wanted him dead. His children – your friends on this crossing – were standing with their mother on the steps of their villa. The killers turned their weapons towards them, but on their chief's shouted order they made do with emptying their magazines into the poor driver before calmly making their getaway in a van. Mendosa's death traumatised Augusta and her mother for a long time; her mother moved to Geneva, where she's lived for nearly ten years now. Her room in the Hôtel des Bergues has a view of the Rhône and the Île Rousseau: she's passionately admired Jean-Jacques Rousseau since she was a girl. Once a month the general manager takes her to the strongroom and leaves her there, and a little while later she returns to her room carrying an old raffia bag stuffed with louis d'or and bundles of dollar bills wrapped in newspaper. From time to time she drops off a packet tied up with string at reception and asks them to let Getulio know it's there. He turns up from who knows where, borne on the wings of hope, and for a few weeks, maybe even a few months, lives like a prince. When his mother forgets him he plays cards. With positive results, I'm told.'

While he was talking Porter had been leading Arthur down a labyrinth of gangways, ignoring the lifts and climbing the companionways two steps at a time. At his last words the two men found themselves at the entrance to the breakfast room. The maître d'hôtel showed his astonishment with an exaggerated pout, and left his desk to block the doorway with his body. With an irritable hand movement Porter gestured him to move aside.

'I'm sorry, Mr Porter, but I have no tables free.'

'What are you talking about? My wife's there and she's waiting for me.'

The man hesitated, deeply embarrassed.

'Mr Porter, it is customary to dress, even somewhat, for breakfast in the morning.'

Porter, suddenly realising that he had come straight from the gym in his lavender-blue dressing gown, laughed loudly. The maître d'hôtel did not know how to react.

'I do apologise—'

'No need! You have no idea how much pleasure it's given me to see how absent-minded I am. I've always envied the naturally absent-minded. Please sit Mr Morgan at my table. He'll keep my wife company while I put on something decent. Five minutes, no more ...'

Minerva, wearing a sort of red fez on her head that was attached to her jet-black hair with safety pins, merely gave Arthur a nod as he arrived.

'Mr Porter said to me—'

'I don't care what he said to you. I detest talking at breakfast. And above all, no bread on the tablecloth.'

Chunks of pineapple swam in the egg yolk on her plate and she spread mustard on her toast with childish gluttony. A giant Victorian teapot being pushed like a shrine between the tables passed close by them. In the waiter's expansive movement to serve Arthur with tea, his elbow nudged the fez, tilting it dangerously to one side. Minerva, attempting to replace it, patted it, but too briskly, and the fez tipped onto her other ear, taking with it her wig and leaving a very bald temple in view. Failing to notice, she continued to munch her toast and mustard. The diners at the next table had difficulty stifling their giggles. Arthur too found it hard to keep a straight face. Porter's arrival would have put an end to the grotesque sight, had he not been the sort of man to pursue an idea, to examine it from every angle, to extract its very marrow without paying the slightest attention to what was going on around him. If the *Queen Mary* had started to sink he would have carried on discoursing fluently, with the ocean rising around his ankles until his mouth finally filled with water and he could only emit a last tragic gurgle. To find himself so absent-minded that morning at the door to the dining room had filled him with delight. He had never in his life been absent-minded before, and he vividly remembered the irritation of his French mother when she had found him absorbed in one of the many puzzles that preoccupy small children: 'Allan … come on … please try and just think about nothing for a while.' It was impossible. How he had envied absent-minded people throughout his life! Because the mechanism of thought will wear out if it doesn't, at some point, drift off into its own little world.

Arthur avoided looking at Minerva, whose toast, spread

with far too much mustard, had sparked a sneezing fit with disastrous consequences for both her fez and her wig, which it was threatening to dislodge entirely.

'My dear,' Allan Porter said, getting to his feet to pat his wife on the back, 'your hair's in a bad way this morning.'

With a hefty tap on her fez, Minerva finally straightened it.

'I don't approve of personal remarks,' she said acidly.

Undeterred, Porter resumed his reflections on the attractions and advantages of absent-mindedness. He would so much have liked to be a poet, to write poems and 'wander lonely as a cloud'. Poets are absent-minded, aren't they? And if they possess genius people forgive them everything, doubtless because uncultured materialists suspect them of receiving secret messages from the Unknown that only they can decipher. A country has to look after its poets, or at least … if not its poets – that divine gift is unevenly distributed and a number of civilisations have fallen so far behind that they will never catch up – at least, if not its poets, then its pleasure-seekers, who enjoy life to the full and without thought of tomorrow. On condition, obviously, that it possesses an elite with sufficient self-denial to be willing to involve itself in politics and remain in the shadows: a quasi-monastic choice.

'So where would you place Getulio Mendosa?'

'Ah, you've surmised perfectly that his appearance this morning is what prompted my thoughts. I find it impossible to forgive him. He's as intelligent as his father and he ought to be playing an important part in his country's future, but instead he prefers to play cards and squander whatever scraps of fortune his mother puts his way, like a dog with its bone. She might die one day, just like that, without anyone knowing the code for her safe deposit box in Geneva, and then you'd need a thermal lance to get into it, and that only after a ruinous court case. And what if there isn't anything left in the damn box? Men of great gifts who the fairies spoil from the moment they arrive on this earth are often drawn to commit a sort of moral suicide. A very bad example for a young man like you.'

'There weren't any fairy godmothers flitting over my cradle. Just my mother and for a very short time my father, before he was killed in the war. I run fewer risks than Getulio. But I'm very curious to know how you know everything about everybody?'

Minerva, who had not deigned to listen to their conversation, wrinkled her nose.

'There's a smell of fish.'

At the next table a middle-aged English couple were eating kippers.

'You can't tell people they can't eat fish for breakfast.'

'Allan, I know no one so slack as you. To hear you, no one should ever say anything to anyone else. And you've also got ketchup on your collar.'

'I haven't liked ketchup for years. It's more likely to be lipstick.'

'You'd be perfectly capable of something so vile!'

'Sadly not. I'm afraid it's just a dab of blood from where I cut myself shaving.'

'In any case it's of no importance ... I'm going to the promenade deck now to join Philomena.'

Porter drank his tea, lost in thought, his hand still raised. Arthur observed with surprise an unexpected finesse in his ruddy, thickset features. He must have been a charming baby and an attractive man in his prime, despite being short and having probably been completely bald since his thirties. He made use of his baldness: his shining, tanned, elegantly speckled head, framed by a horseshoe of white hair, was impressive. His face had one flaw: lips that were so thin you could hardly see them, a horizontal slit between his nostrils and dimpled chin. That apart, he had a handsome nose and vivid blue eyes that could suddenly, with an angry thought, turn iron-grey. Conscious of having been lost in contemplation for a full minute, Porter smiled with genuine humility.

'Pardon me ... I was just struck by a memory: of a slim, wonderfully attractive girl I met forty years ago with a name that knocked me out: Minerva. Never marry a woman whose name fires your imagination ... but to answer your already distant question: out of the thousand passengers and four hundred men and women of the ship's crew, I know three people: you, Getulio Mendosa, and Professor Concannon, who doubtless set you a deplorable example during this crossing but whose singular personality you'll learn to appreciate when he sobers up at the start of term. Three people. Not many, you'll admit. But Noah's Ark didn't contain many either, and if they didn't manage to save the world – which from a purely spiritual point of view is unsaveable anyway, and doomed to every manner of sin – at least they kept it afloat. Arthur – and you call me Allan from here on in – I shan't hold you up any longer. Go find your friends. Here's my card with my telephone number in Washington. I'll be at Beresford in a month's time for a lecture on disinformation. To debunk it and – as you can guess – to give away the recipe ... I don't think you'll be bored.'

The *Queen Mary* was due in the Hudson at ten o'clock. The previous day Getulio had played a last game with the three Americans, who, becoming over-confident, had let their concentration slip. Arthur stayed for a while to watch the game.

Getulio dealt and shuffled the cards with professional verve. Reassured of the result, Arthur went back to his cabin to pack. He had just started when the phone rang. It was Augusta.

'Where have you been? I've been calling you for ten minutes! Do something for me ... go and see if Getulio's started playing yet.'

'I've just come from there. He's playing.'

'I'm frightened to death. If he loses, we won't even have enough for a cab to the hotel.'

'He won't lose ... Anyway, you've got Elizabeth ...'

'I know ... but in France we already ... Let's just say that, like the fabled ant, she's little given to lending. I'm scared.'

'Do you want me to come?'

There was a silence. She was looking in her dressing-table mirror. He could see her gestures, her hand tousling the hair at her temples, her wet finger smoothing the line of her eyebrows, her tongue flicking across her lips.

'I'm in bed, in my nightdress.'

'Madame Récamier received visitors in her nightdress, reclining on her chaise longue.'

'Listen ... I'm horribly worried ... someone has to hold my hand. But swear to me you won't take advantage of me.'

'With deep regret, I swear.'

'And don't let anyone see you. If a steward or a maid notices you, walk past my door as if nothing's happening and wait five minutes.'

She had pulled the sheet up to her chin, leaving her arms and shoulders bare.

'Did anyone see you?'

'No one saw me.'

'Bring the armchair over, hold my hand, and think as hard as you can, "Sleep, Augusta, sleep."'

She closed her eyes. Arthur openly studied the pure oval of her face, in which only her lips gave away the faint trace of her black and Inca ancestors. Across the olive skin of her cheeks and forehead and over her dark brown eyelids there passed brief shivers, like the ruffled surface of the sea, that reached her lovely shoulders and arms and the hand Arthur was holding. An unfamiliar emotion took hold of him. To take a woman in your arms is to deprive yourself of seeing her, to condemn yourself to know only fragments of her, which your memory will later reassemble like a puzzle to be pieced together from scattered images: her breasts, her mouth, that curving dip at the base of her back, the warmth of her underarms, the palm of her hand that you pressed your lips against. But because she lay in front of him like a statue, turned to stone but for those fluttering tremors beneath her skin, Arthur saw her as he felt he had not seen her before. He no longer saw the delicate figure with her unsteady walk on deck, her balance threatened by the rolling of the ship or the fierce gusts that flew into its gangways when you opened the deck doors into the wind. Instead of an Augusta who had fallen from grace in a world of dreadful, vulgar heaviness, he saw a defenceless woman lying in front of him whose body, as far as he could tell, radiated harmonious well-being. In short, she was *also* infinitely desirable, which was something he had thought very little about since their first meeting. Even more surprising was her rapid and complete descent into sleep, as if just the pressure of Arthur's hand had released a torrent of dreams.

In the minutes that followed, two Augustas occupied Arthur's thoughts: one, the living Augusta who dazzled him and who, he knew perfectly well, whatever happened in future, would mark him for ever; and the other, the almost lifeless Augusta stretched out in front of him, her breath hardly perceptible across her half-opened lips, her body shuddering with those spasms that testify to the ferocity of nightmarish images, the other Augusta who was flying somewhere out in deep space, light years away. Like the shroud a sculptor throws over a still damp statue, the lightly draped sheet outlined her secret contours: her barely rounded stomach, the dip between her thighs, her flattened breasts. Her jugular veins beat at the rhythm of her heart, just beneath the transparent skin of her neck, paler than her face. Arthur leant over this impassive mask, as you would lean over an open book without being able to understand what it is saying. A terrible fear gripped him. Was she about to leave this world, which until this moment, by controlling her revulsion, she had confronted with all the panache of a pure and noble soul? Suddenly the idea that Augusta might die there, right in front of him, because he had heard her cry for help too late, made him throw himself onto her sleeping body. Clasping her in his arms, he would wake her and recall her to earth, drive away the cold that was overtaking her, before she cooled and stiffened for ever.

But instead of an icy body he felt her deliciously warm cheek against his, her exquisitely cool neck against his lips.

A thickly muffled voice murmured, 'You swore. Let me sleep.'

Straightening up, Arthur noticed a half-full glass of water and a box of antidepressants. Romantic compassion overwhelmed him. Nine years after her father's assassination, she was still struggling with the horror of the event, the driver opening the car door, the minister waving to his wife and children standing on the steps, calling, '*Adeus, ate sera!*' and at the word '*sera*' his head exploding like an overripe pomegranate, its pulp and pips splashing the bodywork that had been carefully polished just an hour before.

From close up, a woman's forehead can seem like an impenetrable barrier, behind which are hidden anxieties and amazing acts of courage that take men by surprise. And in their surprise is the source of the fear women so often inspire in men and the reaction that fear brings in its wake, of scorn and cruelty, everything that is most cowardly in the male, faced with the threat of an absolute power that he must nip in the bud if he does not want to be its slave. These things are especially noticeable when a woman, giving herself over to sleep, lets down her defences and becomes a child again, capable of inspiring in the most hardened male an immense and urgent desire to protect her from the world's savagery. Mendosa, the great and powerful Mendosa, who had been widely expected in international circles to be appointed to Brazil's supreme court, believed he had provided everything his loved ones needed to be happy and perhaps even triumphant in his company, with his protective arms around them, hugging his wife to his chest, his hand resting on Augusta's black curls, and Getulio standing at his side, straight-backed, arms folded, his gaze filled with extraordinary defiance in one so young.

Arthur was not making any of this up: on a round table in the middle of the cabin there was a photo in a silver frame, a testament to happier days. In Geneva Mendosa's widow barely remembered him. In Brazil his political colleagues had shared out his influence between them. He remained alive only in Getulio and Augusta's memory. His murderers had overlooked that one eventuality: their crime, and its image, engraved for ever on the retina of a daughter who would never come to terms with it.

Years later, during bouts of exhausting insomnia, Arthur would relive this scene. As so often happens when we dig deep into a memory, in the deluded hope of retrieving some stray detail that will illuminate and complete the puzzle, he began to feel less certain that he was not confusing his regrets and desires with reality. Every young man is a Faust who does not know himself, and if he sells his soul to the Devil it is because he has not yet learnt that the past no longer exists and he has entered into a fool's contract. Later, when he wakes up to the truth, he will have no alternative but to lie to himself, which is generally easier than lying to others. A conversation, a meeting, a split-second image all stay in our minds with details and brightness that would not admit of any doubt if the person who had experienced them, or sometimes even made them happen, did not insist – with disconcerting insincerity, or with obvious truthfulness – that they have no recall of them at all. So in which of our previous lives did we live or dream that memory? In the here and now, no one knows or is willing to say. Yet Arthur could not have invented the surge of happiness that crashed over him when, instead of a body he had thought in a moment of panic was already cold, his cheek, lips and hands encountered Augusta's calm warmth and delicious skin. With the brevity of a lightning flash, and just as blindingly, he knew he would never forget that moment, that no other woman would ever make him feel that particular emotion, unlike the more common experience of joy, unfollowed by anxiety. The memory stopped short then, and Arthur could not have said how long he held Augusta's sleeping body in his arms: a second, a minute, an hour? Most likely a second, for he could still hear the voice that said, 'You swore. Let me sleep,' as the cabin door opened and a shocked Elizabeth cried, '*Arthur!* Arthur, leave her alone!' while he, on his knees, watched Augusta bury her face in her hands and turn over, curling up in her bunk with her face to the wall, motionless and wrapped tightly in the sheet that was twisted like a straitjacket around her shoulders. The strangest part of the scene, however, was what happened next, when Arthur, despite his strength, found himself on the receiving end of Elizabeth's fury as she grabbed his hair, dragged him onto his back, and proceeded to kick him energetically and repeatedly in the ribs. Later, when they were able to laugh about it, she insisted she only remembered a single kick and countered by accusing him of tripping her up and sending her flying onto the cabin floor, knocking her half unconscious by the corner of the dressing table. Meanwhile Augusta slept, in another world far away, and his fight with Elizabeth was brought to a sudden halt when they noticed that in turning towards the wall Augusta had uncovered her bottom half and revealed to both of them the sight not of what was most secret but what was most delicious: the dip at the base of her spine, the shaded crack between her generously rounded buttocks that continued into her neatly joined thighs, the pale creases at the backs of her knees, and her feet, which were warmed by a pair of Mickey Mouse-patterned socks. Nothing could have looked less like the sophisticated creature muffled in a coypu coat and cloche hat pulled down to her eyes, who had clung to Getulio's arm on the promenade deck. It could not be the same woman, and Arthur believed it was a hallucination until Elizabeth rushed to the bed and pulled the sheet over her to cover her.

'She's crazy! Two pills after lunch! She's not supposed to have more than one a day. She's scared Getulio will lose. Why can't she get it into her head that he never loses? Arthur, you're a brute! I could have fractured my skull. What did you think you were doing?'

'Don't tell me it's my fault.'

'So what on earth were you doing here?'

'She phoned me. She wanted me to hold her hand—'

'Yes, her *hand*. Don't you see that in this state anyone could rape her and she wouldn't notice? Oh Arthur, I can't keep watching over her all the time! I've got my own life and I need to do something with it; I don't just want to be an idiot sitting on a fortune and looking like a dummy.'

'Looking like a dummy ...' The scene ended there. What followed was unimportant, not worth dwelling on years later. Elizabeth had a bump on her head, Arthur a bruised stomach. Getulio more than made good the losses of his first few days. He appeared at dinner looking bad-tempered, followed by Augusta in a white gown, a rose pinned between her breasts. As they walked to their table a hush fell in the dining room. Getulio enjoyed the attention. Arthur picked up several whispered comments.

'Handsome couple.'

'They aren't married.'

'Obviously not, they're brother and sister.'

'There's definitely a dose of black or Inca blood there.'

'They're father and daughter.'

To which Elizabeth replied, with a sweetly sarcastic smile, 'That's right. He had her when he was five. Brazilians get their first boners when they're awfully young.'

Arthur pulled her away. Professor Concannon joined them. He had not yet reached that distant frontier beyond which he became incomprehensible. It was always a surprise to see how at a certain moment a single glass would propel him over that ideal limit to a place where his power of speech was no longer reliable, but short of that point, what a marvellous chatterbox!

Had he not, since the start of the crossing, written a whole class on the political consequences of Montcalm's crushing defeat of the English at Quebec in 1759 and his appointment by Louis XV to the title of viceroy of Canada? In 1791 Louis XVI had wisely decided not to follow the advice of the traitor Fersen and, instead of fleeing via Varennes, gone in the opposite direction and taken ship for Canada at Brest. Montcalm was seventy-nine years old; he had relinquished his powers as viceroy and Louis XVI, in an unstoppable assault, had swept the French troops forward and kicked out of North America the only enemy France had ever had, Great Britain. Voltaire, in a pathetic *mea culpa*, had beaten his chest, regretted his unfortunate phrase about 'a few acres of snow', and composed a long, pompous poem to the glory of those acres.

Arthur interrupted him. 'If my information is correct, Voltaire had been dead for thirteen years when Louis XVI stepped onto Canadian soil ...'

At this hour Concannon was no longer a man to be halted by mere facts. He dismissed Arthur with a wave of his hand.

What did Augusta think? She was certainly listening. There was merriment in her eyes, an amused smile on her lips, perhaps even a hint of indulgence, as though, already familiar with this speech, she accepted out of compassion for the charming and inventive drunk in front of her that he should go back to it, embellish it and, borne along by the enjoyment and goodwill of his young audience, supply an unceasing stream of new chapters pouring forth from his delirious imagination. Arthur followed the story intermittently, his attention repeatedly distracted by Augusta, sitting bolt upright on her chair like a perfect pupil, chin up, making sure with a nod to the waiter that everyone's glass remained full and that when dinner was over champagne was served in flutes that bore the Cunard crest. Their eyes met again and again. She did not blink. Drowning in her gaze, shot through with flashes of mischief, Arthur was unable to reconcile his two images of Augusta: the glamorous creature who dominated the evening by her grace more than her exotic beauty and the other, pathetic creature who that afternoon had been stuffing herself with antidepressants to calm her fears. The natural, not to say guileless, way she had come back from that imaginary journey was profoundly baffling to him. She watched him move his lips in a clumsy and unsuccessful attempt to hear his own voice and reassure himself that dinner was real, and leant over to him to murmur in his ear, 'Don't you like my dress?'

'I never said that! I like white. White is for the ghosts who come back to haunt us.'

'I always come back.'

As she spoke, Getulio was noisily rejecting the emblem of the Bourbons. The House of Braganza had repulsed the king of Canada and conquered North America.

'Wrong, quite wrong!' Concannon cried in a scandalised voice, pointing his finger at the offending pupil. 'How can you forget the battle of September 1870? Unable to contain themselves at the spectacle of war being declared in Europe between France and Germany, two fraternal nations, ten million South Americans lay siege to the North, defended by three million North Americans. The two armies face each other across a perfect line bisecting the isthmus of Panama along the present-day path of the canal. The southerners, armed only with their machetes, are wiped out by their enemy's bullets. The northerners do not enjoy their victory for long: mired in the swamps, eaten alive by mosquitoes, they fall in their hundreds of thousands. Dawn rises over a charnel house.'

Concannon extended his arm, his transparent flat hand describing to his listeners the jumbled, billowing semicircle of piled-up corpses, disembowelled horses, overturned gun carriages and exploded cannons, their yawning muzzles releasing their final wisps of smoke. His audience was there, in the thick of it. However, he skated over the barking of the coyotes attracted by the stench of dead bodies and caked blood, and the sinister chuckling of the vultures as they tore indiscriminately at the flesh of northerners and southerners alike.

'Capitalising on the shock and horror of the few survivors, the oppressed of the continent rise up, in the North as in the South: Incas, Aztecs, Olmecs form alliances with Sioux, Comanches, Mohicans. They massacre the black slaves or pack them off back to Africa. Very few reach their destination. Meanwhile the Indians of both Americas impregnate the forsaken white widows and found the greatest mixed-race nation on the planet. Can't you see by my bright-red complexion that I'm the son of a Sioux? Like you, Getulio and Augusta, are little Incas.'

'I rather thought we – you and I – were descendants of Irish pioneers,' Elizabeth said.

Concannon was brusque.

'It's one and the same! No thank you, no champagne. Carminative drinks don't agree with me. We'll move straight on to Armagnac if you'll be so kind.'

The frontier was approaching. As they left the table Concannon, staggering slightly, held on to Augusta's arm.

'You four go and dance. Dancing's your thing. I'm thirty years too old to come with you. I was a great dancer once ... back then. Think of the day when that will happen to you. Most importantly, I have an unfinished conversation of the greatest possible interest to wrap up with my friend Paddy at the bar. A very interesting fellow when all's said and done, a sort of primitive intelligence. His uncharted brain is ideal territory for me to sow new ideas, which thrive admirably … I shall see you in the morning, my child.'

Five musicians in dinner jackets glossy with age were onstage, playing jazz tunes from before the war. Blissfully happy women, a whisker beyond middle age and held at a perfect arm's length by their partners, dreamt that nothing had changed since 1939: the same musicians, same tunes, same husbands. With an indulgence it usually refused to show, time had stopped. Six days on board the *Queen Mary* were six days out of time. Sheer fun. In the final reckoning they didn't count. And what if we made everything go back to what it had been? What if that handsome Englishman over there, the one whose wife is holding him by the hand and a shoulder from which there hangs an empty sleeve, what if we gave him back his arm, lost in the landings in Normandy? What if we gave that one back the leg that was torn off at Guadalcanal, Minerva her luxuriant black hair that fell out after a tropical fever, her husband his slim midshipman's figure? They might be dancing for the last time on this liner with its reassuring decor, its triumphant Art Deco style that made everything for ever young. After the great conflagration, the world in which they had lived before resumed its old rhythm, as if it had never tottered. The trumpeter who had once blown his horn almost hard enough to burst a blood vessel in the line's early days, when the Cunarder had competed so fiercely for the Blue Riband with the *Normandie*, that same trumpeter, his hair now snowy white and his lips swollen from years of playing, was back onstage, impersonating

Louis Armstrong all over again. Peace reigned: the captain inspired the same respect as God; society was divided into three classes: the chosen on A deck; the philosophical on B deck; the huddled masses on C deck who waited their turn impatiently, but feared the captain's iron rule. The passengers could sleep easy. The revolution was not coming. Augusta danced with Arthur.

'Will you come and see me in New York?'

'As soon as I've made myself a bit of pocket money. Won't you come to Beresford?'

The band struck up an old tune, 'Cheek to Cheek'. He tried to press his cheek to hers.

'Getulio's looking,' she said.

As she left the dance floor she unpinned the rose from her gown and slipped it into Arthur's pocket.

He asked Elizabeth to dance, a number so slow that she almost fell asleep in his arms. Suddenly she woke up.

'I expect it's already too late … But if you find yourself idealising her too much, just remember the Mickey Mouse socks.'

The classic picture of the young immigrant in a black, too-tight suit, a shirt with crumpled collar, shiny tie, shoes too often mended, cardboard suitcase at his feet, standing alone on the quay by the Hudson, looking crushed by his first glimpse of skyscrapers that, after six days at sea, make him so dizzy he hardly dares look at them, dazed by the boom of the city that rumbles endlessly on above ground and deep in its entrails – that classic picture, capable of softening the hardest heart, is not entirely false. Apart from the fact that the suit is neither black nor too tight, the shirt and collar are immaculate, the shoes new, and a heavy officer's trunk, on which the capital letters are still legible — CAPT. MORGAN, I COMPANY, IST BATTALION, 152ND INFANTRY REGIMENT — has replaced the cardboard suitcase. It no longer belongs, of course, to the captain whose body, riddled with pieces of shrapnel, has lain since 1944 in the military cemetery at Colmar, but to his son, Arthur, disembarking from the *Queen Mary* in a crush of passengers and a tumult of shouts, hugs, porters' cries and yellow-cab drivers' exasperated yells to move out of the way. The image is not false, insofar as the young man, finally disembarking on this foreign shore, has lost sight in the crowd of those friendly faces that for the duration of the crossing helped him painlessly to cut the umbilical cord that attached him to Europe. He is alone. He is not about to climb to the top of the Empire State Building, thrust his chest out, and shout, 'New York, here I come!' Such is not his ambition, and in any case he has, in the space of a few minutes, realised that this country, so often described to him as a paradise, is also the anteroom of a hell devised by human beings. A grey limousine with blacked-out windows stops a few metres away from him. A uniformed black chauffeur and a young man in a teal-blue suit get out, hurry over to a pile of luggage, and load the cases into the trunk. Allan and Minerva Porter materialise out of the crowd, shake hands with the young man and the chauffeur, and disappear into the car, which everyone makes way for. Professor Concannon has also vanished, as have Augusta, Elizabeth and Getulio. At the fourth attempt Arthur succeeds in persuading a cab to take his trunk and drive him to Grand Central Station. He sees no more than a glimpse of the city. Is this really New York, its streets cratered with ruts, its crumbling buildings blanketed with soot, a station that looks like a cathedral, a grimy Boston-bound train that immediately dives into a tunnel? He has seen nothing. He hears

Augusta's voice saying, 'Will you come and see me in New York?'
In his pocket he has Elizabeth's address and the number for Allan
Porter's direct line. Getulio will be getting back to Beresford by
road, at the wheel of an old but very elegant car, a 1930 Cord.
The previous evening, Arthur had decided not to wait for him.
His liking for the Brazilian is as qualified as the latter's liking for
him. They are going to be mixing with each other and Arthur
can already foresee that it will not be easy. There is Augusta, plus
the floating shadow of Elizabeth: is she, will she be, has she ever
been Getulio's lover? At last, emerging from the endless suburbs,
the train rolls on into woods, skirting lovely villages of white-
painted clapboard houses with blue roofs. A train that runs as
smoothly as this opens the door to unruly reveries. Arthur has
Augusta's rose in an envelope. The petals are falling off, already
wilted and curled up.

'You must separate them, then slip them between the pages
of a book you won't be opening for a year or two,' says a hoarse
voice close to him.

On the seat on the other side of the carriage, an old woman
with white doll's hair lights her cigarette with a soldier's lighter.

'I've kept dozens in my life,' she says, blowing out a small
cloud of blue smoke. 'Perfect. Never a problem. Do you like
roses?'

'I like *a* rose.'

'When you pick a rose to give it to a woman for her buttonhole,
you must be careful to remove the thorns without damaging
the stem. If you don't, the woman – I say "woman" if it's a red
rose, because of course if it's a white rose I'd say "girl" – the
woman will prick herself and panic. You'll see a look of profound
irritation on her face and your plan coming to nothing. You'll
sweep her finger to your lips to stop the bleeding. She'll see that
as a lewd invitation – which it might well be – and cry rape.

You'll be arrested, and you'll get ten years in prison and a one-hundred-thousand-dollar fine. Don't say I didn't warn you.'

She rummaged in a huge carpet bag, pulling out empty cigarette packets, a packet of sanitary napkins, two dirty handkerchiefs, and an alarm pistol, before laying her hands on what she was looking for: a small book with a rainbow-coloured cover.

'These are my poems, *Roses For Ever*. You can give them to your friend.'

The train slowed. She put everything else back in her bag, placed a fur hat on her head and, turning to Arthur with a wide smile that deformed a mouth seamed with vertical wrinkles, said, 'That's five dollars.'

'What's five dollars?'

'The book you just bought.'

'I haven't bought anything.'

He slid the booklet back into her bag as the train braked. She nearly fell, grabbing the back of her seat just in time.

'I never saw anyone so badly raised in all my life,' she said with towering scorn, proudly jerking her chin upwards to show him how wrong he was, that she was not just anybody but a poet of renown.

A fat man in whose way she was standing threw a disapproving look at the young man taking refuge in his corner, his forehead against the window, minutely studying the platform and the few travellers alighting on it. The old woman appeared on the other side of the window, straight-backed in her high heels, her fur hat aslant. With her umbrella she struck the window and shouted something Arthur did not understand. The train began to move again.

'Maybe she'll have more luck with the next guy,' a male voice said ironically.

Arthur turned round. On the seat behind him a man in his fifties, with grey hair plastered to his forehead in a fringe and a cheerful face emphasised by a clipped, very white beard, was reading a newspaper he was holding at arm's length.

'You mean she's a trickster?'

The man put his newspaper on his knees and folded it with the flat of his gloved hand.

'A hard word, but that's about the size of it!'

'I've just got here, and I've had the shock of my life; I mean, I've just got off the *Queen Mary* ... I'm French—'

'I can tell.'

'Does she often pull that trick?'

'Every journey she manages to sell one or two copies of her poems, self-published.'

'Are they any good?'

'I've read worse.'

'Did you buy them?'

'Yes ... having refused two or three times ... Out of curiosity. I had a five-dollar bill in my pocket ... I guess you're going to Beresford.'

'Are you?'

'No, I'm long past that age, but I studied there thirty years ago. My son's been there since last year. You're bound to meet him: his name's John, John Macomber. More a sportsman than an intellectual.'

With a smile he picked up his paper again. By the time they reached Boston night was falling. A small bus with a sign saying 'Beresford University' was waiting at the station exit. Ten or so students got on. The driver said he had backache and was unable to lift the trunk onto the roof. Two strapping-looking boys in blue blazers and grey trousers hoisted it like a feather and tossed it carelessly up among the other luggage.

76

An hour later Arthur was unpacking in the small bedroom of the fraternity house where he would spend three years of his life. There was a bed, wardrobe, table, two shelves, a gloomy overhead light, a bedside lamp and, framed and screwed to the door, a list of regulations. He learnt fast – from Getulio first – how to get round them. He identified John Macomber and decided that that excellent football player had not inherited his father's sense of humour. They met in the mornings on the cinder track at the stadium. Arthur signed up to train for the 3,000 metres. He had no intention of taking part in any events but he felt the distance, without overstretching him, suited his physique and heart rate. John Macomber trained at sprint starts, short sprints, and forward rolls. When they met, they slapped palms together and grinned at each other without speaking. Getulio sometimes joined them. Nature had blessed him with the long legs of an 800-metre runner. A hundred metres from the finish he would drop his arms and walk along the verge to the bag that contained his gear, drape a towel around his neck with perfect elegance and stroll back to the changing room, dragging his feet.

'Those last hundred metres ... I'll never do it. It's so stupid, they should just set up a 700-metre race instead!'

'You should send a letter of complaint to the Olympic Committee.'

It was a shame: he had a fine stride, his pulse rate was below sixty, his lungs remained good despite the cigarettes and alcohol. The truth was that being at the track quickly bored him, just as he got bored during classes, where his memory astonished everyone and his indolence drove his teachers to despair. Card-playing was forbidden, but inspections were rare, so he made himself enough pocket money to pay for the garaging and petrol of his superb red and white 1930 Cord.

'I bought it because of Augusta. Red like her rose and white like the blouses she wears in the evening. I have no intention of going unnoticed.'

Allan Porter gave a lecture at the beginning of November. A handful of students were invited. Faculty and other university staff and several teachers who had come out from Boston filled the lecture theatre well before the start. Arthur recognised the young man in the teal-blue suit who had opened the limousine's doors for Minerva and Allan on the quayside. A holster bulged obviously under the left side of his jacket.

'I met Mr Porter on the *Queen Mary*. He particularly asked me to come to the lecture. It looks as though it might be full. My name's Morgan, Arthur Morgan.'

'I'll look into it straight away, Mr Morgan. If you wouldn't mind waiting in the hall.'

A few minutes later he returned and led Arthur to a reserved seat in the front row among the distinguished guests and university authorities. To his discomfort, he then had to endure their appraising looks and whispers. All of them surely knew far more than he did about Allan Porter, whose arrival on the platform the audience greeted by rising to its feet. Porter had lost his tan and possibly a few kilos. Arthur regretted that he was not gracing this stiff academic occasion in his canary-yellow tracksuit. It would have added piquancy to his lecture, which to begin with was dry but took flight when he began to go into detail, dismantling the mechanisms of several campaigns of disinformation, the first being that of the Wehrmacht's intelligence service before the outbreak of war. The Germans, feigning clumsiness and incompetence, had succeeded in convincing Stalin that his general staff was betraying him, prompting the Paternal Genius of the Soviet peoples to purge the Red Army vigorously, first executing Marshal Tukhachevsky, followed by twenty generals, then another thirty-five thousand senior and junior officers. Decapitated and robbed of its best technicians, the weakened Red Army had been almost annihilated in 1941 at the launch of Operation Barbarossa. The Allies had shown similar skill in 1944 when they had convinced Rommel and Keitel that a planned invasion force would land in the Pas de Calais area, so the two field marshals had diverted their divisions there, leaving the Cotentin peninsula exposed. Since the hostilities had ended, the KGB had learnt its lesson and was now instigating wave after wave of disinformation, especially in intellectual and academic circles, and successfully discrediting anyone who spoke out against Stalin's dictatorship, the Soviet gulag, or Communist imperialism.

Concluding, Porter paused, and asked if anyone in the audience had a question they would like to ask. There was the usual moment's shuffling and murmuring, then from the back of the hall a deep, aggressive voice said, 'The speaker would strengthen his argument if he were to offer us some equivalent examples of political disinformation by the United States in the Cold War era.'

'May I at least see whom I'm addressing, sir?'

'No. I'll identify myself when I've heard your answer.'

A gleam of lively amusement appeared in Porter's eyes, as though he might have cried, 'At last!' had he not been afraid of offending an audience that had been remarkably passive up till then. Of course he had an answer! It went right back to the Founding Fathers of the American nation. The President of the United States swears on the Bible to respect and defend the Constitution. His vow is a religious act that establishes a theocracy. American political life is carried on under God's protection, a God who will not tolerate untruth.

It was impossible to discern the irony that Arthur suspected beneath these emollient words, so manifestly intended to confuse the issue. Fortunately the speaker at the back of the room was not satisfied and his baritone made itself heard again.

'Don't make me laugh!'

Not in the least put out, Porter looked suddenly inspired, eyes raised towards heaven, as he said, 'Don't be surprised, then, if I make myself chuckle too. Think, my invisible interlocutor, of the United States as an empire. Oh, not an empire in the classical sense of having territories in every corner of the earth. No: we were a colony of the British Crown and we don't like colonial powers, but our empire is not territorial. It is the empire of the dollar. Can you imagine the covetousness that inspires in the rest of the world? We must therefore defend ourselves, using methods that the puritanical ethic of our government would disapprove of, but imposed by factual necessity. It's never hard for a state to recruit technicians who can organise a coup d'état or train guerrillas, or specialists who know how to foment corruption or disinformation ...'

At these words, Arthur felt Porter's gaze lingering on him.

'... it is clear that these purely defensive operations must be entrusted to men or women who are prepared to sacrifice their eternal salvation to their love of their country. And are also ready to be disowned in the case of a failure or the discovery of their operation. They are the scapegoats who save the face of the people's elected representatives. They can be thrown in jail, they can even be shot, but they will not disclose the names or the plans of their principals. They have a conception of praxis that is infinitely superior to that of civil servants and find it right and proper, in certain cases, to perjure themselves in court. In fact, let me tell you that these individuals belong to a new order of chivalry of which the world has need to preserve its balance. Would you like a list of their names, accompanied by their addresses? In strictest confidence, of course, and not to be passed on to the KGB.'

'The USSR would not hesitate to reciprocate such a generous gesture, and the Cold War would come to a rapid end.'

Porter jubilantly threw his arms wide to clasp to his bosom the enemies of yesterday who had suddenly become the brothers of today, calling on the audience as witnesses with disarming casuistry.

'You see how simple everything is! And no one, not in Washington or Peking or Moscow, has thought of it. Sir, I shall inform President Eisenhower straight away of your generous suggestion. Usually he is none too keen that I bring up politics with him; it's a subject that lacks gravity for a retired military man, but I don't rule out, over a round of golf, persuading him to hear the voice of reason.'

'Bullshit!' the questioner shouted, an African American who by now had clambered up on his chair and was being applauded by the other students.

'B–S–in–deed!' Porter joyfully responded.

Satisfied to have won his argument by laughter, he was collecting his notes when another student who had climbed onto his chair in turn, applauded by those around him, shouted with a definite edge to his voice: 'Mr Porter, aren't you yourself one of those godless and lawless men, ready to cast aside all morals in the name of the supposedly higher interests of the state? You're an alumnus of Beresford, you had a distinguished war in the

Pacific and then in Europe, and now you're rumoured to be the Père Joseph of the President of the United States—'

'You mean the guy who does his dirty work for him?' Porter exclaimed, a broad grin lighting up his round features. 'Allow me, incidentally, to congratulate you on your knowledge of Père Joseph, which appears to show a genuine understanding of French history, for which we Americans have so little aptitude. Well, to be perfectly frank I would have loved to be another Père Joseph in my youth, but sadly the United States had no Cardinal Richelieu. However, I fear we're going off on historical comparisons that despite your professors' great skills lie beyond your current knowledge. We'll have to come back to that later in the year.'

The audience laughed and broke into applause. The speaker slipped his notes into a leather folder which the young man in the teal-blue suit took from him respectfully.

Arthur did not meet Porter after the lecture. He was borne away by several professors who had no wish to see more questions from the floor turn the occasion into a political meeting. He had dinner with the dean and a few members of staff chosen from among the rare Republicans at a university known for its Democratic tendencies. Arthur regretted not having been able to exchange a few words, but the intervention of the athletic young man in the teal-blue suit and his seat in the front row reassured him that Porter had remembered him and intended to maintain their acquaintance. All in good time. The first term was already half over. However fluent his English was, Arthur sometimes felt lost. An entirely new language had come into being on this side of the Atlantic, and he had to assimilate its rambunctious vocabulary, its elisions and simplified grammar, and often its spelling. In the evenings he closeted himself away to fill in the gaps. The evening after the lecture, he was in his room when there was a heavy knock at his door. Concannon was leaning against the doorway, his face flushed, glassy-eyed.

'May I come in?'

'You bet! But I can only offer you coffee.'

Concannon shrugged. He had not come for a social call. Arthur plugged in his kettle and the professor sat heavily on the edge of his bed, his embarrassing, oddly glazed-looking hands palm up on his thighs.

A rumour had been going the rounds at Beresford since the start of the school year that Concannon was going downhill. For twenty summers he had been coming back from his vacations in Europe, and every fall he had pulled himself together and delivered a dazzling series of classes in modern history. But this year he seemed unable to get a grip on himself. As the weeks passed he had got worse. Gripping the lectern as if it were a life raft, his head wobbling, he would stretch out a trembling hand to the water jug and miss his glass; asking the class to excuse him for a moment, he would go outside and, without embarrassment, empty his bladder on the lawn outside the lecture theatre. It was reported that one afternoon, after yawning repeatedly, he had told his students, 'This class is so dull that you'll excuse me if I take a short nap. Wake me up when it gets interesting.' Two porters had carried him back to his room. In the close world of a university like Beresford, news circulates too quickly for such a situation to be hushed up. Concannon would not be sacked, but he was to be sent to a rehabilitation clinic and when he came back his post would be filled. The teaching staff, predictably, did not care for him; the students, however, adored him and continued to do their best to protect him both from himself and others. Unsuccessfully, it seemed: he looked unlikely to be coming back the following term.

Arthur offered him a cup of coffee, warning him that it was hot. Concannon carefully wrapped a cotton handkerchief around the cup, picked it up in both hands, and lifted it to his lips.

'Wait!' Arthur repeated.

'I can't tell the difference between hot and cold any more.'

He drank most of the coffee in a single swallow. His complexion, already more red than pink, turned crimson and Arthur was afraid he might have a heart attack.

'That's very good,' he said. 'Kills the bugs ... You have to ... They're everywhere ... everywhere ...'

'You should come for a morning run with me on the cinder track. Nothing like it for getting rid of the bugs.'

'By far the best way is to drown them before they learn to swim. But I interrupted you. You're working. You're an intelligent, ambitious lad. It's a wonderful thing, ambition ... You'll succeed ...'

Arthur had a strong hunch that Concannon had not just come to pay him compliments.

'You really don't have anything to drink?'

Arthur pointed at the framed regulations on the back of the door. Concannon shrugged.

'That's the theory. There's a big difference between theory and practice. Your pal Getulio Mendosa's worked it out.'

'He could get himself expelled.'

'You don't get expelled for that. Especially if you're as good an advertisement for us as he is. The great Brazilian martyr's son! Our country is charged with a divine mission on this earth ... and

84

a paternalistic one: the education of the sons of kings. You may not be a king's son … but someone saw a coming man in you, a new link to a cohort that will save humanity from the deluge.'

'Someone.'

'You know very well who.'

Invigorated by coffee, Concannon straightened up and began to talk more articulately. He got to his feet, wavered for several seconds, then pointed, without touching it, to the hip pocket of his trousers.

'Do I by any chance have a silver flask in there, filled with miraculous liquor?'

There was nothing in his pocket.

'Is it all that urgent?'

Concannon sat down on Arthur's chair, one elbow leaning on a table heaped with books and papers.

'Urgent? No … Important, yes …' he said, knitting his untidy bushy black eyebrows.

'I'll ask Getulio.'

Along the hall he found Getulio playing poker with John Macomber and two others. Getulio jerked his chin in the direction of the wardrobe. Arthur discovered a flask filled with gin.

'It's for Concannon.'

'I don't think anyone thought it was for you.'

Macomber said, 'You know what? He already had his skinful by six tonight.'

Arthur found the professor sitting in the same place, bending over the photo Arthur always kept in front of him: of St Mark's Square on a luminous day before the war, and a couple holding hands, surrounded by pigeons fluttering around them. The woman was elegant in a provincial way, a little too respectable-looking for her age but charmingly innocent, her face lit up with happiness, dressed in a grey suit, undeniably pretty and above all fresh and regarding her companion admiringly as he offered bread to the pigeons in his open palm.

'You should never touch pigeons. He should have worn gloves. Are they your parents?'

'Nineteen thirty-three. Venice. The classic honeymoon. Apparently I was conceived in the city. I have no memory of the event and I've never been back.'

'Nothing's changed there,' Concannon said, laughing. 'Did you find anything?'

'Some gin.'

'Gin has no mercy. Fortunately I'm made of steel.'

He took two gulps and returned the flask. Arthur screwed the top on and put it out of Concannon's reach. He had not found himself in such an awkward situation before, face to face with a man drowning himself by degrees, a man who was now beyond rescue. And not just any man, but a brilliant contrarian intelligence in a world of conformists, a professor whose lectures, despite their eccentricity – especially because of their eccentricity! – had liberated cohorts of students from their social prejudices and academic assumptions. Physical strength had kept his decline at bay for a long while, but the time had come when, with the saddest demons of all riding on its back, decline was taking its revenge. He was no longer fighting it. He was succumbing. To look at him, you would have sworn that he was enjoying it, that he was ready to greet his own extinction with an enormous gust of laughter. Arthur put a hand on each shoulder and shook him, in the vain hope of bringing him back to earth.

'Why did you come? I can't help you. I don't even know what to say to you.'

Concannon looked up at him out of a stricken face on which

his exhaustion had scored deep, dark lines, like long-standing scars. Whitish lumps had congealed at the corners of his dried lips.

'There is indeed nothing you can say to me, Morgan, but I need to say something to you. Be on your guard.'

'Against who and what?'

'What a foolish mistake it was to let yourself be sat in the front row with all the big shots at Porter's lecture! Everyone assumes that you're his protégé now, some kind of spy from Washington on his payroll. They remember him rooting for your application when they discussed the scholarship.'

'We didn't know each other then.'

Whirling his arm, Concannon dismissed Arthur's feeble protestation.

'What about fate?'

A historian by training, he had stopped believing in logic long ago and drew his scepticism, or, if you prefer, his disillusionment, from the amused observation that for centuries men have gone on attributing to their intelligence, reason, experience and wisdom what is actually the result of capricious happenstance and chance combinations of uncontrollable events.

'There's something else,' Concannon said.

A violent cough made him double up, his whole body shaken with spasms. When he finally raised his head, his eyes were full of water and he had to inhale and exhale several times to catch his breath enough to start speaking again.

'Crisis time!' he said, pulling a paper handkerchief out of his pocket. He blew his nose at length before studying the handkerchief with disgust and throwing it in the waste-paper basket.

'Can I get you another coffee?'

'It's a pity you don't have any Armagnac, or a drop of Calvados.'

'There's gin.'

'No thank you.'

'It would be good for you to go back to your rooms. I'll come with you as far as your door.'

Concannon dug two fingers cautiously into his right-hand jacket pocket and pulled out an envelope that he tossed quickly onto the table. Arthur read his own name, without recognising the handwriting. Doubled up again, the professor appeared determined not to help him, remaining completely absorbed in his elegant Italian shoes. Arthur put out his hand towards the envelope and then, after a hesitation, withdrew it.

'I see what this is about!' Concannon said, in an appallingly hoarse voice. 'You aren't willing to share, are you? One day you too will realise that the only thing a pretty woman wants from a man of my age is to play gooseberry … Can I have another coffee?'

'You won't sleep.'

'Insomnia is the handmaiden of all knowledge.'

What knowledge was he talking about? At this moment, in his present state, doubled up like a broken puppet, knowledge seemed little more than a desperate struggle to connect the fleeting visions that were all that remained of his fine, imaginative intelligence. At last he lifted his head, and Arthur saw a lost expression on his face, as if he had just come back from a long journey round the cosmos. It was an expression of a tragic admission of helplessness.

Arthur cleared a pile of books off a stool and put the cup down.

'I think,' Concannon said, 'I think …'

'What do you think?'

'Oh, you know, it's not really at all important now.'

'I insist.'

He drank his coffee in small sips, then put the cup down so clumsily that it fell off the stool and broke on the bare wooden floor. Arthur was about to squat down to pick up the pieces, but Concannon was quicker, and falling to his knees he swept them up into a handkerchief that he gave to Arthur.

'I'm sorry. I hope it didn't have any sentimental value.'

'Only twenty cents. There's nothing to be sorry about.'

He helped Concannon stand up and, supporting him firmly under the arms, steered him towards the door.

'I'll take you back.'

'No! Twenty years I've been in this shitty university, and you think I don't know my way?'

Just now you said, "I think, I think ..."'

Concannon raised himself to his full height and comically thrust out his broad chest.

'I think ... I think ... in fact, I'm sure that love is a divine punishment ... God hands us over to the Devil ... That's what I think ... I swear it ... It's the truth.'

'I'll take you back.'

'No farther than your front door. I don't want you to know where I'm going.'

'It's a promise.'

A light snowfall was flickering white in the pools of light cast by the lamps along the main avenue.

'A mantle of purity,' Concannon said as they reached the door, after a difficult negotiation of the staircase. 'Why are we condemned to besmirch everything we touch?'

He sat down on the first step, unlaced his shoes and pulled his socks off, comically wiggling his toes.

'For the odd delicate gesture I have made I'll be forgiven much

89

in the final reckoning … I thank you for not warning me that I'll catch cold walking barefoot in the snow. One should always avoid saying pointless things. One more thing … You know, I feel much better after that last coffee … one more thing … it was Augusta who slipped that note into the envelope that's waiting for you on your table. She's afraid that Getulio would recognise her handwriting in the mail … Say, Morgan, aren't you scared of the Devil?'

'No.'

'That's good. Help me stand up.'

Arthur put his hands under Concannon's armpits and hoisted him upright with an exhausting effort. Swaying, Concannon leant against the frame of the door and wagged his finger at Arthur threateningly. 'I forbid – FORBID – you to follow me.' He filled his lungs with air, walked mechanically and hastily down the three steps and started off along the avenue, already covered with a fine sprinkling of snow that was the colour of butter where the lamps cast their cones of light. Arthur gazed after the comical silhouette of the professor hopping joyfully, like a child let out to play, shoes and socks held out in front of him, until he disappeared into a poorly lit area between two rows of houses whose curtains were drawn, their windows letting out only weak glimmers of light.

Augusta wrote: 'Arturo *meu*, think of me. I hope you miss me. See you soon! A.'

A photograph fell out of the envelope. On the back he read, 'This is Augusta Mendosa, aged eighteen, in her youth, three years ago, in Paris, on the Quai des Grands … Augustins (of course). Taken by her brother, a certain Getulio.'

She was still wearing a plait. Behind her, a second-hand bookseller in a blue jacket and Landais beret was leaning into the frame. In the distance were the blurred towers of Notre-Dame. Arthur placed the photo next to the picture of the newly married couple in Venice. The two young women, of course, did not look anything like each other. The face of the new Madame Morgan shone with innocent happiness, while Augusta's showed a put-on cheekiness and the knowledge that behind her a clown-like intruder was trying to get into the picture. Looking at the two of them, Arthur was aware of the infinite distance that separated them; and yet at a particular moment in their life they had felt, if only for a few seconds, the same joy, the joy of being young. Whenever his gaze lingered on the Venice photo, he was gripped by sadness. The young, attractive woman in the picture had known only a brief happiness in her life: it had been less than six years between marriage and the declaration of war. Afterwards she had been left alone with Arthur, too young to protect her or guide her or give her the confidence in life she had sorely lacked. Perhaps worst of all was that, for all the tenderness and passion she showed for her son, she was almost embarrassed when he tried to confide in her. She changed the subject, deflecting his confidences, destroying the intimacy he had hoped for. Even that expression of hers, 'the great and the good', of which she reminded him in every other letter, had become as annoying as it could be. What did she think? That he wouldn't make the most of the opportunity offered by his Beresford scholarship? It showed how little she knew him. He worked hard, harder than the majority of students did, he refused attempts to distract him or get him to go out, and he still knew nothing of the America beyond the university campus. So when she wrote, 'Uncle Eugène is offended that you haven't sent him any news. Remember he's your godfather,' he tore the letter up. What could he say to an old bore who had spent his life behind a bank counter and now, in his eighties, smelling of piss, his grey beard stained with tobacco, sat by his wireless in his slippers listening to brain-rot panel games for twelve hours a day? Or worse still, when his mother kept telling him that 'Our cousin, Sister Marie of the Victory, complains that you don't write to her. When you were little, your letters used to make her laugh till she cried. She would read them to the other nuns, who all enjoyed them, and she would very much like to know what she should think about America.' The thought of all those dear nuns listening thoughtfully as Sister Marie read out his letters at the end of their frugal supper in their glacial refectory decorated only with a Sulpician image of the Holy Virgin above a bouquet of artificial arum lilies, sitting motionless on their hard chairs and nodding their starched headdresses approvingly at the contents of the newspaper or a letter that 'was of interest to the community', the thought paralysed him as soon as, softened by his mother's words, he felt himself about to give in and compose a few lines to send to Sister Marie.

He drew back his curtain a few inches. The snow was still falling. How could he have obeyed Concannon's order so easily and let him go alone out into the night, hopping down the empty avenue, arms spread wide like a tightrope walker? What if the poor man had fallen down? He wouldn't be able to get up. Arthur took the stairs two at a time, and stopped at the front door. The snow was starting to cover Concannon's hesitant steps. He must have walked, legs wide apart, to an asphalted central reservation where the snowflakes melted as soon as they touched the ground. To Arthur's right and left were rows of bungalows, used mostly as accommodation for professors and administrative staff. They were all quiet, already sunk in the night's muffled silence. Arthur could not identify Concannon's bungalow among them. He was about to try to read the names on the doors when the lights on campus went out, as they did every night at midnight. There was snow melting in his hair, a trickle of icy water was running down the back of his neck, and his loafers were filling up with water. Feeling his way in the silent, icy darkness, he managed to get back to the fraternity house, where the door was still open. He walked upstairs; the timer on the light was set so short that students had to run upstairs if they didn't want to be plunged into darkness before they got to the first floor. On the landing, as the light went off, he bumped into Getulio.

'You're soaked!'

'I walked part of the way back with Concannon. It's snowing.'

'Excuse me … I did knock. There was no answer. I took my hip flask. We haven't got anything to drink. It's an amazing game.'

Arthur would have given much to see Getulio's face. 'An amazing game!' – the expression was so unlike him that Arthur was instantly sure he had seen the photo on his table and possibly the short message from his sister too. Sliding his hand along the wall, he eventually found the light switch. Getulio, already several steps away, turned round.

'I also came to tell you that Elizabeth and Augusta will be coming to Beresford for the Thanksgiving dinner and ball. But you almost certainly knew that already from Augusta.'

He vanished into the darkness along the landing. Lost for words, Arthur went back to his room. Augusta's letter lay unfolded on the table, as he had left it, face down. Unless he had shown rare perceptiveness or had an unlikely hunch, Getulio would not have distinguished it from the other sheets of paper lying next to a spiral-bound notebook open at a page half covered in notes. But even allowing for his affected distraction and scorn for everything that did not directly concern him and, by extension, Augusta, his eyes could not have missed the photo leaning against the framed snapshot of the young Morgans on honeymoon in Venice. In the days that followed, he was unable to detect any change in Getulio's attitude towards him.

Protected by the special providence enjoyed by alcoholics, Concannon had not passed out in the snow. His excellent idea of walking barefoot had produced a positive effect on his exhausted body. He got away with nothing worse than painful chilblains, and a couple of days later gave his class with his feet swaddled in straw and newspaper, the most effective remedy, as he explained, discovered by German soldiers pinned down at the siege of Stalingrad. Rumour still had it that his contract would not be renewed the following year, even if he held out till then, which was looking increasingly unlikely, with his inability to stay on the straight and narrow testing the authorities to breaking point. They had so far only refrained from taking action because of his popularity among the students. When his chilblains started to blister and his feet became covered in ulcers, it took three students to lift him onto his chair. After the class, he caught sight of Arthur.

'What a punishment! No ball for me this year. A great loss, as you'll have heard a hundred times, not to have Beresford's best dancer there.'

'No one told me that.'

'I'll be a wallflower.'

'Augusta will bring you glasses of orange juice.'

Concannon rubbed his hand across his face to banish his tiredness. So quietly that Arthur could hardly hear him, he said, 'That would be a dream come true.'

Two hours before the ball, Arthur tried on his dinner jacket. It had been tight during the crossing. Now it looked even tighter.

'My dear chap,' Getulio said when he mentioned the problem, 'it's not your jacket that's shrunk. It's you who've been building yourself up with your 3,000-metre runs every morning. Not forgetting American food, obviously.'

'I look like a removal man in his Sunday best.'

'No big problem. Women love removal men … and lumberjacks. You know, with their famous moans and groans. I'm not joking. Now stop fussing: there's a train full of girls arriving at six o'clock. We'll just have time to meet them and see them to their hotel …'

The 'train full of girls' was a slight exaggeration. Barely a dozen alighted, sisters, cousins and girlfriends who shrieked like parakeets and threw their arms around the necks of the young men who had come to meet them on the university shuttle bus. Arthur and Getulio picked up Elizabeth and Augusta's suitcases and piled them into the Cord. They were sharing a room at the hotel. Getulio and Arthur followed them upstairs, ignoring the desk clerk's protestations.

'They're our sisters, you goddamn pervert!'

Within seconds of their arrival, a shambles reigned. They strewed the contents of their suitcases across two beds, scattering a dozen dresses, twenty sweaters, enough underwear for six months and enough shoes for ten years. Augusta, bursting into tears at a perfume bottle that had spilt in her toilet bag, wanted to ring for the housemaid. There was no housemaid. Augusta vowed on the head of every saint in Bahia that she would not go to the ball but catch the next train back to New York instead. When was the next train? Paying no attention to her, Getulio selected dresses, jewels and shoes for the evening. Inside a few minutes Arthur had learnt more about women than he had in his whole life up to that moment. He felt he was doing the right thing by looking away when they finally started undressing.

'Are you offended?' Augusta asked. 'Or are you scared of girls?'

'Neither.'

'Then please do me up.'

There were still necklaces to be fastened and the red rose to be pinned on, but after its long train journey the rose showed clear signs of fatigue. Another storm of tears nearly followed when stocking seams were found to be awry.

'My bra's shrunk!' Elizabeth wailed.

'Like my dinner jacket.'

'Darling, what do you expect with the breasts you're developing?' Augusta said.

'I know. You have no such problem with *your* bee stings.'

The bra flew into the air and was still hanging from the light fitting when they left to go back to New York. Getulio lolled in an armchair, reading a women's magazine, indifferent in his superior way. Arthur would have liked to display the same offhandedness, but was enjoying himself too much as he learnt that frivolity was a woman's consummate way of charming a man.

The Thanksgiving Day ball was being held in a hall decorated with multicoloured streamers and photographs of the Beresford football team going back to the 1930s. The local police force supplied the band. Tall young men of athletic build – looking slightly less impressive, nevertheless, than in their Michelin Man-style padded football kit – spun their partners around or danced cheek to cheek in a revoltingly sentimental way. The loners pursued anything in a long dress. Without Elizabeth and Augusta's presence the ball would have been unimaginably tedious. They were competed for relentlessly, but were not heartless and kept coming to find Arthur and force him to dance.

'I've got two left feet … go and have fun.'

But Elizabeth dragged him from his chair or the bar, which only served non-alcoholic drinks in a holier-than-thou way that fooled no one, and no one cared anyway, every man having equipped himself with a flask of bourbon or cognac.

'Come on, Arthur, jump in … You're scared of your own shadow. America's for winners! You stamp on people's feet, you don't say sorry. Why didn't Concannon come?'

She pressed her cheek against his, and at the end of each dance planted a furtive kiss on his lips. As the night wore on, the majority of male students, by now seriously tipsy, held their consenting partners ever more closely. Augusta, however, kept Arthur at an unvarying distance. Getulio, hidden behind a potted palm, ran a clandestine bar: bourbon and Coca-Cola, beer, brandy. The band was running out of breath. The trumpeter, crimson in the face, paused in the middle of a number to down a rapid glass of Jack Daniel's. They were only playing slows now. Oarsmen's hands remained glued to the tops of their partners' arched buttocks. Someone opened a French window and icy air gusted into the hall, blowing away the cigarette smoke and the smell of sweat that mingled with the dancers' undistinguished perfumes. There was a brief altercation outside, a student came back with a split lip, and another who had passed out from drink on the stone steps was revived before he froze to death. Augusta gave the signal to leave.

'Let's kill this party, before it kills us.'

'No! … Just a bit longer!' Elizabeth pleaded, entwined with a sociologist who was also a champion swimmer. 'I'm staying! He can see me back to the hotel.'

The sociologist complained loudly that the capitalist system, caring only about profit, did not allow an intellectual to own an automobile.

'You're right!' Elizabeth said. 'It's disgusting. We're going to change all that.'

But Augusta thought their predicament was romantic.

'You can walk back to the hotel with your arms around each other's waists. At the entrance you'll kiss for a long time, but no heavy sighs. Okay? By the light of the moon. I can already see the postcard: moonlight over young love.'

'If you insist on ruining it, I'm going back too,' Elizabeth said crossly. She had, in any case, no intention of finishing her evening with the sociologist.

The band were putting away their instruments. For a few minutes there was an air of unreality, as the lights were switched off one by one. From outside there came the sound of old cars and motorcycles starting up. Getulio gave his leftover bottles of bourbon and brandy to the police band members. As they went outside, icy air clamped their faces like a steel hand, and guests let out ear-splitting shrieks. Getulio's Cord fired up with a scornful rumble. Elizabeth sat next to him, with Augusta behind, next to Arthur, who hugged her to him. She was shivering.

'Why don't you come and spend Christmas week in New York with us? You'll be awfully bored here all on your own.'

In the darkness in the car he could hardly make out her face, but her eyes shone with a cat-like gleam, glinting in the glow of the streetlamps that lined the avenue. Arthur declared proudly that, as he had no money to go on holiday, he had arranged to spend a fortnight with a family in Boston whose son was learning French.

'What?' Augusta whispered. 'Are you really as broke as that?'

'Not quite broke … but nearly!'

Elizabeth, her head on Getulio's shoulder, was humming, 'Oh sweet merry man, Don't leave me …' At reception they persuaded the porter to open the small lounge for them. Getulio pulled a flat silver flask engraved with his initials out of his hip pocket and passed it round. Elizabeth, sitting shamelessly cross-legged, Indian style, threw her head back.

'How lugubrious!' she said. 'Every party ends in a funeral and every time I feel like shooting myself. And what a bunch of hicks! That sociologist wanted me to read Husserl … Getulio, swear you'll never try and lure us into a trap like that again.'

Getulio swore blind, nodding his head vehemently and smoking a fat Cuban cigar whose band he had left on, as Augusta pointed out to him.

'Who do you think you are? Al Capone?'

They had a short, acrimonious exchange in Portuguese. Elizabeth yawned. Arthur struggled to keep the images passing through his mind under control. Augusta was squatting in her armchair, but more modestly than her friend, with her bottom resting on her heels. He said, 'I like your knees.'

Getulio struggled to his feet, teetering, and leant against the mantelpiece beneath which a coal-effect fire was burning.

'I forbid you to make such filthy remarks to my sister!'

'They're not filthy remarks. He likes my knees. Nobody's ever noticed them before he did.'

'Because they're so obvious,' Elizabeth murmured disgustedly.

Getulio took a long swallow from his flask and hiccuped.

'Don't you find it horribly cold?' he said. 'What on earth are we doing here? Tomorrow I'm going to take you all to Rio in my private plane.'

With an unexpected vivacity Augusta uncoiled herself and stood up, her arm outstretched, an accusing index finger pointed at her brother.

'Getulio, you're tight. You don't have a private plane and we're never going back to Rio, as you well know.'

'All right, forget the plane, but why not an ordinary flight with ordinary people?'

'I don't mind you saying what you like when you're drunk, but not that!'

'I have the right to say I want to go back, if I do!'

Augusta, her eyes bright and her mouth tight with anger, grabbed her brother by the lapels of his dinner jacket and shook him furiously before pushing him away. He slumped in an armchair, his head in his hands. Arthur wondered if he was crying.

'This is so tedious!' Elizabeth sighed.

'Arthur, can you drive?' Augusta said.

'Yes.'

'Take him home and put him to bed, and if he resists, knock him out.'

Arthur drove the Cord with a caution he did not know he possessed. Getulio slept with his head out of the car window, muttering to himself, buffeted by icy air. When they reached the fraternity house Arthur had to lift him, then carry him to the washroom and put him in front of a toilet bowl on his knees.

'I don't know how to be sick,' Getulio protested.

'It's time you learnt! Put two fingers down your throat.'

By a happy coincidence, at that moment a half-asleep student in flowery pyjamas arrived and sat in the next cubicle where he released several stinking farts and then defecated with an evident enjoyment which sounded so unrestrained as to be almost sexual. The drifting stench finally made Getulio throw up. The student left, pulling up his pyjama bottoms over his marbled buttocks, and Getulio, still unsteady, got to his feet and leant against Arthur's shoulder.

'Barbarians! We shall teach them to shit with proper shame … Arthur, a great mission awaits. We shall educate America. I'll never forget what you did for me tonight.'

'Yes, you will. I have no illusions about that.'

Lying in his narrow bed, Arthur struggled to prevent images of Elizabeth and Augusta being displaced by the remembered spectacle of Getulio on his knees in front of the toilet bowl. What an emetic and scatological flourish to such a riotously unpredictable evening! Until then the whole thing had been a sort of tongue-in-cheek quadrille, lightened by Elizabeth and Augusta's caprices and careless fancies. Thinking about the two girls, whispering their names to himself, drove away the gloom of Arthur's first term at Beresford. Going back to France in three years' time, clutching a degree that would open doors onto a world that he only understood very vaguely, was not the only thing that mattered, he realised. He felt strongly now just how much he lacked another sort of key, a knowledge that for some was intuitive, for others acquired, of a milieu that was world-weary, careless, and yet often lyrical, and which, if you were not born into it, you could only enter if you were adopted by the elect.

At eight o'clock the next morning he walked into Getulio's room. The Brazilian was still asleep, his complexion pasty, his face hollowed out, breathing shallowly, his dinner jacket in a heap on the floor underneath his underwear, socks and patent-leather shoes. It had all the elements of a realist painting, a still life entitled *After the Party*, down to the empty bottle of white wine next to a dirty toothglass. Arthur shook Getulio, who moaned, turned to the wall, and grumbled, 'Fuck off.'

'You asked me to wake you up. Elizabeth and Augusta are waiting for you.'

'You must be joking.'

Arthur kept shaking him until he consented to have a cold shower, piled a heap of clothes together, and threw them into a suitcase.

'I'll never be able to drive. And we have to be in New York tonight.'

'Elizabeth can drive.'

'Are you trying to rub my nose in it?'

'Yes, I am actually … and not just once but a hundred times over … so you learn how to drink.'

Getulio mumbled something incomprehensible that Arthur, busy opening the window to disperse the ratty smell in the room, decided to ignore. It was snowing. Light flakes swirled in the northerly breeze, melting as soon as they hit the ground.

'It's getting too complicated,' Getulio said. 'The road will be like a skating rink and the girls will start yelling that I'm driving too fast. Come with us; you'll keep them quiet.'

Elizabeth and Augusta were not waiting in the lobby. When they drummed on their door, there was no answer. Augusta opened it eventually, dressed in a nightshirt with a towel wrapped around her head like a turban.

'What on earth's the matter with you? It's too common, being up so early!'

Elizabeth hurled her pillow at them. Arthur pulled the sheet off her and discovered that she slept naked. Unembarrassed, she sat up, laughed and scratched her head.

'Is there a fire?'

'In one!' Getulio said. 'Can't you hear the revolution? It's on its way here now. Thousands of refugees are heading for New York, intending to spend Christmas eating caviar and drinking champagne.'

'Pathetic,' Augusta said, her nightshirt slipping to the floor. 'I have a pretty back, don't I?' she said, not bothering to turn her head.

'Very pretty,' Arthur said, astonished at how free they both were, and almost as surprised that Getulio, who had been so annoyed at his sister showing her knees, was suddenly unconcerned at her showing a stranger her naked back and legs (strong, slightly gypsyish), which contrasted so strikingly with Elizabeth's pale and slender figure.

'Peeping Toms!' Augusta cried, shutting the bathroom door behind her.

'Mad,' was Getulio's only reply as he slumped into an armchair.

When their suitcases were packed and handed to the men, the girls walked downstairs like queens, ignoring the summons of the desk clerk, holding out their bill. Getulio paid. As they were about to get in the car, he held Arthur back.

'Let me have fifty dollars for the gas. I'll pay you back when we get there. The banks are shut this morning.'

Arthur only had twenty dollars to keep him in chocolate bars and bread till Monday. Elizabeth, understanding rapidly, pretended she had forgotten her handbag, put her arm in his and walked back to the hotel. She took a hundred dollars out of her coat pocket.

'Give him this. He won't take it from me if you're there.'

'If he pays me back, where shall I send the money?'

'Don't worry: he'll never pay you back.'

Getulio pretended to find it completely natural that his penniless associate should suddenly have a hundred-dollar bill in his pocket.

'You really don't want to come?' Augusta said, stamping her feet on the pavement.

A gust of misery surged up in Arthur's chest, choking him. He would have given anything to go with them, but he did not have that anything.

Augusta had snowflakes on her eyelashes. As they melted they rolled down her cheeks like tears.

'You think I'm crying, don't you?'

'No, I'd never think that …'

'Getulio will arrange for you to come down for a weekend.'

'I'll start saving.'

Leaning forward to kiss Augusta on the cheek, he held her left hand and pressed her palm with his thumb in the place where her glove left some skin exposed. She responded with a fleeting squeeze back. Elizabeth was more demonstrative, putting her arm around Arthur's neck and planting a kiss on his lips.

'You know that we love you, don't you ... Without any good reason. Fortunately! That's what love is. Completely wild. Irresponsible. You'd better not cheat on us.'

Arthur stood on the pavement until the car was out of sight. A hand waved in the rear windscreen. It was Augusta. Or was he seeing things? The snow was falling more and more thickly.

Thinking about the two girls helped to change his feelings about university life. The memory of his six days on board the *Queen Mary*, of the girls' tumultuous appearance at Beresford and their departure blanketed in snow bound his past and present together, and the two sylphs, blonde and brunette, cheerfully accompanied his days. He could have nursed a thousand regrets at not having been able to go to New York with them, but in fact he had never been so cheerful. His fortnight in Boston with the O'Connor family went by in no time. The O'Connors' touching desire for their fifteen-year-old son to speak French, their curiosity about France, and the aura of respect with which they surrounded Arthur, as if he were a youthful ambassador of a victorious nation rather than one defeated and torn apart by its internal strife: it all conspired to temper his feelings of regret.

When classes restarted in January he immersed himself in work. Getulio was several days late, without explanation, as though worldly powers had unduly detained him in order that he might assist, by his genius, in resolving some problems of intercontinental magnitude. He cultivated such mysteries wilfully, impressing his American fellow students but leaving Arthur cold.

As luck would have it, soon after the beginning of term the

university library asked Arthur to translate a series of recent journal articles. The fee would pay for a weekend in New York. Arthur tackled Getulio, in the hope that he might offer to drive him there. Via a roundabout and confused explanation Getulio revealed that the 1930 Cord was no longer in its garage, but had gone to the breaker's at Christmas. On the return journey to New York after the ball he had fallen asleep. No one had been hurt, and afterwards the three of them had not been able to stop laughing.

'Nothing makes you laugh as much as death when you have a lucky escape from it,' Getulio said. 'It makes you feel like doing it all over again, like a matador with the muleta. We'll take the train, along with the storekeepers. It's amazing what you can hear in a railroad car.'

Getulio's way of living transformed defeats into victories with a touching virtuosity. When he got off the train at Grand Central Station and discovered Augusta was not there to meet him, he remembered that she loathed organ music; and there was the charming old lady with a double chin, dressed in black and with a straw cloche hat crammed on top of her bun, who had been belting it out for twenty years for the benefit of all departing and arriving passengers.

'Bach on a harpsichord, on a flute, piano, violin: Augusta loves him. But on the organ he makes her hysterical. Don't ask me why …'

Arthur was staying at a modest hotel on Lexington Avenue. Having made his disapproval clear, Getulio promised to come by at eight for dinner.

Instead it was Elizabeth who arrived.

'Apparently Augusta isn't well. Nothing serious. Don't make that face! Getulio's staying with her. You're lucky: I'm free tonight.'

Something in her had changed. He could not say exactly what, and perhaps it was only because, wrapped in an old belted raincoat and wearing a military beret, she looked less feminine than she had at Christmas. But at the trattoria she led him to, in the middle of Greenwich Village, he realised that she was offering him a privileged glimpse into her other life. New York was not, for her, a playground for the high-society shenanigans of a spoilt heiress, but the arena for her only real passion, the theatre, which freed her from her oppressive background.

In the first stage of her conversion she had moved from her apartment on 72nd and Fifth and into an apartment above the trattoria where they were eating. The trattoria was a meeting place for many of the Village's artists, which explained how she knew practically everybody at the nearby tables and was kissed a dozen times by new arrivals and as many times by those leaving. For several weeks she had been looking after a handful of unemployed actors and was now looking for a theatre for them that – as she explained at length – would not be a theatre where audience and actors would look at each other mimicking real life, but a space where they would collaborate together in the dramatisation of a play.

Arthur listened carefully to her explanation, which he found not without good sense, despite the revolutionary tinge she gave it.

'And do you know who I'm going to put on first?' she said with a triumphant look.

'No idea.'

'Henry Miller! Henry Miller and Anaïs Nin.'

When he failed to show the requisite enthusiasm Elizabeth went on, with a hint of condescension, 'Oh, I get it! You don't know Miller ... you should be ashamed, you French were the first to publish him. Like James Joyce. And Anaïs Nin, surely you know who she is?'

'I'm afraid not.'

'His lover during his Paris years. She hasn't published much, apart from *House of Incest*. I'm putting on a production that's a dialogue taken from their books. Do they really not mean anything to you?'

'Give me time. I'm discovering your country, I'm a diligent student, and actually quite a boring one. I was brought up on different authors from you, apart from Mark Twain who I reread every year. When does it start?'

'Next month. We rented and converted a loft in the Bowery—'

'Which is not really famous for its intellectuals.'

'That's exactly what we want: to take the theatre to the people.'

A couple stopped on their way out to discuss the sets with Elizabeth. When the woman, who was black, placed her hand on the table, it was extraordinarily fine. The man had his arm around her waist. They did not acknowledge Arthur during the conversation, or as they left.

'It's because you're dressed like a bank clerk: suit, white shirt, blue tie. You don't know how to dress. I wanted to tell you the moment I saw you. Always too neat, with your starched collar, your too-light socks with your dark suit, your ties that are so straight! Liberate yourself. Stop looking like an usher! Follow Getulio's example. No one ever knows what he's going to wear, yet every time he appears he looks like a king. That said, when you come to my show you have to put on all your most disgusting clothes if you don't want to be refused admission. Well, I'm exaggerating slightly, but you get the picture.'

Now she was the way she had been on the boat: acid, cynical, funny, always ready with a cutting remark, and with that ever-present complex that she would never rid herself of. Impossible to live with in the long term, maybe, but very attractive for the space of an evening or a few days away. A hunch, however, told him that the moment had not yet come and he should not force the pace.

'Why did you get your hair cut so short? You look like a lesbian.'

'I had enough of being, you know, the Vassar girl who swings her thick shining hair for a shampoo advert.'

They were finishing dinner when one of the waiters picked up a guitar and began to sing a *canzone napoletana*.

'I suppose they think I'm a tourist,' Arthur said. 'Let's go ... Is there a bar near here?'

'If you can put up with bourbon, my place is better. And you'll get something by Henry Miller to take away.'

She lived in a pretty duplex under the roof. Her bay window looked out onto a scraggy false acacia that was lit by a floodlight at its base, whose cone of blinding white light pushed the surrounding buildings into the shadows.

'Whose idea was that?'

'Mine. Everyone likes it. I switch it off at midnight.'

She poured two bourbons into cups which he suspected her of having chipped deliberately.

'What do you think of my apartment?'

'Where do we sit?'

'On the floor. Progress has abolished couches.'

Poufs and cushions littered the floor, with ashtrays and trays laden with unmatching glasses, an ice bucket, an open turntable, and piles of long-playing records. Three mattresses laid next to each other on the floor and covered in Mexican fabric had to be the bed.

'Yes, right first time: that's where I sleep. When Aunt Helen came to visit, she looked everything over and didn't show any surprise. All she said was, "Well, at least you can't sink any lower."'

Leaning back into a pouf, Elizabeth stared into her cup as if she was looking into a crystal ball.

'I could do without her opinion, but she's one of my trustees, and apart from my monthly allowance I have no funds to put any shows on without her. Since my parents died, she's rarely reined me in, and right now I need her to pay for the cast during rehearsals.'

She might just as well have said 'my cast'. Everything rested on her. From a folder she took out some photos of Henry Miller, Anaïs Nin, and the two actors who would be playing them on stage. Anaïs Nin in person might not have possessed the incendiary beauty of her writing, but the young woman who was to play her was instantly striking, with burning eyes, a small forehead, and a pout of tremendous disgust that dominated the lower half of her face. Arthur saw Miller for the first time in Elizabeth's portrait by Brassaï: his lopsided face, tremendously sensual mouth, superb forehead. Undeniably handsome in his way, and Arthur took an immediate liking to him, a pariah in American literary circles, which were just as closed as those of high society. Elizabeth lent him her two clandestinely imported *Tropics*. They finished the bottle of bourbon, then two cans of lukewarm beer.

'I'd ask you to stay over,' Elizabeth said, 'but I'm dog-tired and George may come back, and in any case he'll be here at the crack of dawn and won't like finding someone else in the apartment.'

Arthur did not ask who George was, and instinctively decided that he was one of those ephemeral men who passed through Elizabeth's life the way he himself would, when the time came. There was no urgency. Elizabeth placed her hands on his shoulders.

'Don't believe half of what Getulio tells you. There was no accident on the road from Beresford to New York. When he parked outside my place to drop me and my cases off, a Cadillac pulled over and a young guy, cigar in his mouth, striped trousers, frock coat, got out holding a chequebook. Bought Getulio's Cord … just like that. For his museum. Getulio pocketed the cheque and that night we went on a spree. He paid a year's rent for Augusta and ordered three suits for himself. Did he pay you back that hundred dollars I gave you?'

'No. But you warned me. I expect it'll be the same story with what I gave him to come down this weekend.'

'Unwise boy!'

'It doesn't cost a fortune and I enjoy being his creditor. Is Augusta really ill?'

Elizabeth stroked his cheek with disarming tenderness.

'It's going to be so hard,' she said, shaking her head with compassion. 'So very hard … But I understand why you feel this way. She's unique. Really unique, whereas women like me are everywhere. If you lose me here, you'll find me in Vienna or Paris or London or Rome, and yes, sure, there'll be some extra detail or a detail missing, a different name, but, generally speaking, the same. So perhaps you can understand why I'm running away from it all by cutting my hair short, living in a loft, putting Henry Miller and Anaïs Nin on stage in an attic in the Bowery where there's nothing but drunks and bums mouldering under the pillars of the elevated subway.'

She kissed him. He went back to his hotel by taxi. Beyond the Village, the city slept.

He waited all the next morning for Getulio, who did not appear. Stupidly he did not know where to look for him, nor where to telephone Elizabeth so that she could give him Getulio's number. If he went back to her apartment he risked putting her in an embarrassing position if he stumbled on the 'George' of the night before. With more courage in the face of defeat than he thought he possessed, Arthur immersed himself in museums and loitered in Central Park and downtown New York until dusk. There was no message for him when he got back. He returned to the trattoria in the Village for dinner, but Elizabeth did not appear, either alone or accompanied. They sat him at a small table by the door where the waiters ignored him. The couple who had talked to Elizabeth the night before – he mainly remembered the young black woman's lovely hand – walked past him without recognising him. The following day, arriving ahead of time at Grand Central Station, he hid himself in one of the front carriages as his sole revenge (Getulio having left him his return ticket). A few seconds before the train pulled out, he saw the Brazilian's scowling face as he ran frantically up the platform from the back of the train, trying to find Arthur. Eventually, as the carriages clattered under the East River, a breathless Getulio, his tie askew and hair all over the place, appeared in the corridor, looking incensed.

'You might have waited on the platform! I looked for you everywhere.'

'I thought you'd be staying with Augusta. How is she? I hope you found someone to replace you at her bedside.'

Getulio paused, not knowing whether to react or pretend he had not heard.

'She's much better this morning, thank you for your concern. Did you get my message at the hotel?'

'I didn't get anything.'

'Truly? That's ridiculous. I called several times, left my telephone number, asked them to put me through. You were never there.'

The truth was that he wanted Arthur to feel guilty for not having stayed next to the telephone and having been so careless in matters of friendship. Several times he harked back to the extraordinary set of circumstances that had kept them apart during their short visit, preventing the Frenchman from seeing Augusta. She had been in tears about it, would you believe? Oh, not much, just the odd tear or two that wash away a sorrow. The conductor came by. Getulio delved in one pocket after another with mounting anxiety.

'My ticket! I lost my ticket!'

Arthur pulled both tickets out of his pocket.

'Fortunately I think of everything.'

From today, he had decided, he would make Getulio suffer. For a week after they got back he did his best to avoid him, and he only came into contact with him because they had to sit the same exam. Getulio, having spent several – very profitable – nights playing poker, had no memory whatsoever of the lecture on the Rome–Berlin axis. Arthur, with princely magnanimity, or perhaps delighted to score a point, gave him the key dates and an essay plan. The plan backfired when the results were announced and the professor held up Getulio's essay at length as a model. Its merit was all the greater, apparently, because he had lived through the war at a very great distance from where it was happening. The

113

essay's author was a marvellous actor when it came to modesty. Failing to thank Arthur, he ventured some advice on the best way for innocent Americans to deal with modern history. This was a mistake, because he did not foresee that the opportunity would present itself again a week later. Enjoying a remarkable run of good luck, he was going to bed at dawn after a marathon series of poker games, which was as good a way as any of displaying the insouciance of a superior being. For the following exam Arthur ruthlessly gave him a prophetic quote by Keynes that was actually by Bainville, unilaterally restored the Austrian monarchy during the inter-war period, and changed by a year the date of the Wall Street crash. The professor of modern history looked dismayed, attributing Getulio's errors to tiredness. At the end of the class Getulio rounded on his friend.

'I suppose you thought that was funny.'

'My turn to, as you say, jerk you around.'

Neither of them being of a disposition to explain themselves, Arthur suggested a basic remedy.

'We haven't done a circuit of the campus for a long time. How about a half-hour jog to get our heads straight?'

They put on tracksuits and set out around the buildings, elbow to elbow. Less fit, his lungs clogged with the accumulated nicotine of his epic card games, Getulio gritted his teeth. On the last circuit, white-faced, he had to sit down. Arthur put on his most pleading tone of voice.

'Don't tell me you're going to die on me, just like that … without giving me Augusta's address and Elizabeth's phone number.'

'So that's it!'

'Yes, that's it.'

His head between his knees, Getulio was silent. When he sat

up, the blood was returning to his cheeks.

'You should have asked me sooner. Don't go bothering Augusta. She's getting married … oh, not for love, but she and I, as you probably guessed, are going through hard times. She wants them to be over, but I'm worried that she's sacrificing herself for me, so that I can carry on my studies. I begged her to wait. In July we'll have the money from the sale of an estate of my father's in Minas Gerais. Till then I'm sending her my poker winnings.'

'What about your losses?'

Getulio laughed loudly.

'I never pay my debts at cards. I can tell from your expression that you find that dishonest. Arthur, you have to start looking at life in a different way. People with scruples are going to have a very hard time of it in future. Why do you want to see Augusta again?'

He remembered what Elizabeth had said.

'She's unique.'

'Yes, that's certainly true. There may be women ten times more beautiful than she is, but as soon as she appears Augusta becomes the sole attraction.'

'Who's she marrying?'

'To tell you the truth, there are two suitors in the picture. We haven't decided.'

'What do you mean, "we"?'

'I have a say. I'm her big brother, almost her father—'

'– and a bit her pimp too, if I'm not mistaken.'

'No, you're very much mistaken, and you understand nothing with your middle-class French psychology.'

'What if, on the contrary, I understand everything? Come on, Getulio, give me her number.'

'Never. What for, anyhow? You don't even have the wherewithal to go to New York for a weekend.'

Arthur turned his back on him and jogged away down the path that ran round the campus. When he passed the bench again, Getulio waved a scrap of paper at him.

'If you're really in need of love, why don't you go and see Elizabeth? Apart from your ties and socks, she thinks you're quite attractive.'

Arthur was easily offended. How could he defend himself by revealing the truth, that it was his mother who bought him his socks and ties? He had suspected her of having bad taste for years, but he would not tolerate anyone making fun of her for believing that she could, by choosing his clothes for him, keep the child who had become a man dependent on her. Arthur loomed threateningly over Getulio, who pulled back, offering his bird-like neck to the hand that gripped it, hard.

'I hurt your feelings,' he said in a strangled voice.

'If Elizabeth wants to tell me, I'll let it pass. But not you.'

'She didn't tell me … well, she nearly told me. Stop, you're hurting me! We're not going to fight, are we, for heaven's sake?'

The tall, handsome Getulio in his blue tracksuit, slumped breathlessly on a bench, could not provoke bad feeling for long. In fact, without his good looks he was pitiful, his eyes widened in fear that Arthur might squeeze even harder. His neck reddened. He swallowed saliva, making his Adam's apple bob up and down ridiculously. A pack of a dozen runners in shorts and singlets passed them. From their measured breathing and lengthened stride, they were training for the 1500 or 3,000 metres. None of them turned his head. They disappeared behind a grove of trees and reappeared beside an artificial lake where their reflections wobbled in the black water without disturbing a pair of swans.

'We look absurd,' Getulio croaked.

'Who did she tell?'

'Augusta told me.'

Arthur let go of Getulio's neck. Men always misimagine what women say about them. When they discover the truth, they find out what a lethal view women have of their weaknesses.

'It doesn't mean she agrees with what Elizabeth said.' Getulio rubbed his neck where it was reddest from the pressure of Arthur's fingers. 'Take Elizabeth's phone number anyway. Go and see her in New York, when you can afford to.'

'I can afford to already. All you have to do is pay back the hundred dollars I lent you the morning after the ball.'

Getulio raised his arms beseechingly to the sky.

'Dear Lord, how can he say this to me? I thought you were the last honest man on this earth of liars and cheats, and now I find you asking me to return money that came from Elizabeth. I saw her give you the hundred dollars. She was paid back a long time ago. I owe nothing to anyone.'

'You didn't pay anyone back. I stake my life on it.'

Arthur pocketed Elizabeth's number without another word and walked back to his room. He had been giving occasional French lessons to two social-science students, and had just enough for a train ticket. He called Elizabeth.

'You forgot me. I shan't be able to see you much, we're rehearsing. But you're a big boy, you can look after yourself. I do have a bed for you.'

'What about your invisible man, your George?'

'George? Oh, he's not around any more. It was too comfortable for him to think, and he never washed. You do wash, don't you?'

Arthur almost backed out. Eventually he took the plunge. Not to start washing – he already had a sportsman's attitude to cleanliness – but to find out where Getulio was hiding Augusta. He arrived at Elizabeth's apartment on a Friday evening during rehearsals.

'Go up to the mezzanine and watch if you like. We're nearly done.'

Sitting on a pouf, with his legs dangling between the balusters, Arthur watched a scene that to him was more comic than unsettling. Halfway up a stepladder, a woman with luxuriant curly black hair, wearing a figure-hugging evening dress, was playing opposite two other actors, one in battledress with a sub-machine gun slung over his shoulder, the other in overalls and wearing a workman's belt full of tools. 'Playing opposite' was a slight exaggeration, as Arthur rapidly became aware that the female lead was endlessly repeating a mantra of which he could only make out two syllables, 'mammon, mammon …' The play's deep symbolism could not have escaped the most intellectually challenged member of the audience. As the worker and the soldier exchanged incendiary slogans about war and peace with each other, their attractive counterpart on the ladder mumbled and shook her head, her face half hidden by her long, thick curls. Behind a high desk Elizabeth beat time like a conductor. A deep monotony descended. Suddenly the woman stopped muttering 'mammon' and began stripping off her costume jewellery, her sheath of black satin and her underwear, which the two men then fought over until they succeeded in killing each other. Having stepped down from the ladder, the woman turned the inert male figures over with her foot and danced over their corpses to a savage rhythmic accompaniment. Darkness was falling, obscuring the buildings outside. The spotlight lit up the acacia, whose branches were already in bud. Arthur saw to his regret that the woman of mammon, posing with her legs apart, one foot on each actor, was not actually naked, although her flesh-toned leotard left little to the imagination.

'What do you think?'

'Superb.'

He was thinking more of the curly-haired woman than the scene itself, of which he had understood nothing except that the flesh triumphed over the trivialities of life.

'Who wrote it?' he felt obliged to ask.

'Nobody wrote it. Theatre is dying under the weight of writers. You're watching a collective work that exists beyond words.'

The actors congratulated each other in terms that Arthur thought excessive. The curly-haired beauty wrapped herself modestly in a dressing gown. Her name was Thelma and she came from San Francisco. The two men, Piotr and Leigh, who had been vegetating in walk-on parts in plays that Elizabeth described as 'backward-looking', had discovered 'theatre *vérité*' under her leadership, a new form that was going to sweep away bourgeois entertainment. Permanent members of the troupe that Elizabeth had been at great pains to assemble, they were both waiting for stardom, one working part time as a valet and chauffeur, the other as a cook, while Thelma helped with the housework. Piotr brought a bowl from the kitchenette full of simmering wild rice. They ate on paper plates, sitting on the carpet Without asking, Thelma poured a glass of milk for Arthur. He protested.

'I'm very sorry but I haven't quite got to that stage yet.'

Elizabeth opened a bottle of Chilean wine, under the disapproving gaze of her troupe. For a while the conversation remained stuck in various professions of allegiance to vegetarianism and a macrobiotic diet. The rice turned out to be inedible. Arthur took out a packet of cigarettes, to the consternation of both the men present. Thelma ran to open a window. A gust of cold air blew into the loft. Elizabeth explained that her French friend had come from old Europe, which was lagging behind in the march of progress. She was so persuasive that her friends began to look at Arthur with kindly pity. There was nevertheless an awkwardness that refused to go away, and that eventually became sufficiently noticeable for Thelma to make a move to leave, followed by the other two. Elizabeth shut the window and lit a cigarette.

'I'm not the only sinner any more,' Arthur said.

'No. And you can go and open another bottle.'

She turned down some lamps and the apartment's edges disappeared in the dim lighting.

'I made them run away.'

'That's fairly easy when they're not hungry any more.'

'You don't take any prisoners, do you?'

She shrugged, got up to put on a record, and went to the bathroom. Arthur felt melancholy creeping up on him. Why, at this time of day, put on the sublimely beautiful Mahler, who trailed such clouds of irremediable sadness in his wake? Elizabeth came back in the dressing gown Thelma had borrowed, her face still damp and shining, bent over Arthur, unknotted his tie, unbuttoned his collar, and threw a sweater at his head.

'Take your jacket off. Won't you ever allow yourself to loosen up?'

'With you it'll happen in a flash.'

Sprawled on the Mexican mattresses, they talked, smoked and drank more Chilean wine. Arthur said, 'Your friends are weirdos. Sweet, but weirdos. Are there many like them?'

'A handful, but they're all evangelists. There are religions that started with fewer apostles. They're not in a hurry. Give them twenty or thirty years ... by the end of the century they'll have

120

come out on top and human beings will be living in a state of harmony and well-being.'

'That'll be exciting.'

'Mm. I won't fit in.'

Later she put on some jazz. Her taste was eclectic: Louis Armstrong, Fats Waller, Ornette Coleman. They listened as they drank more of the rough Chilean wine accompanied by slices of chorizo that took their heads off. Elizabeth lay across a cushion, her head on Arthur's thigh.

'I know why you came to New York.'

'Do you? And what are your orders?'

'Not to give you Augusta's address at any price.'

Arriving at Elizabeth's apartment, Arthur had forgotten about Augusta. Now she returned. Why couldn't you, just by pressing a button, set in motion the scenes you wanted to think about, banish them offstage, arrange intervals for them, and pick up their threads in your memory when you felt like it?

'So you won't give it to me?'

'Of course I will. But she's in Washington for a couple of weeks and you don't have time to go there. Give me your hand.'

She took his hand in hers and slid it into the opening of her dressing gown, between her breasts.

'I badly need a man to feel my heart beating tonight.'

'It's beating. Feel better?'

'Yes. We can talk about Augusta as much as you like.'

Arthur was not sure he wanted to. Although his experience of love was limited, he felt that one couldn't dig deeply into the life of the object of one's love with impunity. Elizabeth had the brutal directness of a spoilt child; she could easily reduce Augusta to nothingness, leaving just some lovely pieces of wreckage, but wreckage all the same.

'Don't say anything bad about her. I don't want to know what she is, I want to keep her the way I imagine her, the way I first saw her on the *Queen Mary*'s promenade deck with you and her brother—'

'And in the cabin? When she showed you her bottom! That I didn't expect.'

Arthur hadn't expected it either. In his daydreams about Augusta he berated himself: instead of standing with his mouth open on the second occasion when it had happened, more intentionally, in the hotel room at Beresford, he should have thrown her a towel to show his disapproval and make clear to her that he had different, not purely physical feelings about her.

'Oh, stop worrying!' Elizabeth said. 'I never say bad things about girls like her. Or men like Getulio. I'm friends with them both. When I took the train to Le Havre, the first thing I saw was the perms of a dozen of my old aunts, my mother's cousins, making their way home after a tour of the Paris jewellery stores and a lot of dinners at Maxim's. That was their idea of Paris. I started to panic, and then I saw this bizarre couple. I thought they must be married. Getulio wears a wedding ring sometimes, Augusta too. It's their smokescreen, their way of saying "Leave us alone!" That's all: there's nothing ambiguous about it, don't worry. They just don't want people asking questions. And did you notice how Getulio's so set on being the only source of information about them? No contradictions, things so easily verified that you never think about bothering to check them. And there she is, in perfect unison, but watch her carefully and you'll see her eyes start to glitter whenever Getulio goes too far with his boasting. Never forget, none the less, that the two of them are in cahoots and even if she's aware of her brother's showing off, she'll always stand by him. One day when he really needs some money, he'll marry her off handsomely. Which is a way of saying that you're not the man for her. I like them, yes, I really like them. On the train, and on the boat, they opened their arms to me, as if we'd known each other for ever. Right now our paths are intersecting in a way I'm hugely enjoying: they're entering American society and I'm doing my level best to escape from it. They haven't quite arrived, and I haven't quite freed myself. As their elevator goes up, mine's going down. We're at the same floor, but Getulio's dying to push the button.'

'Just tell me one thing.'

'What? I can't promise I will.'

'Is it true that she's going to get married?'

'How could you believe that?'

Concannon was lying on his back, his eyes closed, his head supported by a large pillow, the sheet tucked under his arms. A tube connected his right arm to a drip. His immobile left arm ended in a half-open wax-coloured hand, as if the blood had stopped circulating in it. The professor's face, its veins usually flushed with the first glass of alcohol, had taken on a grey-mauve pallor and yet, crowned by his flossy white hair and accentuated by the line of his bushy black eyebrows, his features seemed singularly calm, although at each exhalation his cracked lips swelled barely enough to open and make the whistling sound of a steam engine about to come to a final stop after a few last pathetic hiccups.

Summoned by a bell, the nurse left Arthur alone with him. The room's lowered blinds diffused the bright orange-red rays of the setting sun.

'Professor!'

Could he hear, lost amid the confused images that filled his sleep? Arthur held his waxy left hand and squeezed it. The nurse had said, 'We don't understand. The haemorrhage is localised on the left side and shouldn't have affected his language or thought processes, but the patient is apparently aphasic.'

'Professor, it's Arthur Morgan,' he repeated in the ear of the motionless figure.

An eyelid fluttered open, revealing an unmoving blue eye, veiled but more lively than might have been expected. The lips tensed into a smile. Concannon extended his right hand as far as the drip would let him. The fingers flickered, beckoning Arthur closer.

'I'm … dying …'

Arthur had no time to protest.

'… I'm … dying … of thirst.'

A muffled laugh set off a horrible mucous cough. Arthur handed him a glass of water and a straw without getting up.

'Sweet heaven! Ugh!'

The voice was dramatically hoarse.

'Either it's a miracle, or you're putting on an act with the doctors.'

'Hush!' Concannon said, opening the other eye.

'I only found out when I got back last night. I was in New York.'

'With her?'

'No. With Elizabeth.'

How could he think about that in the state he was in?

'Why are you refusing to talk to the staff?'

'Nurse too ugly … doctor an idiot … want them to leave me be … Not you … I've always liked the French …'

He closed his eyes after the extreme effort. Arthur tried to think of something to say. Sunk into himself, Concannon let out a long, deep sigh. From out of his self-imposed darkness his words came more clearly.

'I knew, very early on, I'd end up … gaga …'

'You're not gaga at all.'

'I'm pretending to be gaga … it's worse. I feel sleepy …'

'I'll leave you to rest.'

Concannon shook his right hand so abruptly that the drip came out.

'I'll call the nurse.'

'Did you know … I was the best dancer … in the whole university?'

'Yes I did. But I prefer to hear it from you.'

Concannon started to snore, so noisily that it sounded like wheezing. Arthur pressed the call switch and the nurse appeared immediately. She was, as Concannon had said, a woman of average physical looks but an incontestable authority.

'This is the third time he's pulled the drip out.'

'He's started to snore.'

'With lungs as clogged as his are, I'm not surprised.'

She put an arm around Concannon, and with unexpected strength lifted him to plump his pillow and settle his head, which was lolling.

'Did he talk to you?' she asked suspiciously.

'No,' Arthur lied.

'Don't be misled … he's still in shock. In a semi-coma. But he knows you're here. You mustn't tire him.'

Arthur held Concannon's working right hand and squeezed it tightly, receiving in reply a slight pressure from his fingers. His cheeks swelled and his lips parted, exhaling a gust of rank breath. Arthur was sure that the gesture was directed at the nurse.

'The most painful thing,' the nurse said, 'is when they want to speak and they can't manage to find their words. The doctor's on his way. He said no visits. I have to ask you to leave now.'

A night with Elizabeth had changed nothing in his life. A few minutes at Concannon's side had changed it much more. Back at his room, he wrote to his mother, to his uncle Eugène, to Sister

Marie of the Victory, moved by a feeling of remorse at having neglected those who loved him in all their naivety, his mother especially, who was so good and so clumsy.

His classes had almost ceased to interest him. He had the feeling that he knew all he needed to know and that he was just marking time. There was an incredible amount of information available at the fingertips of students who hardly used it. Everyone specialised in very particular areas. John Macomber, whose father Arthur had met on the train that brought him to Boston, was only interested in the battle of Gettysburg. Within ten years he would know more than if he had taken part in it as a staff officer. Beyond the topography of the battlefield and General Lee's shattering defeat at the hands of Union forces, John was a member of the university football team and played cards regularly with Getulio, who usually wiped the floor with him. One day John would take over running his father's Massachusetts dairy company and steadily drive the board of directors to distraction by likening every commercial decision to the battle of Gettysburg.

With Getulio, Arthur's relations had become increasingly formal. If the Brazilian had read the message from his sister that Arthur had left on his worktable while he was away from his room, he would just have to make sure it did not happen again.

With Concannon's death, Arthur lost a generous supporter. The professor's funeral was remarkably gloomy. The dean and a small group of students assembled at the crematorium. A short address summarised his university titles and achievements and minimised his tormented personal life. He could not be praised as an example to his students: the scandals had been too many and too noisy. Among the group that dispersed sadly after the ceremony was a stocky young woman wearing a black straw hat with a ribbon. She came towards Arthur and he recognised the nurse from the hospital. Had she, beneath her brisk exterior, a heart after all?

'Perhaps you were his only friend,' she said. 'After his stroke we found a handwritten card in his papers that said, "In case of accident, inform Arthur Morgan." That's why I phoned you. He spoke to you, didn't he?'

'Yes. Only a few words.'

'He wasn't aphasic, I was sure of it. A few minutes before his heart stopped, he looked me in the eye and said, very distinctly, so that I wouldn't forget, "Tell my friend Arthur: *Ad Augusta per angusta*. He'll understand." I expect you know what he meant.'

'Yes, perfectly.'

'Is it Italian?'

'No. Latin. It's a Latin play on words.'

'Is it indiscreet to ask what it means?'

'"To greatness through difficulties."'

'Was it a kind of code between you?'

'In a more specific sense Augusta's also the name of a girl we both found attractive and who does seem to be a difficult nut to crack.'

'I feel I'm being indiscreet.'

'Yes.'

'I didn't mean to be. I've often seen people die. You get used to it … and then one day a man dies who you don't know anything about and who means nothing to you, and it breaks your heart. I imagine Professor Concannon was an admirable man.'

'You're right, he was.'

*

At Easter Arthur spent two days with Elizabeth. When he questioned her about Augusta she was stubbornly vague: she was away or she was sick.

'I'm not refusing to cooperate, I promise.'

'That's a pity. I'd have been flattered.'

'Liar!'

He was lying, a little. Elizabeth was alive in the pleasure he gave her, and she him. Once he was back at Beresford work took over and he was content, no more. He forgot her for a time and instead wrote long letters to Augusta and put them away in a locked drawer. Getulio treacherously offered to go with them both to Chicago.

'I can't afford it.'

'Augusta will be disappointed.'

'You know perfectly well that I can't.'

'Borrow.'

'Who from?'

'I'm sorry I can't even lend you a quarter. I'm very short right now.'

After he came back from the Chicago weekend, which was probably pure invention, Getulio received a phone call from the general manager at the Hôtel des Bergues. Madame Mendosa had left a package for him. He was away for a week and came back with his pockets bulging. In a moment of loneliness Augusta, freed from brotherly surveillance, had sent Arthur a postcard.

> Arthur, where are you? I think of you … You mustn't
> lose heart. Concannon's death is so horribly sad that I
> feel I'm in a black hole. Getulio bought me a very pretty
> Balenciaga suit, but who am I ever going to wear it for?
> Arturo, you don't make any effort to see me … Love. A.

*

The most noteworthy event of that last term was a summons from Allan Porter. He was inviting Arthur to Washington. The envelope contained a return air ticket.

The secret adviser – so un-secret that everyone murmured his name, endowing him with extraordinary powers – received Arthur in his office at the White House.

'What are you doing this summer?'

'I was thinking of going back to France for two or three weeks, to see my mother and a few friends, so that I can tell myself I haven't gotten too Americanised yet. At the same time I'm not sure I'll have the money to get over, and even if I do, maybe it would be better if I saved it. I'm wasting too much time with bits of translation and French lessons.'

Porter, in striped shirtsleeves and a scarlet bow tie, wearing gold cufflinks and wristwatch and seated behind a massive reproduction Chippendale desk, played with a paper knife that punctuated his questions.

'You wouldn't like to work during the months of July and August?'

His tone was imperious.

'Doing what?'

'Oh, nothing too strenuous. Friend of mine, a stockbroker in New York, is looking for an intern.'

'I'm not terribly well up on stockbroking.'

'Another good reason. Let's have lunch; you can think about it.'

Senior White House staff ate lunch in a private dining room. Porter did not shake hands, moving briskly and making do with a wave in response to the salutations that greeted him from table to table.

'People are pretty happy with your results at Beresford,' he said, having ordered both food and wine without consulting his guest.

'What "people"?'

'The authorities. You'll find the second year more interesting.'

'I hope so.'

'I'll admit there's nothing more boring than studying. Life is a teacher of a more amusing stripe. If you spend time as an intern at Jansen and Brustein, you'll learn things no university will ever teach you.'

Arthur raised an objection that he realised, as soon as he uttered it, he no longer believed in.

'My mother's waiting for me to come home.'

'Your future's waiting for you too, and its love is a good deal more fragile than a mother's.'

'That's rather cynical.'

'Cynical? No. Lucid, yes. Put it this way: we can work something out. Every day we have planes leaving for Europe. In September I'll get you a return flight that'll cost you no more than the inconvenience of travelling with military personnel.'

Arthur, if he was being entirely sincere, had to admit that his reservations had less to do with filial love than with his fear of leaving America, which was where Elizabeth and Augusta were, even though he had not managed to see the latter for many months. Invisible, she was an obstacle whose foolishness he was fully aware of.

'In that case I accept. Gratefully,' he said.

'I require no gratitude whatsoever.'

The dining room was full. Latecomers waited at the bar for a table to become free. Diners talked and laughed so loudly that Porter and Arthur almost had to shout to hear each other, robbing their conversation of nuance. A faintly hygienic scent hung over the room, and it was hard to say whether it came from the men's aftershave, their scented handkerchiefs, or the air conditioning. Two or three times the uproar stopped dead for a few seconds for no reason, then resumed just as suddenly.

'An angel passing by,' Arthur said.

'I'd be very surprised. There are no angels in Washington, DC. They gave up. No one was listening.'

After he had signed the bill Porter paused and looked straight at Arthur.

'You'll learn plenty of stuff at Jansen and Brustein. The majority of it mustn't leave the office. A single indiscretion can scuttle a deal that's been months in preparation. But I believe you'll enjoy swimming in shark-infested waters for a few weeks.'

'Shark-infested?'

'Certainly, to your European eyes. Didn't Concannon warn you on the boat over? The United States has one god: money. It absolves all sins. Do you know Washington?'

'No.'

'It's a modern-day Rome. My chauffeur will give you a tour this afternoon, then take you to the airport. I've suggested he avoids the black areas … they're not our proudest achievement. Are you stopping in New York before you go back to Beresford?'

Arthur thought about it. He wanted to. He had not seen Elizabeth for a month.

'My secretary will change your return ticket. At least Elizabeth Murphy will give you a slightly less conventional idea of our society than I can.'

Arthur stiffened. Porter saw.

'Tell yourself that there are no secrets,' he said, 'and read nothing into it except a mark of interest in your person. Miss

Murphy always makes me think of a fable of your great La Fontaine: for the cicadas to go on singing, the ants need to carry on storing up food for winter. I represent the most rigid part of America's character; I do it so that inside the citadel the cicadas, like your friend, can go on singing … or putting on a show. Let's take a short walk, shall we? The car will follow.'

Not just the car but a young man in a beige alpaca suit followed them, the same one, Arthur recognised, who had been at the quayside when the *Queen Mary* docked and at Beresford the night of Porter's lecture.

'Good,' Porter said. 'I see you have an eye for detail. Take it from me, I have to have him. Others feel it's important. It serves Minerva's purpose too. She's convinced that that young man with his P38 under his jacket will make sure I don't step out of line, as if I have nothing to worry about except chasing hookers in a town where everyone spies and rats on everyone else. Can you see me in my underwear in a hotel room with some broad, and a photographer and journalist suddenly bursting in? The next day there I am, front page of the *Washington Post*, the strict guardian of politicians' virtue but not always my own, followed by some court appearance into the bargain, with a judge fining me for my conduct. I can just see the President's face, forced to limit the damage from the scandal … You're lucky to be French, to be free in a country where it's more of a point of honour *not* to go sticking your nose in the private lives of public figures …'

Porter walked with a military stride, stopping dead in the middle of the pavement without paying any attention to other pedestrians, gripping Arthur's arm, to underline the force of his words and convince him of society and the press's narrow-mindedness.

'I'm not saying that you'll ever find yourself in such a position,' Porter said, as they parted. 'But maybe one day …'

133

'I'm a long way off.'

'That's what we all think … The chauffeur will take you now. It's nothing like New York. A cold town, even at one hundred degrees, as befits the seat of power. Power's like ice. Still, there are some things to admire. I'll let you be the judge.'

When he got off the plane at LaGuardia, he called Elizabeth.

'Arthur! You've come at just the right time. Come straight away. I have a surprise for you.'

The surprise was Augusta. Later Arthur was annoyed that Elizabeth had not warned him. She had doubtless done it deliberately, in the interests of proving how generous she was, of reminding him – though he had not forgotten – that the two of them were free and only shared, when they met all too briefly and rarely, a pleasure that the angels envied. But the meeting with Augusta was such a shock that he was speechless and stood frozen, his overnight bag at his feet, as though she had caught him red-handed. Six months of not seeing her had transformed her into a myth, an idea whose body and even voice had grown more indistinct from day to day, leaving behind a fragile statue that was swept away, brought back, erased by the slightest gust of wind. It took him several seconds to recognise her: she was standing with her back to the window, her face in shadow (Elizabeth, liking things to be close to the ground, had only lit one low lamp). We are made so that the abrupt fulfilment of a secret desire leaves us disarmed, no longer sure whether we want what we have so desperately wished for; instead we feel stripped of what previously doubled our life's value and filled it with enchantment, to the point where the one we love turns into an unreal being all over again, whose reappearance overturns the order of things. And how could Arthur not be dismayed by the reality of a meeting he had so wanted taking place under Elizabeth's roof and scrutiny, plunging him into a confusion that for some reason neither of the two women seemed to be aware of?

The low lamp lit Augusta as far as her knees. The rest, her waist and bust, the straight and noble way she carried her head, became clearer as Arthur's eyes got used to the apartment's half-light. So she was really here, and he finally recognised her as she was, both in his memory and his imagination, as a flesh-and-blood woman, her body sheathed in a tight dress of black silk, wearing a simple pearl necklace and two delicate shell-shaped gold earrings, and with her waist belted with a silver sash that hung from her right side. Even if one suspected from her laconic postcards that Augusta felt for Arthur only a small fraction of what he felt for her, the meeting was too unexpected for them not to be equally disconcerted. Was it actually happening? Had they invented it? Arthur was already no longer young enough to harbour ideas of romantic love. The reasons for his attraction to Augusta were hard to explain, and even if he had possessed a clearer sense of his own mind, he probably could not have admitted them. The fact that she had responded at all, even by hints and implications, still seemed incredible to him.

'Well,' Elizabeth said, surprised by their silence, 'I thought you were at least going to throw your arms around each other! Is there something I don't know?'

Arthur brushed Augusta's cool cheek with his lips.

'You don't make any effort to see me,' she said.

'Getulio makes every effort so that I can't see you.'

'When will I see you properly?'

'Now! Look, I'm here! I kissed your cheek, and I stroked your arm as I did it.'

'You violated her neutrality!' Elizabeth said.

Augusta only had five minutes. A car was coming to take

her to a party. Where? She didn't know exactly. Or whether Getulio would be there. She would not have had anything to wear without Elizabeth lending her a dress. An impossible dress, actually. You couldn't walk up or down stairs in it, which was all the more disastrous in a three-storey building without a lift, and in a working-class neighbourhood. Why didn't Elizabeth come back to 72nd Street instead of living in the Village, which was a really dangerous area? And look at how people dressed in the streets here, in jeans and polo shirts, and every few yards there were those choking smells of frying food from Italian trattorias and French bistros. Worse, on the stairs you'd bump into a couple of gays holding each other by their pinkies and stinking of patchouli, 'you know, that scent maids use for underarm deodorant when they do the housework'.

'Are you finished?' Elizabeth asked.

'Yes.'

And Augusta, in tears, threw herself into Arthur's arms.

'Save me, if you're a man.'

Elizabeth flicked the switch and in the courtyard garden the acacia blazed.

'That's all that was missing. It's enough to make a stone weep.'

Arthur stroked Augusta's neck shamelessly as she nestled against him. He wanted her. Past her bare shoulder he could see the courtyard, the tree, the neighbouring buildings, one dusky red, the other apple green. Lights were going on in the windows. An arm lowered the blinds on the floor opposite.

Augusta pulled away from him, hiding her face in both hands.

'Oh, I look horrible!'

'That's the very least one can say,' Elizabeth answered, taking her by the hand and leading her to the bathroom, where they locked themselves in.

The overnight bag, abandoned in the middle of the loft, was an invitation to leave. Arthur hesitated. There was still time to break with the two of them, to make his escape and live the life Porter had described so well to him. He could hear them murmuring in English: Elizabeth's well-modulated voice calming Augusta's excitement. On the sofa there lay a sequined dress, a dancer's tutu, and an old, creased suit. Elizabeth must have rummaged through her actors' costumes before she found the black silk dress. The tenant downstairs put a song by Elvis Presley on his record player. There was the noise of an altercation on the stairs, which ended in the sound of hurrying feet. The neighbour turned down the volume. Augusta was the first to emerge.

'It's awful, I'm late now … Arturo *meu*, it was wonderful to see you again. You really haven't changed a bit … yes, I promise you, you're just the same; you don't look your age at all! It's so nice just to see each other once every six months. We don't have time to get tired of each other. See you in six months' time … you promise, don't you?'

'I'll be in New York in July and August.'

'Call me then. But don't say anything to Getulio. You know how odd he is. You never know how he'll react. He's the impulsive one. I think he's slightly afraid of you. He told me that one day you nearly knocked him out. You know that I would never have forgiven you if you had.'

'Give me your phone number.'

'It's 567 … it's not important, I can never remember it. I live with friends on Fifth Avenue. Elizabeth knows exactly where it is. She'll tell you.'

She held his face in both hands and placed a rapid kiss on his lips. When she had gone through the door she turned round, her hand already on the banister.

'I felt very bad when Concannon died. Getulio didn't want me to go to the funeral.'

'He didn't go either.'

'Getulio didn't like Concannon. It would take too long to explain. Actually he doesn't like anyone. Yes ... me ... maybe. Poor little me. Always crying. And ridiculous. Arturo, don't ever forget me.'

They heard her going down the steep staircase. Elizabeth walked through to the room that overlooked the street.

'Arthur, come see!'

In the street a white Rolls-Royce was parked, with a black uniformed chauffeur standing next to it. He opened the door for Augusta and she disappeared into the car without looking up.

'Ye gods!' Elizabeth sighed. 'Have we lost her already?'

Two months later the answer came: yes, and no.

After passing his exams without mishap, Arthur returned to New York and started work with Jansen and Brustein. For the first few nights Elizabeth looked after him. They agreed that they would not impose on each other, especially since she was starting rehearsals of a new play, about which she remained secretive. In Rector Street, not far from her, he rented a small room on the top floor, which was just about comfortable: bed, wardrobe, table and chair, shower, old engravings of Austrian monarchs on the wall. Captain Morgan's trunk was Arthur's only addition. His landlady, Mrs Paley, who was Hungarian, had known better days and claimed once to have been a star in the corps de ballet at Budapest, before the dismantling of the Austro-Hungarian Empire. She spoke French with an attractive guttural accent and from time to time wielded a vacuum cleaner with the air of a princess somewhat down on her luck but with wonderful pluck in the face of adversity. The spire of Trinity Church loomed outside the window. Jansen and Brustein's offices were round the corner. Arthur arrived at eight o'clock and left at five, when, after a frenetic day, the district relapsed rapidly into somnolence and tons of paper churned out by telex machines littered the roadway and pavements of Wall Street outside the Stock Exchange. Mr Jansen was rarely seen, remaining in his office and receiving visitors as sparingly as possible. He aped the City of London brokers: pinstriped double-breasted suits, blue shirts with starched white collars, plain ties. His associate Brustein, who was permanently scruffy, in corkscrewed trousers, a crumpled jacket with shoulders snowy with dandruff, and his tie askew, brimmed with vitality: he always had a joke on his lips, called the employees by their first names, shook hands ten times over, and possessed dazzlingly fast judgement and a decisiveness of mind that had made the firm's fortune. Rumour had it that he had been a codebreaking genius during the war. His friendship with Porter dated from that time.

The employees were squashed into a round room from where the view swooped down an enfilade of skyscrapers towards the yellow waters of the Hudson. A dozen of them worked in the glass-walled room, which sweltered at the slightest ray of sunshine. It did not take Arthur long to become aware of their hostility. He had not climbed the ladder, and senior figures, who were theoretically loathed, protected him. To begin with, he found it hard to concentrate in the clamour of conversations, the shrill nagging of the telephone and the continual interruptions, and then, little by little, he managed to follow Mr Brustein's advice and keep himself apart.

'They're idiots. Ignore them; they'll respect you for it. Wall Street's a jungle. You don't defend yourself here: it's attack, attack every time, as if your life depended on it.'

'But I'm only here temporarily.'

'Don't forget that we might offer you a permanent post, then one of them will have to go. Whoever gets the short straw. Be especially careful of one of the two women, Jenny. She thinks the whole world's against her. Twenty-five, and already divorced twice. Sounds like fun, doesn't she? The other one, Gertrude, wears a hearing aid under that great wig of red hair. She's deaf, and so naturally she hears very well. She's got a great future.'

The employees took it in turns to break for lunch, but some stayed in the office, munching sandwiches and drinking Coca-Cola over their typewriters and calculators, making do with taking the phone off the hook.

'They're scared to death that someone'll take their place,' Brustein said, chuckling. 'Come and have a bite with me. They won't be able to sleep for six months when they see us leave together.'

At a table in a little bistro pretending to be a Parisian bar, Brustein opened up a bit more.

'Allan Porter's wrong to make himself so noticeable. Someone'll take a shot at him one day. He was much more effective when he stayed in the shadows. But we're all like that! One day we itch to stick our nose outside. At the same time we never quite shake off our old loyalties. But don't get sucked into his set-up, except with the greatest of caution: once you're in, it's hard to get out again … Enough said. Did you know that I have a very great pretension? Which is that I am the greatest connoisseur of Cézanne in the whole United States. You like Cézanne?'

'Yes, but I'm afraid I may need to brush up on him if I'm going to have to talk about him to a fanatic.'

'Okay, then let's meet up again in two weeks and I'll blitz you. Start getting your answers ready.'

The employees who did not stay in the office would go down to the shade in Battery Park and sit on the benches and watch the estuary and sky above it, filled with a myriad seagulls that chased the cargo ships, liners and tugs in and out of the docks. Arthur became fond of Battery Park. In the morning he was up at six to run there: half an hour's jogging helped him put up with a day sitting at his desk.

In the evenings he would sometimes look for a cinema or a theatre, but most often he would stay in his room, getting ready for the second year at Beresford. Elizabeth surprised him by beginning to come to his room after midnight. The rehearsals were exhausting her. Having fired Piotr and Leigh, who did not understand 'anything about anything', she had taken on Jerry, a young black student at New York College who was 'terribly handsome'. She would undress in front of Arthur, as freely as she did everything else in her life. It was a joy to see her take off her clothes, so close to perfection in her nakedness that you forgot to desire her. Yet contrary to appearances, she remained extremely shy at the most intense moment. Coming back from his jogging in Battery Park and finding her still asleep, he would make her tea with fresh croissants. In the sweltering city, immobilised by the summer's heat, the pleasure that they shared with each other was Arthur's only link with real life. To the rest of it he was indifferent. This world would never be his world.

But where was his world? He started to write to his mother more regularly, trying to repay her by his attentions; he urged her to see a cardiologist after she told him she was suffering from dizzy spells. He would come in September. She lived for his return and wrote to him that 'you'll never know how much your success at your exams has delighted the family. We're so pleased about your lovely job with the stockbroker.' If only she could have seen where he was working, the cramped conditions, the noise, the runners constantly coming in and out dripping with sweat, and at the end of the day the waste-paper baskets overflowing with printouts, empty mineral-water bottles, out-of-date tables, scrap paper … She would not have added, 'That's it, my dear little one … to me, even if you become an important financier, you'll always be my "little boy", playing with the great and the good.' What sort of illusions must have been going through her head? 'You don't talk about your Brazilian friends any more. I suppose they're with their family for the holidays. And what about that pretty American? You don't say anything about her either. I know how much you like secrets. Is there something going on that you're not telling me? You know you can't hide anything from me. I can read between the lines!'

As the two months went on, the gulf grew wider, filled with shame and heartache. Work helped take him out of himself; his nights with Elizabeth brought him a too-fragile peace that vanished into thin air when she rolled away from him and drifted into sleep, as stiff as a statue. A stranger, a passer-by. If he took her hand for reassurance she would pull it away and desert him until New York shook itself awake and bayed again. The murmur would grow and amplify, and then crash like a torrent over lower Broadway. Jogging in Battery Park, he imagined an ideal conversation with Elizabeth. 'Carrying on being as cautious as we are, keeping our two existences properly separate so that they never collide with each other, you know that what we have could last a lifetime ... I hear you say, "How awful!" but think, we never lie to one another, and how many people can say that? Anyway ... I'm just theorising ... Have you noticed, despite the fact that you don't pay any attention to such things, how we never use the word "*aimer*"? It never passes your lips. Has it ever? It doesn't spring to mine either, and even if it did when I wasn't looking, you'd start laughing and I'd soon stop. It's easier in English: "I like you" is immeasurably more attractive than the banal and threadbare "I love you". Italian has a marvellously appropriate phrase you won't find in any other language: "*Ti voglio bene*". I wish you well. You wish me well. We wish each other well. It's a jewel of civilised behaviour; there's a mountain of tenderness behind those words: respect, generosity, friendship. I come back; I don't forget the croissants. You drink your tea sitting up in bed. You have beautiful breasts which will never look tired, by the way. Then you get dressed and vanish. You possess the only key to our meetings. You won't entrust it to me, and you won't do anything to help me see Augusta again.'

There he was mistaken. Brushing her hair one morning, she said, 'Before I forget! Getulio wants to have lunch with you on Saturday.'

'To tell me Augusta's getting married?'

'No. She'll be there. Along with a Brazilian friend who'd like to meet you.'

'I doubt that.'

'Arthur, do try to like yourself a bit. A tiny bit.'

'I can't see what interest I might offer to someone from the milieu that Getulio frequents.'

'Will you go?'

'Of course I'll go, just to see what sort of trap Getulio wants to lure me into.'

What do we retain of that impalpable, possibly non-existent thing we call the past? Hardly more than a few words that we're no longer sure were really said or whether we simply invented them in the naive desire to justify ourselves, to believe we really existed on that day, at that crucial time, whose memory haunts us. There are only images – sometimes linked together like a film in which a censor has cut the best or worst scenes, stripping the sequence of all logic – images that surface and allow us to reconstruct an episode from the past that we are convinced was a fatal crossroads. That was where everything changed. A step to the left instead of a step to the right, a minute later, and an entire life tumbles into the unknown.

Why does Arthur recall, of that July Saturday morning in New York, firstly his long walk through the city from Rector Street to 72nd Street, along the furnace of Broadway and then Fifth Avenue, the burning pavements, the traffic lights that break his rhythm, the lost couple who ask for directions in a language he thinks might be Lithuanian, the scraggy yellow dog that follows him from the Stock Exchange and leaves him at Times Square, a girl on roller skates in blue shorts and singlet spinning like a top around Rockefeller Plaza, pretty, bursting with health, her skin like burnt bread, her dyed hair tied back in a ponytail? After this there is a gap, as if magically Arthur is transported by what the Italians call "*ministero angelico*" from the roller skater on Rockefeller Plaza to the glass door of the Brasilia, which a doorman holds open so that he can receive the full force of Augusta's anxious look, sitting at a table facing the door, opposite two men whose backs are to him. One has a circle of thinning hair, like a monk's tonsure: Getulio on the way to being bald. The other, in contrast, has hair that curls over his collar and, crow-black, is plastered to his temples by a lavish application of brilliantine: the Brazilian wheeler-dealer who is the reason for this meeting. These two disparate hairstyles are accessories in the film which has already started and whose beginning will be revealed little by little. The soundtrack is missing. On the screen there is now only Augusta's blue eyes in a succession of close-ups that enlarge to the point of eliminating both the restaurant's splashy decor and the waitress in a costume of Bahia who, with a sweetness devoid of irony, takes Arthur's hand to guide him through the maze of occupied tables to that of Getulio, who gets to his feet and, after Augusta has offered her cheek to the Frenchman, introduces Luis de Souza and Arthur Morgan to each other. The latter still has no idea of what is going to be asked of him, he only knows that he is running a risk because of Augusta and her bare arms, her pretty dress of orange twilled silk that reveals her shoulders and her throat, the musicality of the Brazilian voices around him: the girl from Bahia, the maître d'hôtel, who is a Carioca, and the wine waiter from São Paolo. The soundtrack is plugged in: a light-hearted Brazilian song drifts through the room. Cocktails arrive, gin with passion fruit, and a bottle of cachaca is placed in an ice bucket in the middle of the table, to clean their palates between courses.

The details are, as expected, tedious. In short, de Souza is seeking information that Arthur can supply from a file held at

Jansen and Brustein's, concerning a company traded by the two brokers. Arthur protests: he's an intern, the twenty-fifth and smallest wheel, and he only sees the files he's given.

'Come on,' Getulio said, 'no false modesty. At a dinner last week at the Lewises', Brustein was singing your praises.'

'I bet he was.'

Augusta's leg is pressed against his. He is not the nothing he pretends to be; she is there at his side, facing the two schemers and Getulio's lies. They pour him a glass of cachaca. It is firewater. Arthur tries to think about something else, about Elizabeth walking naked around his room and lifting her arms, showing her cool blond armpits as she brushes her short hair. He wonders if Luis de Souza is the man Getulio wants to sell his sister to. He wants to run out with her, smack the flashy de Souza, call Getulio the pimp he is, or kill the pair of them. He feels Augusta's thigh against his. In Elizabeth's apartment she had nestled against him. The mere memory of it makes him feel superior to these two men who think they can manipulate him.

There is a jump cut then, a blank whose length he cannot work out. He is walking on Fifth Avenue with Augusta. Luis and Getulio have driven away in a cab. By leaving him alone with her, they think they are playing a decisive trump card, but perhaps this last card is one too many, like the extravagant tips de Souza dispensed to the restaurant's junior staff. Suspicious and proud, Arthur will not let himself be lumped in with a restaurant's minions. His hand squeezes Augusta's bare upper arm. Suddenly she craves shops.

'Don't worry, Arturo *meu*! I shan't buy anything. I'm a voyeur.'

Mostly she wants to have fun catching the salesgirls off guard with falsely innocent questions. At Tiffany's, in front of a showcase containing a ruby necklace, she asks, 'In your experience is it the husbands who buy this kind of jewellery, or the lovers?'

In the lingerie department at Bloomingdale's she questions a girl with shingled hair: 'Don't you have anything in pink and black? My husband prefers black, my lover pink. I can't be expected to change three times a day.'

In a bookshop: 'I'm looking for the *Kama Sutra* in Braille. It's not for me. I read it twice already, anyway. Did you read it?'

The air conditioning in the shops makes the air in the street even more unbreathable. Augusta's hand flies to her throat.

'I am going to die, for sure. Wouldn't that be better for everybody? For Getulio, who can't make ends meet and spends every day dreaming up fabulous schemes that keep us off the street. For you too, darling, who say you love me.'

'I've never said that to you.'

'I can see it as clear as the nose on your face. Where do you live?'

'Lower Manhattan.'

'I want to see your apartment.'

'It's not an apartment, it's just a room I rent from a Hungarian ex-ballerina.'

'I want to visit your garret, then.'

'It's nothing like a garret and it's just round the corner from Jansen and Brustein's and not much further from Elizabeth's.'

A cab drives them to Rector Street. The black chauffeur smiles in his rear-view mirror when they speak French.

'I'm Haitian ... I like hearing French spoken. And even more when people say please and thank you to me.'

The man's hair is a frizzy black ball. He wears blue sunglasses. Arthur wonders why today he is noticing the hair of all the

147

people he meets. On the landing they come face to face with Mrs Paley emerging from Arthur's room with a duster and broom in her hands.

'I had a feeling you'd have a visitor today. I just gave it a little dust. Everything's always so tidy in your room! A real treat.'

'Mr Morgan told me so much about you,' Augusta says. 'You should write your memoirs. Very few women have lived through what you have.'

Arthur smiles: he hardly mentioned Mrs Paley's name, and the fact that she was a dancer. He notices with amazement, because now he cannot get it out of his thoughts, that Mrs Paley is wearing a grey wig with long dangling ringlets.

'What language you think I shall write my memoirs in? I don't speak Hungarian since a long time. German, I hate it. French? But I lisp.'

'Mr Morgan told me you had an affair with a royal person—'

Mrs Paley waves vaguely with her free hand.

'It's very possible! In those days no one asked for your papers on every street corner.'

Anxious that the conversation will drag on, Arthur opens the door to his room, goes in and looks around the very restricted universe where there are no signs of any presence besides his. Elizabeth leaves as she came. The table, the books stacked on his trunk, the bed neatly covered with a cretonne bedspread printed with horsemen and young women bathing in a pool: it's a very average place to welcome Augusta to, but she wanted it. On the landing she is still working her charms on Mrs Paley with a calculated candour.

'Did you ever think about giving dancing lessons?'

The delighted Mrs Paley is trapped. Her tenants are not nice, always complaining about something. She mentions Diaghilev, Lifar, Balanchine. The Russians hogged everything. She never liked the Russians. Arthur is perfectly well aware that Augusta, frightened by her own temerity, because she was the one who asked to come, is putting off the moment when she will find herself alone with him. When she finally steps into his room and he shuts the door behind her, dispatching Mrs Paley to her gloomy musing on vanished greatness, Augusta – he sees from her embarrassed and mechanical attitude, from the nervousness of her hands, clasped together so as not to give herself away, from her inflamed cheekbones and her inspecting the room's dingy decoration in order not to meet his eye – Augusta says in a toneless voice that he doesn't recognise, 'How lucky you are, Arthur! You make do with so little! You'll find it easy to be happy. Getulio is just the opposite. He wants everything he hasn't got. It always surprises me that you two are friends.'

'Don't be quite so wide-eyed. Getulio and I aren't friends.'

'He talks about you so warmly. He introduced you to a great friend today, someone who can be useful to you in the future.'

Arthur wants to tell her that he will look after his own future, a long way from Getulio, but he has seen too many examples of the animal complicity between brother and sister to take that risk. Augusta leafs through some pages of Arthur's notes, opens a book, and looks up at the engravings on the wall.

'Who's that?'

'Archduke Rudolf.'

'And that?'

'Empress Elisabeth of Austria-Hungary. Perhaps you'd prefer me to say Sissi, the way they do in ladies' novelettes.'

'That was such a tragedy! In Geneva they showed me the place where she was assassinated.'

Then, sitting on the bed, smoothing out the bedspread with the flat of her hand, and with her head tilted and not looking at him, she says, 'What's happening to us?'

'For six months I've despaired of seeing you again. Getulio's always been standing guard.'

'Not today.'

'There's a reason for that.'

'Yes. I wanted to see where you live.'

'I don't live here.'

'Where do you live then?'

'In my head, and my head is full of lots of different Augustas all going round in circles.'

From the street comes the litany of New York, a police siren. Planes glide across the sky of lower Manhattan making their way to LaGuardia where, like black kites, they wheel in tighter and tighter circles when the runway is busy. The neighbourhood is deserted. People have left in their thousands to bake on the beaches of Long Island. Arthur, leaning on the windowsill, has his back turned to Augusta. Her voice reaches him as if through a screen.

'Am I getting in Elizabeth's way by being here? You're close to her, aren't you?'

'She's just a friend. We see each other when she's free.'

'You don't need to hide anything from me. She's your lover, isn't she? Oh, don't answer! It doesn't cost her anything—'

'You'd have to ask her that.'

He turns round. Augusta is on her back on the bed, her hands behind her head. All that is between her and Arthur is her light summer dress, which falls into the gap between her legs, outlining them as if she were naked.

150

'Arthur, do you ever play the truth game?'

'No, it's a game for liars.'

How much time passes like this? It's difficult to remember. It feels as if they talked a lot and were often silent. The evening gradually draws its shadows over Manhattan. A gust of warm air that smells of sea and oil comes up from the Hudson, flies along Rector Street, raises a billow of dust, magically picks up cardboard boxes, newspapers, and paper bags that dart up to the lower floors of the building and fall back to the roadway with a thump or rasp. In the pink and grey sky, which looks strangely innocent above the all-consuming megalopolis, the winking lights of transatlantic airliners trace, like meteorites, smoky parabolas.

Augusta says, 'Getulio thinks you're stupid. He's the one who's stupid. You understand everything. I saw straight away that you didn't like Luis, not because he's dishonest, which he is, but because his tips are too big.'

'Does Getulio want to sell you to him?'

Augusta bursts out laughing.

'What an idea!'

'Who did the Rolls-Royce that picked you up from Elizabeth's belong to?'

'Nobody, Arturo *meu*. Getulio paid a fortune to rent it for me to go to a party in New Jersey. I was supposed to make a big impression. Sadly there were already thirty Rolls in the car park when I arrived, late. All the latest models. So humiliating!'

*

A while later she swings her legs off the bed, stands up, walks back and forth across his room, switches on his bedside lamp, opens the cupboard that contains Arthur's only two suits, then the trunk that holds more books than clothes, a tennis racquet, walking boots, and the photo of his father and mother on their honeymoon in Venice. Augusta picks it up and takes it over to the light.

'Don't tell me … I've already guessed. You look like them. Were they happy together?'

'I think so. For a short time.'

'It must be wonderful.'

'Yes, at least my father had that before he died.'

Arthur can feel her hesitating, that her walking around the room is delaying the moment when small talk will no longer be enough to cross the gulf that divides them. Augusta's lovely face, so animated since their meeting at the Brasilia, has become closed. He wonders if this will be the moment when her childhood's drama surges irresistibly to the surface and chokes her, when the night falls that brings the world to an end.

'You've got something to tell me.'

She stops and looks at him, her hand to her throat, where red spots have appeared, as though an invisible force was trying to strangle her before she can speak.

'I heard you were the only one to have seen Seamus in hospital.'

Between themselves they always said Concannon, Professor Concannon, just to avoid the oddity of his first name, which was not pronounced the way it was spelt.

'Who told you?'

'Getulio.' Augusta shrugs. 'He never liked him. Is it true that Seamus couldn't talk?'

'He pretended he couldn't to the doctor and nurses.'

'Not you?'

'No, he asked me for something to drink. I gave him a glass of water and he said, "Sweet heaven! Ugh!" but he still drank it, then he reminded me that he'd been the best dancer in the university.'

'Nothing about me?'

Was that what she had been building up to? He would never have guessed.

'Yes. He wanted to know if I'd been to New York to see you again. Are you crying? The first time I saw you you told me, "A woman who cries is ridiculous."'

'Then I'm ridiculous.'

She wipes away a tear which is about to roll down her cheek.

'He left the nurse a message,' Arthur says. 'She gave it to me without understanding it: "*Ad Augusta per angusta*". It feels as if it was meant for us.'

She walks over to the window and leans on the sill with Arthur. Two seagulls have ventured into the narrow canyon of Rector Street and they rise above the buildings to vanish into the sky.

'I need to get back. Getulio will be waiting for me. I was supposed to be back at five o'clock. God knows what he will be thinking. If he had your address he'd be here already, pistol in hand, determined to avenge my dishonour, and you'd be a dead man.'

'A dead man would do nothing to avenge your dishonour, and by the way I'd like to remind you that I haven't made a single move to compromise your honour.'

'I know you haven't.'

He moves to put his arms around her. She pushes him away with unexpected gentleness and determination.

'Have you made a decision?'

'About the business with your friend Luis?'

'Yes.'

'I'm coming back down to earth … I'll decide on Monday.'

'I'm not putting any pressure on you, but you'll tell Getulio that I asked you to, won't you?'

'I promise.'

'Come and find a cab with me. I don't want to leave you.'

The elevator is ancient, uncommonly filthy and covered from floor to ceiling in obscene drawings and inscriptions. Augusta reads them out with great seriousness as they descend.

'I recognise your writing, but honestly I didn't know you were so good at drawing.'

'I know, it's a bit boastful of me and a bit naughty … but when I can't sleep it helps me to shut myself in the elevator and write to you, maybe showing off a little too much sometimes.'

They come to rest with a thud at ground level. Arthur takes Augusta in his arms this time and kisses her. She presses the button for the twelfth floor and they reascend, redescend several times, seeking each other's lips. At ground level one last time, she pulls away and holds his face in her hands.

'Now this dirty elevator is sacred. Every time you take it you'll have to think of me. Everywhere we go in our lives we'll turn ugliness and obscenity into something beautiful. Nothing will touch us.'

They walk towards Broadway, hail a cruising cab driven by a gnome whose head is hardly higher than the steering wheel. He is chewing on a cold cigar. Bald, Arthur notes.

'Arturo … this is a secret: in September Getulio is leaving me for two weeks. He has to go abroad. Without me. Don't leave me alone. Take me wherever you want. Don't kiss me in the street … I have to go.'

The gnome fidgets impatiently, revving his cab in neutral.

'Dear Prince Charming, I will get into your superb carriage if you let me say two words to Mr Morgan, with whom I have, this afternoon, undertaken to turn all the ugliness crushing the modern world into something beautiful. Isn't that so, King Arthur?'

'With this guy and his smelly crate, it's not going to be easy.'

'What's wrong with my crate?'

'I adore your crate,' Augusta says. 'Listen, Arturo, I want you to remember one thing: if you'd taken advantage of my innocence this afternoon to have your way with me, I wouldn't have stopped you.'

'We'll talk about your innocence another time.'

'Where will you take me?'

'It'll depend on what I can afford.'

'I'm done here!' the gnome belches.

'Listen, Arturo *meu*, if you're very poor we'll just go to a very cheap place, and to forget our poverty we'll make love like the gods.'

'What if I take you to a luxury hotel?'

'We'll try not to make it too sad. Elizabeth will let you know when I'm free.'

'What about your address?'

'Don't tell me you want me to lose all my mystery in one go.'

She runs the tips of her fingers along his lips and climbs into the cab, which pulls away with a squeal. Out of the passenger window a hand and arm appear, waving a pink handkerchief.

So what part of all this is true?

Brustein ate with his fingers, clamping a chip between thumb and index finger, carrying it greedily to his pink, fleshy mouth. He did the same with the lettuce leaves, having sprinkled them lavishly with salt. Paper napkins he had used to wipe his hands were strewn across the table.

'I spent,' he said, 'a spellbinding year in Marrakesh. During the day I worked in an American bank and I spent the evenings with Moroccan friends I'd made who were mad about cooking. They convinced me that you can only taste the most delicate things by plunging your fingers into the dishes. Between courses a big jug and silver bowl goes round with rose petals or rose-geranium leaves floating in it. Compared to that advanced stage of civilisation, we're degenerates. Jansen's my most trusted friend, but when I eat with my fingers he has great trouble not being sick. He's super-sensitive, born in Sweden where everything's so clean, so hygienic and correct that he'll never manage to be completely American.'

Arthur wondered exactly who had lived in America thirty or forty years earlier, when Brustein, who had been born in Prague, was in Morocco, Jansen in Sweden, the Mendosas in Brazil, Concannon in Ireland, Mrs Paley in Hungary. In the luncheonette the broker was fond of, and to which he had taken Arthur, Latin Americans easily outnumbered blond northerners. At the next table the conversation was in Portuguese. The two waitresses were Asian, plump and heavy-calved, with legs bowed like elderly cavalrymen. Out of the hatch to the kitchen emerged the head of an enormous black man, grinning delightedly each time. Where had that Lithuanian couple come from, on the Saturday morning when Arthur had walked to the Brasilia restaurant? He looked around vainly for real Americans, for those Native Americans with copper-coloured skin of whom he knew only two examples, immune to vertigo as they cleaned the windows of the building where the stockbrokers had their offices.

'I'd like to meet some Americans,' Arthur said.

'For that, my friend you'll have to leave New York. This is America's back room. Look on a map, see how narrow Manhattan is. It's all appallingly compressed between the two branches of the Hudson. As soon as you get out of it, you see that the United States begins where New York ends and that it's very sparsely inhabited indeed, contrary to what one thinks. I was your age when my parents left Czechoslovakia for reasons you can guess. I was seized by a craving, and for a year I travelled all over the country in every direction, in Greyhound buses that cost me practically nothing. I had fifty dollars a month, not a king's ransom. I washed dishes, baled hay, sold newspapers on the street in Chicago, was an extra in a Cecil B. de Mille movie. I fed myself on strawberry ice cream and hot dogs. In short, the perfect career path for the future American multimillionaire, apart from the small detail that I didn't become a multimillionaire ... well, maybe ... if one day I sell my art collection, my two Cézannes, my Renoir, my Modigliani, a fine series of Picasso watercolours, and of course, for tradition's sake, because I did after all grow up in Czechoslovakia, a unique collection of Mucha drawings and posters.'

Brustein was going round in circles. It amused Arthur to wait patiently for the moment when he would come to the point.

'Porter told me plenty of good things about you. It always surprises me that he can be so well informed and then trust only his intuition. He claims to have a gift for it, a completely irrational sixth sense.'

'You had a gift too, when you were a codebreaker.'

'Ah. He told you. I had two strokes of luck, breaking the Japanese code and then the *Kriegsmarine*'s. By pure chance: I tried a key and the lock opened. Let's get an ice cream to get rid of the taste of these greasy hamburgers.'

Short-stemmed glasses as tall as vases were placed in front of them containing extravagant multicoloured combinations of ice cream, candied fruit and whipped cream topped with a parasol held aloft by a sugar doll.

'There's a moment when bad taste becomes art,' Arthur said.

His remark plunged Brustein into deep contemplation.

'About,' he said, his spoon suspended over his dessert, 'about this Sociedade mineira de Manao, I think we need generously to encourage Mr Luis de …'

'… Souza …'

'Mr Luis de Souza to take it over. It's been vulnerable for three years; its results have been a disaster. The shares are as low as they can go. Confidentially, however, there are rumours going round that recent drilling has indicated there might be oil there.'

'And if there isn't any?'

'If there isn't any, Mr Luis Whatever will take a bath. It's the sort of risk wheeler-dealers like him encounter from time to time. He'll recover from it or he'll go to jail.'

'I'm not out to ruin him.'

'Be sure that in our racket we're not out to ruin anyone. We want to create wealth that circulates; we want a planet full of millionaires who don't know what to do with their money. How will we be able to function without them? You're a quick learner, Arthur: we don't create anything, we speculate on stupidity, vanity, greed and lack of insight. Even so, I'm surprised that this man chose an intern who is still a complete novice, without worrying that he'll let the pussy out of the bag. And yet … after all, maybe Mr de Souza is right. Your call. I'm not talking about your conscience. Things move too fast on the New York Exchange to have time to examine consciences.'

'So?'

Brustein smiled, swallowed a spoonful of ice cream and pushed his plate away. A mischievous gleam shone in his light-coloured eyes.

'Don't put pressure on him. Let him make his bid. He'll relieve us of a lame duck. Jansen and I will find a way to show our gratitude.'

'And what if there's really oil in Amazonia?'

'Don't make me laugh.'

In the afternoon Getulio phoned Jansen and Brustein. Arthur gave him a green light, partly because Brustein had charmed him, partly because he had loathed de Souza's manners. When the contract was signed he found, on top of his salary for that month, a discreet envelope that resolved the material question of his escape with Augusta in September. Brustein looked contrite when he thanked him.

'I'm sorry for Mr de Souza, though. The rumours about test drillings for oil are more than premature. It would be more accurate to say they're non-existent.'

'Did you know?'

'Does one ever know anything with absolute certainty? I've always lived on doubt and chance.'

*

Elizabeth continued to appear late in the evening, irregularly, with a casualness that he did not hold against her any more than her absences or her unannounced appearances. Finding Arthur in the middle of working for his October exams, she would undress in a twinkling.

'You're too serious. It'll be your downfall. I'm beat. Goodnight.'

Rolled up in his sheet, she fell asleep immediately. An hour later she was lying on her back with the sheet thrown off, a hand across her bust, the other across her pelvis like the coy Eve on the Foscari Arch at the Doge's Palace in Venice. What was she looking for when she sought him out? In the morning when he came back from his jog in Battery Park, she was either still asleep or gone. Slowly Arthur began to do as she did. He took what she offered, which was both very little and a lot: she was a presence in a gargantuan town that paid him as much attention as a gnat. When they found themselves talking to each other, their conversation stayed suspended between them in a kind of no man's land, even when Getulio and Augusta's names came up. Rehearsals went on. Jerry, the new recruit, was learning everything with disconcerting ease. Thelma showed no imagination, but was an adornment. As soon as she appeared a fragrance wafted across the small stage that had been set up in the apartment, where the play was slowly taking shape. Piotr and Leigh were now on tour on the West Coast in a bourgeois production, lost to the real theatre. Their departure meant that Elizabeth had given up their diet; she also, Arthur suspected, occasionally drank more Chilean wine than she should. As to where they would stage their show, Elizabeth had decided on a disused warehouse at the docks.

'You can't imagine how beautiful the space is: huge beams,

broken windows, a sort of sticky dust all over the walls and the corrugated-iron roof, packs of rats that fight all night, squeaking like mad. All the imagery of a dead civilisation on a dead planet. The audience will feel completely at home. It's the world they live in, carefully averting their gaze to forget that they're trampling filth and ruins underfoot.'

'Sheer madness!'

Who would she end up with? One morning, as he showered with the door of the small bathroom open, she called out, 'You have a nice back, and real cherub's buns.'

He admired how supple and perfectly muscled she was, without ever doing any exercise. She could do the splits and headstands. They teased each other like children. As she drank coffee and ate fresh croissants (whose scattered flakes he would carefully brush out of the sheets after she had left) he said to her, 'I'm unbelievably lucky. I've discovered the mythical androgynous woman in you. I'm simultaneously your lover and your mistress.'

'Who are you with Augusta?'

'We're still in the world of make-believe.'

'Be careful when you fall.'

'You'll rescue me.'

'Don't mistake me for a nurse.'

He had no illusions about this chapter in his life. He knew that Elizabeth would disappear when he was least expecting it, and then maybe he would start to understand her better. But what an odd introduction to life's ambiguity it was, this affair without passion, possibly even without love, certainly without lies, if not without omission. Why didn't she want him to come to her apartment? When she did invite him, no more than twice during that long summer, he had the feeling that before he arrived she had hidden all traces of a stranger's presence, apart from the props for her play: a screen, a hospital bed, a wobbly chair.

Later Arthur was to remember these two months of suffocating summer in New York as a turning point in his life. At Jansen and Brustein he experienced the aggression of the business world and the ferocity of the competition. His colleagues hardly spoke to him, mostly because they felt anxious about the friendship shown by Brustein to a young foreigner who was too quick to learn everything, and a little too because they feared he would stay, even though he had on several occasions tried to quell their fears by talking about his second year at Beresford and his trip back to France.

Gertrude Zavadzinski, the colleague who concealed a hearing aid under her thick red hair, had been the only one to exchange a few words with him outside the office. Everyone called her Zava, an easy, androgynous nickname that matched her sturdy figure: broad shoulders, wrestler's hands, a round face and flattened nose covered with freckles, mannish manners, an air of being always on the defensive. With the natural politeness of the milieu in which he had grown up, Arthur had stepped aside in a doorway to allow Zava to pass. To his surprise, she spoke to him in French with an accent that had no American twang.

'I recognise French manners.'

'You could have let me know sooner.'

Shortly after five o'clock they were sitting in a bar on lower Broadway, drinking beer.

'I was born in Warsaw in 1930. We all spoke French at home.'

Her family had been in New York for a holiday the month before war was declared, and had stayed.

'My father worked in a bank in Warsaw. Here he has swept streets, driven a cab and a bus and been a janitor. My mother has been a lady's companion. I studied at Brooklyn College. We still live together, and speak French together.'

Her hand kept going to her hair to make sure that it hid her hearing aid, as she spoke in short little sentences that left no room for replies.

'I'm a black belt in judo. Twice a week I box at a ladies' gym. People know. No one jerks me around for long. In any case I hear much better than people think. Come and have dinner with us one night. My parents will be so happy to talk to a Frenchman.'

He had gone, touched to find in the family's misfortune such loyalty to a European education that America, with all the weight it carried in the world, its jeans, its chrome-plated automobiles, its Coca-Cola, its museums stuffed with masterpieces, its galloping technology, made – poor Europe! – a bit more obsolete each day, abandoning its pitiful wreckage at the side of the interstate highways of its new civilisation. It had taken barely fifteen years to crush Mr and Mrs Zavadzinski, who had perhaps been refined once, and in any case, thanks to their command of French, proud to belong to a privileged Europe without frontiers, the Europe that Stendhal and Joseph Conrad had known. Now closeted in a cramped three-room apartment in Brooklyn, opposite a neon sign whose red light inflamed the dining room every ten seconds despite the strip of black linoleum that covered the window in an attempt to block it out, the Zavadzinskis were awaiting a minor apocalypse. Their only reason for going on was the daughter who had triumphed over her disability, destined, they hoped (with their taste for fairy tales that was so typically Polish), for a great future that would avenge their failure in the land of plenty.

'The American dream … the American dream!' Thadeus Zavadzinski repeated in a voice full of rancour. 'What a very great lie for people like us, who had two maids, a car, and a house in the country!'

His wife grasped his hand and stroked it with her thumb to calm him.

'You're being ungrateful! If we'd stayed in Warsaw, we would be dead or destitute by now. Gertrude is our happiness. She'll be everything that life hasn't let you be.'

The somewhat painful evening had ended on a note of melancholy. Gertrude had seen Arthur to the bus stop. No one could sleep in the damp, unhealthy heat. Whole families squatted on the steps of apartment buildings or just lay down on the pavements, hoping for the slightest breath of fresh air.

'That was nice of you, Arthur. They'll talk about it for a long time. They don't see anybody. Our relatives all left for the West Coast. One of my two cousins is at West Point, the other's a surgeon in San Francisco. They don't speak French or Polish. We don't see them any more. We don't live in a smart enough neighbourhood.'

When they got to the bus stop he had wanted to see her back to her door.

'Then I'd have to show you the way again. We'd be going backwards and forwards till the morning.'

'I'm perfectly able to find my way around, and if I get lost, to ask someone's help. It looks like everyone's sleeping outdoors tonight anyway.'

She burst out laughing.

'You might survive, but two minutes after you closed your eyes you'd find yourself in your underwear, without a cent, and not having the faintest idea what happened to you.'

'What about you?'

'We understand each other. I've knocked down two or three of them, and now there's peace. I walk around with my hands in my pockets ... Don't tell anyone at the office that you've met my family. I may be no beauty, but it won't stop them making up God knows what stories to ridicule you, to ridicule me. We don't deserve it. We're better than they are ... aren't we?'

She was made of granite, physically and morally built with the determination to survive in a pitiless world. She would not go under; she had her secret garden, that dreary apartment in Brooklyn where her parents brooded over their defeat, with her their only hope.

'Why do I want to confide to you the things that even my father and mother don't know? An ear, nose and throat specialist examined me six months ago. There's an operation that can cure my deafness. Another two or three years and I'll be able to afford it ... One morning I'm going to walk into the office with my hair cropped, and everyone will see I don't have a hearing aid any more.'

So that was her dream. Arthur compared it to the poverty of his own. What was daydreaming about Augusta in comparison with the victory Gertrude had set her heart on? Nothing. The bus was coming. They hugged each other like two warriors. Through the back window he saw, cut in two and distorted by the reflection of the neon signs, Gertrude's tall, masculine form marching away like a grenadier.

*

As it opened, the lift door's yellow light revealed Elizabeth sitting in the darkness on the top step of the staircase, her head resting on her arms.

'You're home late!'

'It's not midnight yet.Mrs Paley could have let you in.'

'And told me her life story! No thanks.'

He hardly had time to shower before she was curled up, naked, wrapped in the sheet as she always was, sleeping or feigning sleep. On his return from Battery Park the next morning, already gone, she had left the smell of her chic and expensive perfume behind in the bed and a scribbled note on the table: 'Thank you. E.'

For what? How she protected herself! They had not exchanged more than three words, and not a single caress. The fact that at some moment that evening she had had the sudden urgent need for a presence next to her while she slept bothered Arthur more than if she had dared to risk an admission. A shadow had crept between them, when they had naively thought themselves above such mawkishness. But then one never is; experience proves it. We barricade ourselves against our feelings in vain. A suspicion passes, pauses, seeps in, digs subterranean shafts, and then erupts like a ferret flushed out by a terrier.

Arthur had a bad day, his work routine haunted by an unease that he would banish for a time only to feel it returning as soon as he raised his head. He waited in vain for a sign from Gertrude Zavadzinski. Engrossed in the Stock Exchange telex feed, she appeared to be as unaware of him as every other day, and at five o'clock, leaving the building ahead of him, she disappeared into the crowds streaming out of their offices. The storm that had been threatening since the morning burst as he was walking back to Rector Street via the docks. Within minutes the streets were transformed into torrents as women dashed for the subway, their light summer dresses clinging indecently to their bodies as a result of the rain and the jets of dirty water the cars were splashing up from the potholes in the cratered streets. Arthur arrived at his room soaked. Mrs Paley was waiting for him on the landing.

'Give me your suit, I'll dry it out in the kitchen. The lady from the other day, you know ... the Spanish one—'

'She's Brazilian, actually.'

'Oh! I'd have thought ... from her accent ... She left a note for you.'

Arturo *meu* ... it's happening ... Getulio is going away on 1 September for two weeks. I've told Elizabeth; I'll meet you at her apartment with my suitcase. Do you know where we're going? The best thing would be a desert island with all mod cons. I shan't say I love you, you would start being horrid straight away. Miss Augusta Mendosa sends you fondest regards.

The rain had come in through the window he had left open that morning and made a pool on the parquet floor, soaking several books and a notepad on the table where he worked. Following hard on his heels, Mrs Paley rushed to the mess with a cloth and bowl in her hand.

'It's my fault ... I should have known. Let me do it.'

On her knees she mopped the floor, displaying a bottom that Arthur fleetingly thought must once have received its fair share of compliments.

'I hope the letter that came in this morning's mail isn't too wet.'

Arthur recognised his mother's handwriting. The rain had begun to dissolve the ink on the envelope with its French stamp, smudging his name and leaving only, on the left, the words 'America, by airmail'. Despite having been lectured several times about her error, Madame Morgan continued to believe firmly that a single 'America' existed, the one where her son was being initiated in the ways of the great and the good.

'Don't stay there dripping like that! Get changed, come on. No need for modesty! I'm not of an age to take it as an invitation any more.'

Wrapped in a bath towel, he handed her his soaked shirt and suit. The storm stopped as abruptly as it had started, leaving the ordinary sounds of the city to start up again: the fire department's sirens, the droning of a long-haul flight descending to LaGuardia, the foghorn of a tug going up the Hudson. Mrs Paley wrung his soaked rug out in the basin.

'In New York,' she said, 'even the storms are oversized. Ten years ago there was an earthquake in California, two hundred dead, ten thousand homeless. Last summer a cyclone hit Florida: a hundred dead, millions of dollars' worth of damage. They don't know how to do anything like everyone else. When I met Stephen in Budapest in 1920, he told me he was a diplomat. Eventually I found out he was just the ambassador's bodyguard, but it was too late ... I'd followed him to Wyoming where he owned thousands of acres ... The truth was that he lived with his parents on a little farm with two cows and two pigs. No pearl necklace for me! I left him, my dear Stephen, and went to work. After the war I'd happily have gone back to Hungary if it hadn't been for the Communists. At least I can tell myself that I've known love ... Do you know what love is, Mr Morgan?'

'I'm learning.'

'If you'd seen me in the yard of that farm with the toothless old man, the mother who read the Bible all day long and my diplomat Stephen who didn't wash any more and drank ten pints of beer every night … me, ex-star of the Budapest ballet, who had packed my ballet shoes and my tutus and pink tights in my suitcase! To dance in the yard of that farm among all the pig manure and cowpats! I left it all behind when I ran away.'

Elizabeth was right, you didn't want to get Mrs Paley started. Even on her knees, with her sleeves rolled up and her skinny, spotted arms working away, she was ready to tell you everything that had happened to her. Arthur stopped listening, turning the envelope from his mother over and over in his hand, and, with his silence failing to supply the necessary encouragement, the ex-star of the Budapest ballet got to her feet, her joints cracking joyfully.

'That's how it is! Life goes on … We get older.'

'At every age.'

She darted out of the room with her bowl, cloth and sponge and Arthur's clothes.

The letter weighed more heavily in his hand after she had gone, demanding to be opened.

I wasn't very well last week, but the thought of seeing you arriving here soon perked me up. [she was the only person Arthur knew who used expressions like 'perk up']. I've had your bedroom painted. Your suits are back from the dry-cleaner, looking like new. I hope you're not overdoing it with all those exercises. When you're back you'll be able to play tennis again. A string on your racquet had popped [did she think she was coming down to his level by using the word?] and I took it to

169

get it restrung. The man in the shop fixed it and didn't charge me. He asked after you. You'll be able to play at the de Moucherels' [how had she managed, living in military circles, not to learn that you leave out the 'de' when you just use the surname?] with Marie-Ange and Marie-Victoire, you haven't seen them for years. We've also been invited to spend a week-end (is that how you spell it?) at Laval with our Dubonnet cousins. Antoine Dubonnet has gone into politics – you must remember him, he's a town councillor now – and he's very interested in America and wants you to tell him about it. His daughter Amélie, who you met on holiday at Bénodet, is about to become a nurse specialising in "geriatrics". I expect you know what that is. She's cut her hair – do you remember how you used to pull her plaits when she was little? The pensions for widows of officers who died on active service have been increased. I managed quite well before, I'll manage better now. What do you need? You told me you were earning a good salary at that Jansen and Brustein (with that name he must be Jewish). So it won't hurt you to pay for your ticket back home. Sending you all my love, my darling son, for me you're still my wonderful companion in my great loneliness, Jeanne, your Maman.

Arthur almost cried. Just as she would cry when she got his letter announcing that he would not be coming back to France until the following year. Their lives were going in different directions, but why did it have to happen so cruelly? The worst was that she would hide her enormous disappointment under a mask of cheerfulness and face it with a smiling bravery that had never fooled him and only intensified her son's remorse. Disappointed? No, of course not, not a bit. But his cousins would be, and so would all his distant relations who were so looking forward to seeing him – every time she said so she believed it a little more – Arthur, her messenger from the modern world, America its beacon. He picked up the accusatory photo of the young newly-weds on their honeymoon in Venice and turned it to the wall.

In the trattoria, still half empty at that hour, the waiters in aprons and striped waistcoats wandered nonchalantly between the tables, picking their nails and teeth. He chose an isolated table at the end of the room and called Elizabeth from the cloakroom. The telephone rang on, then, 'Oh, it's you, Arthur … where are you?'

'In the trattoria downstairs. Come down.'

'I can't.'

'Make an effort.'

'Is it important?'

'Yes.'

There was a silence. She must have been covering the mouthpiece with her hand.

'I can't hear you.'

'All right … I'll be down in a quarter of an hour.'

He ordered a bottle of Frascati that he had almost finished by the time she appeared, in a lavender-blue dress and wearing silver-blue eye shadow, coral-pink lipstick and a Native American headband. Utterly different. And visibly pleased by Arthur's slack-jawed reaction.

'I can make an effort. For important occasions.'

'Then I'm afraid you may be disappointed.'

'I was outside when the storm started. I got soaked.'

'Me too.'

'I got dry and curled up in bed. I was fast, fast asleep when the phone rang.'

'You come back down to earth easily.'

'And now I'm hungry.'

The trattoria filled up with the usual Village wildlife. Elizabeth knew most of the couples and Arthur enjoyed their surprise at seeing her in her make-up and girlish blue dress, she who had pioneered, long before it was fashionable, the uniform of jeans and bleached singlets and exotic necklaces and silver nails.

'There's nothing more reassuring than a woman who's hungry. Marie-Ange and Marie-Victoire are never hungry.'

'Do I know those particular Maries?'

'Two skinny nags. No, and you never will. They live in Laval and they'll never leave.'

Elizabeth lit cigarette after cigarette, taking a few drags before stubbing them out in the rapidly filling ashtray.

'Don't you worry about your voice?'

'My voice is too sharp. I need to make it more throaty. An artist's life is full of such pleasant sacrifices. How do you think a Murphy can hold an audience if she talks like some affected girl from Park Avenue?'

'It depends on the role.'

'Trust me. This one's not an affected girl.'

Some time later, after a third bottle of Frascati that was no improvement on the previous two, Elizabeth took Arthur's left hand and placed it, palm upwards, on the table to study it with knitted eyebrows.

'Do you read palms?'

'Madeleine, my old French nanny, is really good. When she was twenty she used to go to fairs and earn her living by telling farmers' fortunes.'

'Did she read your palm?'

'She always refused. She doesn't want to know, or me to know.'

Arthur was not sure he wanted to know either. He tried to withdraw his hand. Elizabeth held it tightly.

'Now's not the time to pull away. Anyhow you can't any more. I've seen.'

'What?'

She ran her index finger along his lifeline, which extended well past his palm.

'No complications. A perfectly geometrical curve. Who wouldn't envy you?'

'Me.'

No complications? He could see plenty multiplying along his future path.

One of the waiters, sitting sideways on a table, was tuning his guitar.

She was still examining his open hand.

'A happy love life—'

'Thank you, you're too kind.'

'Wait … short relationships.'

'That's a happy love life, by definition. Come on, Elizabeth, please let's go before he starts singing "*O sole mio*".'

A couple entered: a young Asian woman with her neck in a surgical collar, and a man in his thirties wearing a beige corduroy suit and a shirt that was unbuttoned to reveal his hairy chest.

They both gave the same hint of a wave in Elizabeth's direction and sat down at a distant table.

'Those two love each other,' Elizabeth said. 'She was a dancer, he writes novels which all the publishers have turned down. A month ago they were so desperate that they made a suicide pact and hanged themselves. The beam broke. He fell down and broke his coccyx, the dummy. He called for help. The neighbours came and cut her down. It's possible she'll have to wear a surgical collar for the rest of her life, and she'll never dance again. But a publisher read an article on the hanged couple from Greenwich Village and offered to publish the novel he had turned down six months earlier. You see, love can be useful.'

The waiter strummed his guitar, repeating over and over again '*Capri, petite île …*'

'To us?'

'Not to us, no.'

She smiled innocently and laid her palm on top of Arthur's.

'I don't know where I am any more,' Arthur said.

'In your hand I can see evidence of a rare duality, as if you have two men living inside you.'

'I'm not two men. I'm sometimes one and maybe sometimes another.'

She took her hand away and with her index finger traced a line that cut across another line that was very faintly marked.

'But there's still a minute or an hour or a day when the two men are the same man. What's happening this evening?'

'I'm a monster. I'm going to hurt, horribly, the only woman in my life. And she'll forgive me and send me an unwearable sweater that she's been knitting on the long summer evenings, looking at my photo. Have I said enough?'

'More than enough. Not everybody's lucky enough to be an orphan. But apart from that – which you've already decided and which is done and will spoil, just a bit, your pleasure at having Augusta all to yourself – apart from that, do you know what's waiting for you afterwards?'

'I have no illusions.'

'It's a big risk.'

'I'm ready for it.'

'You're brave.'

In front of the steps up to the brick building, whose door and window frames were painted an aggressive green, she put her hands on Arthur's shoulders.

'I'm not going to ask you in.'

'You can come to my place.'

'We have to let some time pass.'

He wanted to tell her that he found her infinitely more desirable like this, in a shift dress that left her neck and arms bare and a headband that made her look ten years younger. How old was she actually? Twenty-five, twenty-six at the most, and outspokenly mature.

'The first of September, she'll be upstairs. In the morning, around eleven. Don't come before and don't keep her waiting. I don't want it to be too difficult. Do you know where you're going?'

He had no idea yet. Brustein's envelope would not be big enough for any extravagances. He had thought of a few days at Cape Cod or, even more simply, Long Island, but she hated the sea.

'If you like, I've got a bungalow at Key Largo that I inherited. I'll phone and they'll get it ready for you. The beach is thirty yards away and the yacht club two hundred. The restaurant's all right.'

'She doesn't like the sea.'

'Just make it so that she only sees you. She wanted a desert island with all mod cons. Key Largo in September is just about that. Aren't I heroic?'

'I'd like to say all sorts of sweet things to you, and plenty of them, but I'm scared you'll laugh and it won't work.'

'You need to wait. I don't know what's going on either. We'll see each other at the end of September. Or in October. Don't forget, my premiere's around 30 October.'

'I'll be at Beresford.'

'So skip your classes. Arthur, sometimes, just sometimes, you're too serious.'

She had already climbed two steps and stood a head higher than he. Her slender, lavender-blue outline had a candle-like grace in the feeble light over the steps.

'You're very lovely,' he said stupidly, then shrugged because he was so ashamed at the platitude.

'People don't often tell me that, but it's not important … I prefer not to be. Lovely women are ten a penny. Dolls. The United States is a huge warehouse of dolls of all ages. Can you see me at a widows' club with purple hair, festooned with glass jewellery and reeking of Parisian perfume? I want to escape all that. I'm trying a different sort of life.'

'At least promise me you won't hang yourself like that Chinese woman.'

'That takes two.'

She climbed the steps quickly, and as she did the hem of her dress lifted, revealing the back of her fine bare legs. At the door she turned round and placed two fingers to her lips to blow him a kiss.

'*Adios caballero!*'

*

Was that all they talked about that evening? Definitely not, but Arthur did not forget the essentials, her hand laid on his palm to cover up the lines that said too much, her unequivocal firmness in drawing a boundary between them from now on. In a game as free as theirs had been there is always one who without warning, and to the other's complete surprise, refuses to go along with the rules when they suddenly become aware of their dangers and artifices. Arthur no longer doubted that Elizabeth's arrival the previous night, her sitting on the stairs outside Mrs Paley's in the darkness, their night together without touching or speaking, the empty bed he had found on his return from Battery Park holding croissants that suddenly felt ridiculous, had a significance far beyond any words they could have exchanged. The picture of Elizabeth was magnifying. At the outset it had been little more than a sketch, but slowly she had added to it here and there, some delicate touches, some harmonies to the colours and nuances to the vibrato of her voice. How much did she regret having pretended she was impervious? Born with a silver spoon in her mouth, she had never stopped trying to make people forget who she was or how rich, or her American society background that she rejected so vehemently. Once – Elizabeth had told him – when she and Madeleine had had a heart-to-heart talk, her nanny had said to her in her rough, provincial, country way, 'Just don't go getting too far ahead of yourself, young lady.' Elizabeth had hugged her fiercely, hidden her face in her large bosom and, clinging to her warmth and wisdom, wept and wept. 'Oh you're lucky, my duck,' Madeleine told her, 'so lucky to cry properly and let everything out! Lots of people can't really cry and they just pretend. You're a proper girl, you know how to cry when you need to, and I know I'm the only one you dare to show your tears to.'

Apart from Arthur, with whom Elizabeth occasionally let herself go, telling him about her nanny with sudden unguarded candour, nobody knew about her relationship with the mythical Madeleine, whose common sense had never been shaken and whose goodness had remained as it always had been, stern and all-encompassing. Being French, he was the only one who could understand Elizabeth's boundless attachment to, and appreciation of, Madeleine, who had not only taught her to speak the perfect French of the Loire valley but a string of startling colloquial expressions that sounded irresistibly comic in a foreigner's mouth.

Arthur returned to Rector Street on foot, breathing the smell of wet dog and flint that rose between the buildings after the lightning and the storm that afternoon. From the roadway and pavements the tons of heat that had been stored up over the past two months began bursting out of manholes and basements in clouds of vapour pierced by the headlamp beams of automobiles and yellow cabs creeping uptown to the theatres and music halls. Drenched by the violent rain, the town was now tipping silently into sleep in the resplendent night, refreshed, cleansed of its miasmas, hardly disturbed by the rare pedestrians who emerged like ectoplasm out of one cloud of vapour and disappeared into another that immediately closed over them.

There is nothing like walking in a city at night for talking to yourself, rebuilding your life and the world at the same time, writing yourself the perfect speech, saying the perfect words to the girl you left a moment before without giving her a chance to come back at you, or composing with magical ease a particularly hard letter. 'Dear Maman, I'm afraid that I'm going to disappoint you very much. Everything was arranged for me to come and see you in September, and now, firstly, Mr Brustein has asked me to carry out an inquiry into an investor in Miami, and secondly, the Beresford term starts earlier than I thought. If I came, it would be for two or three days at the most, which we can't really justify financially. Much better to put it back to Christmas, which we can both spend in Paris without having to visit Uncle Whatsisname and the Thingumajig cousins. Believe me when I say ...'

It was not so terribly hard to lie at a distance, and she would be proud of his conscientiousness and of the confidence that Jansen and Brustein's was already showing in him after such a short time. He was moving among the great and the good! With Elizabeth things were not so simple. She answered back, for a start, and her answer did not have to cross the Atlantic before it reached Arthur, and then everything about her self and her character announced her readiness for combat, for aggressive defence. She might have been more of a woman than she wanted to be, but she clung to that privilege. 'You should have talked to me,' he said, 'and I should have talked to you. We thought we were being clever, and in the end our paths hardly crossed at all. I felt we'd invented an exceptional relationship, between two people with no hang-ups ...' No hang-ups? It was trite, and wide of the mark. He had hang-ups galore, despite Elizabeth's behaviour having swept them aside from the first time they met. He was not even sure that he didn't blame her for having, with her disarming spontaneity, invited him into her bed (after her initial procrastination with the vanished George). 'Surely you can see how annoying it is for a man of my age to realise it's you who decides everything: the day, the time, practically the way we're going to have sex. You come to my place without warning.

Tonight, when you wouldn't ask me in, I'd never felt as close to you as I did during dinner, despite that guitarist singing, "*Capri, petite île* ..." Do you want us to slide into clichés, staring into each other's eyes and murmuring sweet nothings like Mimi and her student? Oh, and if I hadn't found Augusta so attractive, would you have paid me the slightest attention?' The answer was missing. He discovered that he was incapable of making it up.

In the lift that took him up to his twelfth-floor room, with Augusta's accent and tone of voice in his head he scanned the obscenities that defaced its panels. What had she really thought of the drawings: a rash of obelisks, piled-up heaps of stone archways, here and there an obelisk diving into a stone archway? Mrs Paley claimed that she knew the author of the graffiti, a retired accountant who had four locks on his apartment door and went out, summer and winter, wearing a raincoat and carrying a newspaper. One evening they had met on the stairs and he had twitched his newspaper aside, revealing the limp trace of his already elderly pretensions. 'I told him I didn't mind. Everyone needs to get some fresh air once in a while. He looked very disappointed, and since then he doesn't say hello to me any more.'

Sliding open the lift door, Arthur saw, in the dim light, Elizabeth sitting where she had sat the night before, on the top step of the stairs.

'You took your time! I'll bet you walked.'

In his room, she said, 'Don't turn the light on ... it's so much nicer ... undress me ... don't say a word ... stay where you are ...'

In the morning she was asleep when he got up and, barefoot and in silence, tidied up, folded her blue dress and laid it on the back of his one armchair, put her underwear on a chair next to her high heels, and pinned a note on the door that said WAIT FOR ME in capital letters.

*

She did not wait for him; she was already in the street, her arm raised for a cab, when he appeared in his tracksuit, sweating, with a paper bag of croissants in his hand. He offered her one and they ate them standing there, next to the taxi's open door.

'Tonight?' she said.

'Yes. Not before midnight. I'm having dinner with Brustein.'

'Wonderful! You're already having business dinners. My little Arthur will go far.'

'It's not my doing.'

She stroked his cheek tenderly.

'The boring thing,' she said, 'is that our lives aren't going in the same direction.'

'I have no talent at all. I mean, none like the ones you like.'

'Yes you do. You do have one. A major one. We'll talk about it tonight.'

She laughed and was suddenly shy, like a child who has said something terrifically rude. She blew Arthur a kiss on one finger, got into the cab, and gave him her croissant paper.

'A souvenir. Arthur and Elizabeth ate croissants in Rector Street and said goodbye to each other after a night of love.'

Brustein surprised Arthur with the news that Allan Porter and Gertrude Zavadzinski would be dining with them.

'I invited them for a while later. We'll have a half-hour to ourselves. My wife's not ready. She's Spanish and she lives in New York City the way she lived in Seville. Getting up's as hard for her as going to bed, and her all-round unpunctuality used to drive me crazy when we were first married, but I got used to it eventually. Now I find her lateness restful. If by some miraculous happenstance she decided to be on time, I think I'd be profoundly disturbed. Allan deals with these things differently. He pointed Minerva towards the Seventh Day Adventists, a wholly idiotic sect but one that has nevertheless put a spell on her. She's a pain in the ass. Also a tireless proselyte. She avoids the poor neighbourhoods, obviously, and expends her energies on Washington's smartest districts. When I teased her about it one day she said, "You know, wealthy people also have souls to be saved. Nobody thinks about them." See what I mean? Come in, come in. I call this room my oratory. I have some lovely things to show you. I know you won't say anything dumb when I show you my treasures; in any case you're not the sort of guy to say dumb things. You'll get the point straight away: that my collection's alive because I love it. Every painting represents a stage in my life. If they were in a museum, these paintings and drawings would never breathe the love they do here. We'll have to be quick, before Porter and Zava arrive and start talking business and politics. I see you're surprised to be meeting Zava here. Allan's interested in her … no, not like that, obviously. Wrong sort of figure. On the other hand, although she's a strange girl she has an attractive intelligence. Her brain's like an elegant, silent mechanism. Not a squeak! Her unswerving loyalty to the US makes her an interesting person from a point of view that we care about. You're beginning to understand, Mr Morgan – or rather Arthur, if you'll allow me, since from the day after tomorrow you'll no longer be an employee of Jansen and Brustein – you're starting to understand that it's the Americans of most recent date who are the most loyal servants of their new homeland, and it's the ones who've been settled here for generations who, as a result of a perfectly natural reaction that's part of the fundamental ingratitude of human nature, are the first to betray it.'

Brustein took a key out of his waistcoat pocket and opened the door of a circular room whose bay windows overlooked Central Park and the Metropolitan Museum.

'It's no more than an amateur's first attempt: a homage to my father. Wherever his soul may be, I hope it's opening up and marvelling. In Prague he was the top expert on Impressionism. He couldn't afford to buy even the smallest sketch, but when I made my first real money on the Stock Exchange he ordered me – *ordered*, do you hear – instead of buying myself a new automobile, to buy a Cézanne drawing that was being offered in a public sale. I did as I was told. That same evening I showed him the drawing. He died in the night. I never saw his face so happy. I keep the door locked not because I'm afraid of burglars, but because I'm sure that my father – well, his soul at peace – comes here day and night to wander at liberty in front of these walls. He's at home here, doesn't want anyone disturbing him, and even likes seeing his name painted on the ceiling, despite the fact that it's a tad kitsch, as the Germans say …'

Arthur looked up. In a plaster rose was a painted inscription: 'Jacob Brustein Museum, Prague 1892–New York 1945'. Arthur would have liked to linger. Brustein did not give him the time.

'You'll be back: this painting and the pen drawing of the Montagne Sainte-Victoire in morning mist are enough for one day. One mustn't overdo it.'

He closed the door and reset the alarm.

'Now that you know me better than my wife, better than Jansen, who's been my partner for ten years and collects nineteenth-century door knobs, better than Allan Porter who's nevertheless my best friend, and better than my colleagues at the Stock Exchange whose nickname for me is the Fox of the Balkans, which is not all that geographical but as you'll have noticed the Americans don't know a lot of geography, am I that much more cunning than they are? My wife will tell you not. It's a wife's job to cut her husband's reputation down to size. Because she was dedicated at birth to the Virgin of the Begonia, she gets called Begonia more often than Maria. This enchants me. I married a flower. Not every man can say that. In a moment or two she'll make her entrance – entrance is the *mot juste* – adorned, lacquered, her hair styled, perfumed and wearing something deliciously low-cut, so lovely that despite my height I've felt like a gnat next to her ever since I converted to Catholicism and married her in Seville.'

He led Arthur into the sitting room and poured him a stiff measure of bourbon without asking him.

'And you're French! What kind of a visiting card is that! You'll find out how much credit that's worth in our world! Make the most of it. Be shameless. In a crowd you always pick out the Frenchman from all the rest. Yesterday it was Porter showing an interest in you, today it's me … and Miss Zavadzinski.'

'*Zava?*'

'And there are plenty more surprises where that came from.'

There were. During dinner Porter, Brustein and Zava exchanged a series of remarks that just seemed obscure to a bewildered Arthur. Maria de Begonia presided, imposing, silent, a tortoiseshell comb encrusted with rhinestones fixed in her heavy coil of black hair, only repressing with the greatest difficulty, it seemed, her desire to sing, '*Si tu ne m'aimes pas, je t'aime / Et si je t'aime, prends garde à toi …*' But perhaps that was a cliché of Arthur's imagining, and she was merely intent on supervising the serving of dinner by a hired waiter who looked even blacker than he was because he was wearing a white jacket buttoned to his throat.

'Coffee will be served in Karl's office' were her first words as she got to her feet after the dessert.

When she left the room, accompanied by Zava, Brustein assured Arthur and Porter that his wife might say very little in their presence but soon caught up when she was alone with him. Obviously the questions they had been discussing during dinner held little excitement for her. In the melting pot of America, there are those who start to assimilate the second they set foot on the dockside in New York; there are also those who will remain strangers in a land of immigrants where everyone, apart from the Native Americans, is an intruder. Begonia spent all her time among Spanish women, and Andalusians at that. At a pinch she accepted into this restricted female circle – she knew no men – the occasional Latin American, despite a snobbish reticence towards them that took many forms. Brustein was delighted by this reticence, which placed him and her above the rest in a society that was horribly stratified. By contrast, their sons, aged six and seven, already behaved like Yankees born and bred, were mad about baseball and cartoons, keen on rock 'n' roll, stuffed themselves with popcorn every time they went to the cinema, and were incapable of saying a word of either Spanish or Czech.

'They're happy! Why should I complain? The funny thing will be that if they have kids, those kids one day are going to want to go looking for their roots, learn Spanish and Czech, and track down the tombs of their ancestors in Prague and Seville.'

The hired waiter came into the office-library with coffee, followed by Begonia and Zava.

'The children are asleep,' Zava said with heartfelt relief.

The little hooligans had ambushed her with enema syringes filled with water.

'They are devils,' Begonia said proudly.

Arthur silently willed her to grab some castanets and dance a seguidilla. Sadly the performance was not forthcoming; everything the imposing Mrs Brustein had to say was brisk and to the point.

'Karl never has sugar with coffee.'

The gravity of this habit was not lost on anyone, and Brustein's display of satisfaction at having this albeit hardly secret aspect of his forceful personality underlined made Arthur like this endearing and happy man all the more.

'Where are you at with your plans for the next few weeks?' Porter asked abruptly, rather less inclined to go into raptures about Mrs Brustein's pronouncements.

Arthur almost blurted out that for now the future was limited to the prospect of Key Largo, which was not without a faint shadow hanging over it, in the form of Elizabeth's ambivalence. It seemed clear, however, that Porter would not be interested in that in the slightest.

'What do you really want to talk to me about?' he asked, irritated by what was being said and not said among this motley group of dinner guests.

'Do you intend to stay in the United States?'

'No.'

Begonia rang for the hired waiter, who must have been listening behind the door because he appeared immediately.

'The liqueur tray, Benny.'

Benny disappeared.

'He's interested in our conversation,' Porter said.

Brustein smiled.

'No danger there. He goes back a long way. In fact, didn't you recommend him to me, Allan?'

'Ah, that's it. I knew he reminded me of someone.'

Then, turning to Arthur, he said, 'I asked the question because it's a significant one. We offer a number of foreign students the chance to stay and study in the US, so that they take back to their respective countries our way of doing things. The problem is that unfortunately sixty per cent of these scholars then decide to stay here when they finish university, and our investment's totally wasted.'

'Why don't you make them sign an agreement that after their studies at Beresford, or Yale or Harvard or wherever, they'll go back to where they came from and apply all the American lessons in morality and economics that they've learnt here?'

'It would be against our principles. We need friends in the world.'

'Even after winning a world war and saving face in Korea?'

Porter raised his arms heavenward, waving his fat little hands like a man drowning.

'I often wonder whether the worst fate that can befall a nation is for it to come out of a war the winner.'

'All over Europe where the Allies fought you'll see graffiti saying "GIs go home!"' Brustein said. 'Our policies are openly criticised in Paris and London.'

Benny came back with the tray of cognac and liqueurs. Begonia sprang back to life and served her guests one after the other, then, Benny having disappeared, sat down again and stifled a yawn. It required far more than this to divert Porter from his speech. In his view, the most problematic issue was the home-grown one of an entire class challenging the system, a phenomenon that was currently making itself felt at the highest levels of state and the universities. McCarthyism was not without a basis in reality, but it was using the tactics of the witch-hunt, incompatible with the principles of American democracy, and dragging through the mud the administration of a country that held its freedoms in high esteem.

Arthur began to see the direction Porter was going in, and was irritated by his circumlocutions.

'What are you trying to suggest to me?' he said, with an abruptness that made Zava smile in amusement.

'Nothing at all, my friend. And you, what are you hoping for?'

Arthur did not hope for anything; he was merely surprised at the interest these two men were showing in him. There were hundreds of candidates as clever as he was, and he would never consider himself to be 'one of them'. Porter's solicitude made him feel uncomfortable. Brustein's character, however, so direct and warmly friendly, penetrated his defences completely. He was about to reply with a wisecrack when he caught Zava looking at him, mutely entreating him not to lose his temper, to stay with them and with her in this discussion, which was still so ill-defined but which she intended to take advantage of in order one day to get her own back on everything life had inflicted on her: parents unable to recover from their misfortune, her deafness, her giant's hands and feet, her frizzy red hair that had got her so bullied by her classmates. And back in Paris, wasn't Madame Morgan expecting her son to take his place among the great and the good?

'However hard I try, I just can't make myself seem important,' Arthur sighed, profoundly convinced that in the current state of things he wasn't.

Brustein came to his aid.

'Don't think any further than tomorrow and the day after tomorrow. We'll help you.'

Begonia, more and more obviously bored, stood up to push back a book whose leather spine spoilt the alignment of a shelf. Her gesture was taken as an invitation to leave. In the hall Arthur helped Zava on with a light cape that covered her shoulders. She had said almost nothing, but as he did so she discreetly took his hand and squeezed it unequivocally.

Like the afternoon he had spent with Augusta in his room in Rector Street, what remains of the two weeks in Key Largo? A string of short films, lazily edited together, whose scenes Arthur will replay again and again in the years that follow, each time with infinite regret and a remorse that is no less enduring.

The opening scenes: the cab stopping outside Elizabeth's building, Arthur racing up the stairs two at a time to ring her bell. The door opens and there is Augusta, a suitcase at her feet, her face consumed with anxiety. She seems so paralysed that he wonders if she has gone back on her word and only come to the rendezvous to tell him that they won't be going away at all because she can't leave New York as Getulio has postponed his journey.

'What's wrong?'

Her lips are trembling, as if she has just got out of an icy bath. He suspects she might break down and takes her in his arms. Nestled against him, she becomes calmer. What is unfolding at this moment is the start of an adventure from which they both know very well they will not emerge unscathed.

'Let's go, right now.'

'Isn't Elizabeth here?'

'No … of course not. You expect too much of her.'

*

The next sequence takes place at Miami. Stepping off the plane, they are surprised by the air's hot humidity. Autumn has come early to New York. In Florida the summer is lingering. Men are wearing shorts or light trousers and brightly coloured short-sleeved shirts, women light dresses, their legs bare and tanned. Everyone looks as though they are on holiday. Augusta's suitcase is the last off the chute and she fidgets. A car drives them to Key Biscayne. Augusta asks the driver to stop at a clothes store and leads Arthur inside. It must be said that he is hardly dressed for Florida. She chooses two pairs of swimming trunks and some linen trousers and T-shirts for him. She needs nothing, just some saris. It is Arthur's turn to worry as he watches her pick out three saris. At this rate they will have to cut their holiday short by a day, possibly two.

Then other images follow: Elizabeth has organised everything. At the dock the white launch from the Key Largo Yacht Club is waiting for them. Sitting nonchalantly on its bow, her long brown legs dangling from each side, a young woman in blue shorts and a yellow polo shirt is smoking a cigarillo which she tosses into the dock's oily water when she sees them. Her tanned face wears a look of profound boredom that may just be her contempt for the tourists wandering aimlessly, admiring the berthed yachts. Her hair, bleached by sun and salt, is kept in place behind her ears with a red ribbon.

'Hey there! Was the plane delayed?'

'No, we delayed ourselves.'

Seeing the chauffeur take their shopping bags out of the car, she smiles.

'So I see! It's not really worth it ... No one wears a lot of clothes at Key Largo: shorts, slacks and a sweater for the evenings. There's no one there. Except at the weekend. I run the club bar and look after Elizabeth's bungalow. It's not hard: she comes once a year. My name's Mandy. What do I call you?'

'Augusta and Arthur.'

Competently she stows their suitcases in the cockpit and holds out her hand to help Augusta aboard.

Mandy's presence stamps the next rapid sequence of images, which calls out for a soundtrack to accompany the harmonies of the dark-green islets and mangroves, the pale and hollow sky, the steel-blue sea, and the flat Florida coastline, washed out and quivering in a mirage of misty heat. Wearing a blue, light woollen hat, she sits with her back to them on the Bertram's bridge deck, piloting it cautiously through the channels marked by black and green buoys. Suddenly-woken tarpons leap and dive in the launch's wake. Augusta lies down in the cabin. Arthur sees her bare feet and legs, which she crosses and uncrosses.

Three hours later Mandy lowers the double throttle to idle and the Bertram's bow dips as it glides between red and green signal lights that are already winking. Night is falling. A few yachts swing at anchor, their sails furled and stored in covers already shiny with condensation in the twilight. Mandy goes alongside the jetty, disturbing two pelicans sleeping with their heads under their wings, and draws up to a wooden gangplank. A pot-bellied man in oil-stained singlet and shorts, his arms tattooed with green snakes, comes towards them, picks Augusta up by the waist, and puts her down as if swinging a feather ashore. Arthur jumps and goes to help with the unloading of the baggage, but the man motions him aside.

'Leave that, that's my job. It's quicker. My name's Cliff.'

Night has fallen in these few minutes. A cool breeze rustles the branches of the wild pines and the leaves of the frangipani trees, whose sweet scent perfumes a gust of salty air. Carrying the suitcases, Cliff and Mandy walk ahead of them down the dirt path that runs away from the port along the top of the beach as far as a white bungalow. Mandy switches the lights on on the veranda and in the living room, bedroom, bathroom and kitchen. The furniture is Philippine rattan, the armchairs covered in pastel-coloured toile de Jouy. Audubon lithographs cover the walls and there are corals and a few polished shells and pieces of driftwood behind glass on the shelves.

'A desert island with all mod cons, isn't that just what you wanted?'

'Do you intend to hold me captive here for fourteen days?'

'And fourteen nights.'

Mandy quickly shows them how everything works: refrigerator, cooker, where the bedlinen is kept, napkins, breakfast tray if they want to have it at the bungalow.

'That's lucky,' Augusta says, 'Arthur's a wonderful cook, like all French people.'

Cliff's face lights up. Despite his piratical appearance, week-old beard, cheerful paunch and docker's arms (swinging idly at his sides now that he has put the cases down), there is a touching vulnerability about him, something that makes you wonder whether, of the two, it's not the female who wears the trousers. His face brightens because he is the club's cook as well as factotum.

'Cliff's made you dinner.'

'Marseille fish soup and duck breasts à la Monclar.'

He says 'Ma-ar-zeille' and 'Moon-klarr.'

'Miss Murphy phoned and said you'll choose the wine. There's champagne in the cooler.'

Mandy and Cliff have gone. Augusta inspects the bedroom, pressing her fist into the mattress.

'What about you? Where will you sleep?'

'I spotted a chaise longue on the veranda.'

'You can't sleep outside! You'll be eaten by snakes, alligators and mosquitoes.'

'Don't worry about me.'

'I don't want to wake up a widow tomorrow morning. What would I do?'

They have the clubroom to themselves, with its varnished wood panels, mahogany tables and chairs, a full-length photo of the founder, Patrick Murphy, Elizabeth's father, the inevitable ship's wheel transformed into a chandelier, the storm lamps that shed no light whatever, model half-hulls under glass, photos of the Bermuda Race and the reconvened America's Cup of 1920, with

Resolute overtaking *Shamrock IV* to win. Mandy has changed into black trousers and a white blouse with a bow. Behind the counter she is filling an ice bucket, fetching champagne and flutes, and switching on a record player. The voice of Sinatra. Later, from the kitchen's swing doors, Cliff appears, shaved, in a white tunic and chef's hat, with a red handkerchief around his neck. Augusta and Arthur are sitting at a table next to a big bay window. Outside, in the blackness, the green and red lights wink at the end of the dock. There are no ship's lights visible in the strait between the keys and the Florida coast. It is a strange atmosphere, like waiting at the theatre for a late curtain to go up. Without Sinatra's voice they could be on board a ghost ship. Staring into the thick darkness, they begin to make out the tall palm trees, their crowns moving in the freshening wind.

Mandy brings the bowls of bouillabaisse.

'It looks like the cyclone's heading for Cuba now.'

Cyclone? They had no idea a cyclone threatened.

'It's been on the wireless for the last three days,' Mandy says.

Augusta turns pale.

'What if the wind blows the bungalow's roof off?'

'There are plenty of blankets in the cupboard in our bedroom.'

'*Our* bedroom? We can't do that to Elizabeth!'

'I love your sense of humour.'

They invite Cliff and Mandy to sit down with them. Another bottle of champagne is opened. Mandy smokes a cigarillo, then another.

'Havanas … The launches come at night. We barter petrol for cigarillos. Don't worry if you hear any noise. Stay indoors.'

Cliff has taken off his chef's hat. He is sweating from the kitchen and mops his forehead with his not particularly clean apron.

'I know France. Twice after the war, I stopped over at Le Havre on a Liberty ship. There was nothing left standing.'

Arthur tries to deflect the conversation away from the ex-sailor's memories, but Augusta leans forward, feigning lively interest in his visits to Le Havre as a Liberty ship's engineer.

'We were plumb out of luck,' Cliff says. 'The first time, the cathouse had been flattened by an English bomb. The second time they'd passed some new law banning cathouses.'

'That must have been so sad!' Augusta says, in such a desperate tone of voice that Mandy starts laughing.

'Well now, that's funny, because last year I was telling Miss Murphy about my stopovers at Le Havre and she said the exact same thing as you!'

'Does she come often?' Arthur asks.

'Didn't see her for a year. I get the feeling Key Largo doesn't interest her too much. You know better than I do, she's more of an intellectual type.'

Mandy, torch in hand, sees them back to their bungalow.

'Tomorrow you'll know the way by heart.'

Augusta closes the mosquito panels, draws the curtains and locks the French windows to the veranda.

'What are you afraid of?'

'What if they came to murder us? Them or their smuggler friends—'

'Do Cliff and Mandy look like murderers?'

196

'Well, of course it's only after the crime that a murderer looks like a murderer.'

He sees in her face that she is genuinely afraid and puts his arms around her. She pushes him away gently.

'Let's wait … Do you mind? I'd like … I'd like you to sleep on the couch with a knife next to you … I saw some big carving knives in the kitchen. Leave the door open. If anyone attacks me you'll hear them.'

Arthur takes too long to answer, hesitating between playing along with her and teasing her. She opens her suitcase and wails that she has left her nightdresses behind. Arthur gives her one of his shirts. When she comes out of the bathroom she is buttoned up to the neck and the shirt tail just covers her bottom.

'I look hideous … You won't love me any more.'

'I'm afraid you may be absolutely wrong about that.'

She offers him her lips and lies down, pulling the sheet up to her chin.

'Is it true that the cyclone's heading for the Caribbean? You don't think they said that to make us feel better?'

In the middle of the night she calls to him.

'Arturo *meu*, Arturo …'

'Here I am!'

'Were you asleep?'

'Yes, and I was dreaming that you were calling me for help.'

'I don't even know where we are.'

'At Key Largo.'

'Where is it?'

'In Florida.'

'Let's go back to New York tomorrow.'

'What if Mandy doesn't want to take us?'

'We'll steal the boat.'

'I don't know how to operate it. But you ask her. I get the impression she wouldn't refuse you anything.'

'Do you mean that you'd stay here on your own, without me?'

'I'm not blasé. It's paradise here: champagne every day, the club to ourselves, a doll's house in the jungle, and last but not least of this island's enchantments, you wearing my shirt.'

'I would never have thought you were so cynical.'

A few minutes' silence. Augusta's voice is heard again.

'If I ask you to come over here, will you swear to me that you won't take advantage of the situation?'

'Don't demand the impossible.'

'I thought you were a gentleman.'

'A profound error.'

Several more minutes pass, and she emits a plaintive cry.

'I can hear someone moving around the house. I'm sure it's Cliff.'

'There's no one there.'

'How do you know? Peep through the shutter without opening it.'

Arthur gets up and tilts the shutter, ignoring Augusta's instructions. Grey and blue clouds are marching across a sky lightened by the moon.

'Can you see him?'

'I can only see a fabulous night.'

'Since you don't want to come to me, I have to come to you.'

She is standing in the doorway. He can only make out a white shirt, without head or legs. She runs to the couch and wraps herself in the blanket.

'What about me?' he says, stretching out next to her.

She turns her back to him on the narrow couch. At dawn he pulls a corner of the blanket off her and curls up against her, slipping an arm over the top of her bare bottom. He doesn't know what he is expecting, bliss perhaps, or for a wave to sweep him away to a new life that will begin at sunrise. Augusta is, or is pretending to be, deeply asleep, ignoring or pretending to ignore Arthur's desire for her. She makes no movement when he draws away, feeling more bruised than if they had made love all night. It is daylight. He makes tea and fruit juice and goes into the garden to look for a red rose. A few steps from the bungalow, the shore curves away in a slender half-moon of tan sand. The sea laps onto the sand, and from the water there emerges a head, hair plastered flat, a shining face, and the naked breasts, stomach and legs of Mandy. Standing still, she offers her body up to the trembling light filtering through the palms and wild pines.

'It's the best time,' she says. 'You should do the same.'

She picks up a towel from the sand and wraps it around her.

'Where were you?' Augusta's groggy voice asks.

'In the garden. A goddess, as naked as Eve, rose out of the water to meet me.'

'Mandy?'

'Well, I don't think it was Cliff.'

'She did it deliberately.'

'That would be too flattering.'

He puts the tray down on the veranda's low table between two armchairs. Augusta sits, crosses her legs. A flash. As he stands there, shocked, she says, 'Voyeur.'

'Prick-teaser.'

'Your shirts are too short! Don't you have enough money to buy shirts with proper tails? What's she like, this Mandy?'

'Blonde.'

'I always had a feeling you preferred blondes. What am I doing here? You knew I don't like the sea ...'

She does not like the sea, that much is true, and she will never swim. She sits on the beach in a sari, hugging her knees, following Arthur with her eyes, calling him back if he goes too far, and is on her feet waiting for him with a bathrobe when he comes out.

'You're frozen!'

'Let's not exaggerate. It's cooler on the beach. The water's twenty-seven degrees.'

He likes the way she dries him, rubbing him through the towelling bathrobe, his chest, right down his back, his stomach and the tops of his legs. She becomes bolder, and he springs shamelessly to life under the bathrobe.

'You're so disgusting! It takes nothing at all to get you started.'

'Nothing? Well, I know someone looking for that nothing ...'

The saris she bought in Key Biscayne protect her from neck to ankles. When they go for a walk Augusta wears a wide panama hat Mandy has lent her. One afternoon, during their siesta, she lowers her last defence. Their pleasure is immense, and they consume it like famished teenagers, everything else retreating into the background, even the sight of Mandy emerging naked from the water every morning, her body gleaming with oil, wrapping a towel around her before she walks lightly back to the club.

Yachts arrive from Miami and Flamingo for the weekend. The club wakes up. Two Asian waiters serve them. Where did they come from? In the kitchen a young woman, ebony-skinned and verging on overweight, helps Cliff. 'He keeps her locked up during the week,' Mandy says. On Saturday night there is dancing. A group goes for a late-night swim in front of the bungalow. The women's shrieks and the men's coarse laughter wake the sleeping egrets in the nearby creek. On Monday life returns to normal and the club and Key Largo belong to them once again. Cliff's helper and the two Asians have vanished. Mandy walks past the bungalow after her swim. Augusta is right, Arthur is a voyeur, although it is not because he finds Mandy attractive but because the enigma she represents has taken root in his brain. Rising from the water, she is like one of those bronze boy-statues discovered after lying submerged in the Mediterranean for three thousand years: the narrow pelvis, square shoulders, face helmeted in wet curls. Rarely does a smile cross her lips. Her voice, with its hoarse rasp, betrays a certain timidity. She says very little, and it seems likely that she uses a rough vocabulary because she doesn't know any other.

With the impressive insight that women possess about their rivals, Augusta says, 'I never saw someone love themselves so much and look after themselves so well.'

Arthur feels Augusta doesn't love herself enough, at least not as much as he loves her.

'Lucky you're here then,' she says, resting her head in the hollow of his shoulder. 'You need to love me for two, otherwise I'm going to go under. Do you think you can?'

In the afternoons the full heat of the sun hits the bungalow. The coast of the Everglades is smudged and hardly visible in the mist rising from its swamps. Augusta is stretched out on the bed. He unties her sari and looks at her without touching her.

'Are you comparing me to Mandy? I'm not as beautiful as her. I know I'm not. I shan't age well.'

'She won't age at all. She's made of marble. Marble is like ice. But you're a flower. You need to be picked quickly ...'

And as he breathes all of her in, she slips into unconsciousness, eyes closed, fists clenched, not a word passing her lips, then, coming back to herself, pulls him towards her, kisses his forehead, strokes the back of his neck. Their separate pleasures spill over with dreams.

The days pass. They don't count them, so delicious is it to live only for each other. Key Largo is a well of forgetting. One evening Elizabeth phones. They are in the clubroom and Augusta picks up the receiver on the bar counter. Arthur only hears her brief, it seems to him embarrassed, side of the conversation.

'Do you want to talk to him? ... No! ... He's sending you a kiss

'… What's the matter, Ellie? Everything's absolutely wonderful, thanks to you … We're coming back in four days' time … No, we can't stay here for the rest of our life. Getulio will be free on the 15th, he'll need me to be there … No, no, please, don't say anything … Don't do anything … We love you …'

She returns to their table, her head lowered, avoiding Arthur's gaze.

'Elizabeth sends you a kiss—'

'– and won't talk to me.'

'We're asking too much of her, I told you already.'

He does not want to think about it, nor does he want to be asked to. He feels that this is a moment in his life when he needs to ignore all obstacles, even though, from Augusta's embarrassment, he guesses she is concealing an important piece of the truth. At this instant he would scale mountains to reach her, if only she would stop refusing to look at him, staring down as stubbornly as she can, in a last-ditch effort to protect herself against too harsh an interrogation.

'Augusta, we're big enough to be able to say everything to each other.'

'You're big enough. Not me. Tell me: were you Elizabeth's lover?'

'Yes.'

He does not hesitate for a second. But how he should have done! He knows it, knows that his 'yes' has travelled like an arrow, impossible to summon back unless he counter-attacks, not now but later, when they are alone in the bungalow and Augusta is undressing in front of him with the same delicious shamelessness as Elizabeth at her apartment or at Rector Street. At that moment she is exquisite, shaking free her night-blue hair, unknotting her copper-brown sari that reveals her body's every contour, a body of such femininity in comparison with Mandy's, although it is not Mandy who Augusta is comparing herself to now but Elizabeth, and the idea that Arthur has enjoyed with Elizabeth the same pleasures as with her has cast a sudden cloud over the innocence in which they have spent these happy days.

'I suppose,' she says, 'she does it much better than I do.'

'No. Differently.'

Brushing her hair, sitting naked on a pouf in front of the dressing table in the bedroom: this is how he would like to remember her, her lower back proudly arched, the shoulders of an adolescent, reflected down to her belly button in the glass that frames her face and her lovely, mature breasts that quiver with each stroke of her hairbrush.

'I don't know enough "things",' she says.

'I didn't expect to hear you of all people say that. And anyhow, let me tell you there's no such thing as "things", as you call them.'

He is on dangerous ground, he knows, but he too has a burning question. The need to ask it has become irresistible, and the only reason he hasn't already isn't because he fears the answer but because the picture he has of Augusta is so flimsy. The slightest thing can tarnish its poetry. Who can say what instinct leads her to anticipate him? Unless it's the feeling, shared by both of them, of standing on the edge of a precipice since Arthur's open admission about the nights he spent with Elizabeth.

'You never asked me if I had another man before you.'

'I don't need to.'

'I knew he wouldn't have the strength of character to keep it to himself.'

'You're talking in riddles. Do I know him?'

'You did know him.'

'Is he dead?'

'Yes. Almost in your arms.'

The brush has stopped at Augusta's neck. Her gaze turns to him and waits, unflinching, perhaps seeking an answer, any answer, so long as it can chase away the cloud that is growing, magnifying, concealing them from one another. Concannon himself had murmured words to Arthur that had made him think, but was it really likely?

'Getulio didn't know anything. He would have killed him. Don't go thinking—'

'I'm not thinking anything.'

'He tried. He talked a lot … He was so intelligent. I was scared of his hands … you remember. Afterwards … afterwards I imagined those "things" … He pulled me onto his lap.'

'That's enough.'

That night they sleep apart. At first light he wakes up and watches out for Mandy. A blanket of mist drifts elegantly over the water, hiding the Florida coast. Mandy walks down to the beach, unwraps her towel and walks slowly out into the wavelets, her arms held wide, like a tightrope walker. She vanishes in soft bubbles and reappears a few seconds later, swimming a long breaststroke, which attracts a silver and white barracuda the size of a large pike. With a sharp windmilling of her arm, she drives it away and lets herself be carried on her stomach towards the sand, her mouth open, taking in mouthfuls of water and blowing them out again like a whale. Catching sight of Arthur, she waves to him before she puts her feet down and then, standing deliciously in front of him, winds her discarded towel around her belly. Augusta is sleeping on the left side of the bed. He nestles next to her and pulls her towards him.

There is no more talk about Concannon. They speak about other things. Such as:

'You didn't make a fuss when I said we were going to fly to Miami. I thought you hated flying.'

'When you're there I'm not scared of anything.'

'And you were happy to come to Key Largo, when you don't like the sea?'

'You like it. Isn't that enough of a reason?'

Or one afternoon:

'Unless you're hiding it very well, I haven't seen you taking any tranquillisers.'

'You're my tranquilliser. Never leave me, and I won't be scared of anything ever again.'

'I shan't leave you. It's you who'll leave me.'

How can she not know it? And if she does know it, why does she pretend not to believe it?

Next day a storm breaks. Tons of water pour from the sky. The roof cannot withstand the onslaught. A wet patch spreads across the ceiling and they have to put a bowl by the bed. Water drips into it, slower and then faster. Augusta hates the noise and stuffs cotton wool in her ears. Cliff comes jogging along the path in a yellow oilskin and climbs onto the roof. His footsteps are so loud they expect him to come crashing through. The sea, which is usually a milky blue, turns the colour of molten lead. When the rain stops, the wind hurls itself into the space the clouds have left, shaking the bay window that looks onto the garden as if it wants to rip it out, uprooting the most ancient pines and blowing the skirts of palm trees up over their crowns. A whirlwind of red and white petals spirals up like butterflies over the rose bed as they pretend to read magazines – he *National Geographic*, she *Vogue* – while their thoughts wander, attracted and repelled by the tempest that has whipped up the sea around the keys, usually as flat and dull as a lake. Cliff, having repaired the leak, climbs down the ladder, which a sudden blast of wind knocks flying as soon as he is back on the ground. He takes off his oilskin and joins them. Arthur offers him a glass of bourbon. Cliff clucks his tongue; his trousers, which have slipped down over his paunch, and his flapping singlet reveal the crater of a belly button encircled by frizzy black hairs.

'A little breeze,' he says. 'The tail end of the cyclone that ran out of puff all on its own off the Cuban coast.'

'You have a funny belly button,' Augusta remarks.

He pushes his index finger into it and wiggles it happily.

'My girlfriend loves it. She's always rummaging around in it to check I didn't hide anything there.'

The bourbon makes his cheeks flush and lights up his eyes, two grey gimlets in his puffy face scored by wrinkles.

When the wind has blown itself out, a deathly hush falls. The horizon clears and over the Everglades fluffy greyish cumulus clouds lower a curtain of rain. Cliff puts away a second bourbon and leaves, sloping off with his rolling orang-utan-like gait, his arms swinging. On the beach a pair of white egrets flap their wings and chatter hoarsely.

In the night Arthur suddenly feels Augusta so tense and distant from him that he raises himself up to study her face, which is full of fear and disgust.

'I can't help it,' she says. 'I can't get the image of Cliff's horrible belly button out of my mind. All that curly hair … I think I'm going to throw up.'

'You're crazy!'

She retches and throws her head back.

'We're never going to be able to make love again, ever. There'll always be that horrible belly button, and his girlfriend's fat finger—'

He shakes her; she retaliates by going completely rigid, stiff as a board. He grips her shoulders and presses her flat on the bed's tangled sheets.

'Stop it!'

Her head lolls limply on the pillow, on the point of nervous collapse. He grips her chin and she wrenches herself away. Pulling back, he looks at her and slaps her, twice. She remains motionless, her eyes huge.

'You hit me!'

She jumps at him and hugs him hard. Two tears of happiness roll down her cheeks.

'You do love me …'

They stay like that, entwined, holding each other tightly, until dawn.

*

They only have one day left. In the wake of the storm the weather has cooled. The sea surrounds Key Largo with a ring of churned-up water and washes driftwood up onto the beach, the sort Elizabeth likes to collect and put in glazed cabinets. Arthur falls asleep at first light. Augusta shakes his arm.

'You're going to miss Mandy swimming!'

Mandy: of course. But Arthur's dreams have been of Concannon, on his deathbed, his pale, transparent hands lying on the sheet, hands that stroked Augusta and probably shocked her, but she had not had the strength to defend herself. We all have our ghosts. Sweep them aside and we're naked.

'You're not the same any more,' she says.

'Yes I am. The only difference is that I didn't know who I was before I met you.'

He has made a breakfast tray, the way he does every day, and goes outside to pick a rose, but the storm has laid waste to the flower bed whose fragrance once enveloped the veranda.

'It's a sign!' Augusta says, her face sad for a few seconds before she starts to laugh, tugging on his too-short shirt to cover her thighs.

She has forgotten her terror of the previous day. Arthur remains the sole guardian of that memory.

Early next morning the Bertram noses out of the dock. On the jetty Cliff waves briefly, cross with Augusta for flinching with repugnance when he tried to lift her on board and preferring to take Mandy's hand. He tidies away the fenders, and then only his crouching form is visible. Nobody looks back, except Arthur. The club is merging with the trees and laurel bushes; it is the bungalow's turn next, in the long shadows of the pines and palms. He catches sight of Cliff's girlfriend, blacker than ever in her white tunic. She has already hung their bedsheets and blankets over the veranda rail. Things are fading. A few minutes before they departed, Augusta, having left two of her saris behind in their bedroom wardrobe and not noticed that Arthur had packed one in his suitcase, had dressed in a suit for the journey. Suddenly she went white: they were going to miss the plane; forewarned by a treacherous Elizabeth, Getulio would be waiting for them when their plane landed and would kill Arthur. Searching in her handbag, he found some tranquillisers, which she took with childlike docility. On board the launch she takes herself off to the cabin again, wrapping herself in a blanket the way she had on the way out. The sound of two weeks of stolen happiness swinging shut behind them is almost audible. Their lives are in Mandy's hands now. Sitting on the Bertram's bridge, she navigates it down the channel, the buoys at arm's length. Over her yellow T-shirt she wears a thick, wide-ribbed navy-blue sweater. Her wool hat is pulled down over her ears. As the sun rises higher, she sheds both sweater and hat, and Arthur enjoys seeing the fine sculpted shoulders of the Greek statue again, the narrow waist and blond curls that flutter in the wind. She turns round and offers him a chocolate bar. He will not forget the puzzle she represents, nor the flat, wide opal sea that laps the islands.

His key had hardly turned in the lock when Mrs Paley appeared in the hallway, a letter and a telegram in her hand.

'I didn't know where to reach you. You should have left a forwarding address. It may be urgent—'

'Nothing's ever urgent.'

'Are you here for a few days?'

'Till the end of the month.'

'I don't have anyone after you. If you need a room, just say.'

'I don't think so. My classes start on 1 October.'

'I cleaned yesterday, but you left everything so tidy—'

'Thank you.'

He regretted his curtness and smiled at her. She was doubtless waiting for him to open his telegram and desperate to know what was in it.

'I hope it's nothing serious … Anyway, the sun and sea have done you good.'

'I'll see you tomorrow.'

He read the telegram standing by the window. He stared out at the roofs, the reddened sky, the towers already winking with lights. From the streets rose a dull rumble of traffic, a sound he had forgotten during the last two weeks. He reread the telegram.

Mother died suddenly 10th at 4 p.m. Heart failure. Funeral 12th. Waiting for you. Condolences. Émilie.

Émilie: his mother's friend, who brought the news of another death with such relish. Five days ago. Where had he been at that moment? Had she called for him a last time? Why wasn't he crying? As though he was being punished by remorse, refusing him even tears. The sloping, slightly old-fashioned handwriting ran across the envelope of the letter. The franked stamp gave the date and time it had been sent, the 9th at 3 p.m. from the post office in Rue des Saints-Pères. The day before she died. Who had found her? He tore up the letter without opening it. Moments such as this refuse ever to be forgotten.

From his landlady's he called Allan Porter in Washington. Porter was in his office and Arthur was connected almost immediately.

'I'll take care of it,' Porter said. 'Hang up. I'll call you back.'

'You're so alone,' Mrs Paley said. 'But your friends, those young ladies, will help you through this terrible time.'

'I doubt it.'

Porter called back less than five minutes later. A military transport was leaving at 8 a.m. for Le Bourget. Without his helping hand Arthur would have stood no chance of getting to Paris on his last fifty dollars. At Miami airport Augusta had fallen in love with an antique silver bracelet. Where would his problems end? The phone at Elizabeth's rang on. He hoped he might find her at the trattoria below her apartment. At the trattoria they told him she was away until Monday. He made do with a sandwich and coffee in a drugstore that was about to close and walked back to Rector Street. On his way past the customs building that was his usual route back he noticed, for the first time, a remarkable statue that decorated the entrance: the rounded figure of a woman who was leaning one elbow on a sphinx's head, the other on a lion's mane, and tilting her expressionless face forward as though she was softly calling to the passers-by. Naked to the waist, she thrust out two very modest breasts that pointed in different directions. A joker had painted the toenails of her huge right foot red. Arthur had walked past this mysterious allegory of customs and excise without ever noticing the woman, an apparently ideal woman of the 1900s. Hadn't the municipal sculptors ever seen a Greek figure like Mandy's, hadn't they ever seen the unsettling willowy adolescence of an Augusta?

He stopped the lift at the eleventh floor and took off his shoes to walk to the twelfth without rousing Mrs Paley and her enveloping compassion. The suitcase that had come back from Key Largo with him was waiting on the bed. He tipped its contents out: trunks, shorts, brightly coloured shirts, and Augusta's sari, the one she had worn on their last evening, still steeped in her perfume. He hung it on a hanger in the wardrobe, threw everything else in the trash. Then, sitting on a chair in front of the open window that bounded a rectangle of star-studded night, he waited for the dawn, buffeted by merciless images from his past and racked with sudden sobs that choked him almost to the point of suffocation.

When he got back from Paris, he finally reached Elizabeth by telephone.

'You're lucky I answered, I forgot to take the phone off the hook. We're in the middle of rehearsing. Where have you been?'

'Paris. My mother died when I was at Key Largo. I only found out when I got back.'

'It's difficult to know what to say to news like that.'

'Don't say anything.'

'Are you unhappy?'

'Yes. Have you seen Augusta?'

She was silent, and he heard muffled background noise, a man's voice then a woman's. He repeated, 'Augusta?'

'I need to talk to you about her. Come by tomorrow morning. Are you on your own this evening?'

'Yes.'

After a short, murmured conversation with the two distant voices, she said, 'Come in an hour.'

He arrived early, just after nightfall, and walked up and down outside her building. A young woman skipped down the steps: he recognised Thelma, the curly-haired actress who had played the crucified woman up a ladder. She was followed by a tall, svelte young black man in a pink jacket and green bow tie. They kissed each other quickly on the cheek and walked off in different directions. Arthur waited a few minutes before going up. Elizabeth opened the door in a dressing gown, without make-up, her face shining with cream. Was she trying to discourage him? He had not come for that.

'Did you eat?'

She made a plate of sandwiches in the kitchen. Arthur contemplated the spotlit acacia with its autumn leaves.

'I haven't thanked you for Key Largo.'

'Augusta did. Here ... open this burgundy.'

'Have you stopped drinking your terrible Chilean wine?'

'Chauvinist!'

'You have to admit this is better.'

'I do.'

She arranged some cushions round a low table and put the glasses and plate of sandwiches between them.

'Is Augusta in New York?'

'I don't think so.'

'She wouldn't tell me her address. She flew off on her cloud afterwards. We live in different worlds. At Key Largo the princess granted me an interlude, or maybe I should say a playlet, the kind of thing you put on as a matinée for the underprivileged.'

Elizabeth walked over to the record player and picked up an LP.

'No! Please. Music paralyses me. I need to talk.'

'I don't suppose you understand any of it,' she said.

Understand? What was there to understand, except that no one can keep hold of anything, and that love, death, peace, success, and every defeat are crouching in the shadows and will spring at your throat just when you least expect it? It's a game of blind man's buff with no one in charge. He had gone into their holiday blindfolded, and everyone had understood everything before he had. At Key Largo he had isolated Augusta, and nowhere else existed. As soon as he let her go, she had put herself out of reach again.

'You're right, I don't understand anything.'

Elizabeth enlightened him. Not totally, but a little. Getulio had not gone abroad. He had spent three weeks in prison. Convicted of what? Practically nothing. Speeding, and a ticket he'd paid with a cheque that bounced. His friend de Souza, the Brazilian wheeler-dealer, had got him released. Was de Souza broke? Far from it. Arthur saw danger looming. Do we sense these things? When they materialise, is it because we sensed them? 'One upset leads to another,' his mother used to say, always ready to find courage in adversity and forever drawing comfort from the inexhaustible wisdom of nations. But was this just an upset?

'I'm happy to tell you the short version,' Elizabeth said quietly.

'What sort of version is that?'

'It depends on you. It might comfort you or it might drive you to despair.'

'I'll risk it.'

'One day she'll say you were the only one she ever loved.'

In truth he had never expected to keep her. Almost as soon as they stepped off the plane from Miami she no longer belonged to him. It was all fading. A stranger and her assignation. Not even a wave as her taxi drove away.

'Did you know about her fling with Concannon?'

Elizabeth burst out laughing.

'Everyone knew. He was crazy about her. But imagine him deflowering a Brazilian virgin! He'd never have been able to do it. I expect he cuddled her, and she was so impressed by him that she let him, but to go the whole way would have needed a different kind of man. No, my little Arthur, you are her first. A bit too much in awe of her, apparently. But maybe that was exactly the way to go about it with her. She's an extraordinarily strange person. It was the one thing she wanted, and the thing she was most scared of in the world.'

'It was the last thing I needed to do to become a man.'

'I wouldn't worry about that. But do toughen up. Fast … When are you going back to Beresford?'

'The day after tomorrow. I have to drop by Jansen and Brustein. They may hire me again next summer. Brustein's being very decent. Why? I've decided not to ask myself. Goodbye, Mrs Paley; so long, New York. Though … I'll be coming back for your play at the end of October. I brought a bit of money back from Paris. Not much. My poor mother counted every penny. And believe it or not, she actually kept it in a woollen stocking at the bottom of a drawer … I nearly let it go with the removal people who were taking everything to a sale. There are a few other souvenirs, photos and letters, in a trunk I left with an old uncle who I'll never see again. Tomorrow's the first day of the rest of my life.'

They kissed like brother and sister, but in the hallway she called him back.

'You know I don't go in for sentiment much, but I liked what we had. And giving you Key Largo was me being generous in a way that's not really me. What I'm saying is, I look at myself and I'm pleased with myself. Let's stay the way we are; it's rare for people of our age. And don't come and see my play; I have a feeling you won't like it.'

'I'm going to come.'

'You do like taking risks ...'

She stroked his cheek with her fingertips.

'Mind how you go in the next few weeks. You're not cured yet. When you are, you'll see ... it'll be your turn to do the breaking up.'

His appointment with Brustein was not till the end of the afternoon. He emptied drawers and cupboards: a suit, a sheepskin jacket, underwear, books for his classes and his preparatory notes, Augusta's sari that would carry her scent until the end of time. He presented Captain Morgan's officer's trunk to Mrs Paley: it was too big, heavy and impractical. He bought himself a kitbag instead, which he deposited at the left luggage office at Grand Central Station. Towns think that we love them. This is a major misapprehension. What we share with them is our moods. Arthur's mood was simultaneously light-hearted, critical, and close to despair. Somewhere in this termite heap of concrete, steel and glass, Augusta was breathing, resting her forehead against a windowpane and watching, without seeing them, the first autumn russets of the foliage of Central Park. From Columbus Circle Arthur made his way to Broadway and in two hours walked down as far as Battery Park. Here, all through the summer, at daybreak, he had run, breathing steadily, thinking he was breathing the air of the open sea. Isn't everything an illusion? The trees had shrunk, the lawns had been worn threadbare. On benches moribund figures threw bread at pigeons. A sticky easterly wind blew waves of unidentifiable decay over him. Oil-stained seagulls skimmed at ground level along the dockside, screeching like children whose throats had been cut. Erect on her island, lapped by black water, Bartholdi's Liberty, idiotically victorious, held up her pistachio ice-cream cornet. After his run he would buy some croissants at an Italian bakery where he was served by a girl with a mop of platinum hair and a lisp. 'Two croithants or four croithants?' When it was four croissants it meant he had someone to share his life with, and she would laugh. Croissant crumbs in the bed, and then the last croissants they had eaten together on the pavement, with the taxi waiting: '... Arthur and Elizabeth ate croissants in Rector Street and said goodbye to each other after a night of love.'

Had it been his fault he had lost her? Not imagining that Elizabeth could be vulnerable, he had not known that he could be so vulnerable either. On this autumnal late afternoon, everything suddenly seemed extraordinarily painful. He turned round and headed back towards Broadway. He was walking twenty paces behind a tiny old woman in black, her shoulders rounded, her back stooped by the weight of years, when two boys on roller skates overtook him, flanked the old woman, knocked her down, and snatched the shopping bag she was trailing in the dust of the path. The skaters raced away with long strides. She shook her mittened hand at them.

'*Mascalzone! Mascalzone!*'

Arthur helped her to her feet and dusted her down. She wrenched her elbow away and threw him a look of hate.

'*Vai affanculo!*'

Other passers-by ran or limped up to them.

'What are you doing to her? Can't you see she's just a poor old woman? Leave her alone.'

'Some hoodlums stole her bag.'

A fat, vulgarly made-up woman said, 'Did she only have one bag?'

The tiny old woman carried on shouting and waving her fist.

'*Mascalzone! Mascalzone!*'

More pedestrians arrived. They were laughing. A young man in a Davy Crockett jacket and a Stetson took charge of her.

'I know her. There's nothing in her bag. She's crazy and her son looks after her. He has a bakery on Bridge Street. Come on, Signora Perditi, you need to go home now.'

'*La mia sporta! La mia sporta!*'

'You should have run after those hoodlums,' the fat, over-made-up woman said to him.

'You try chasing kids on roller skates, lady, then tell me what it's like.'

'There are no real men left, you're all losers.'

The man in the fringed jacket shrugged, took the little old lady's arm, and led her, still grumbling, towards the park's exit. The fat woman made her way to a bench shaded by a copper beech and sat staring out at the estuary, her patent bag firmly gripped across her bulging thighs.

Arthur followed the unsteady couple at a distance. Stopping outside the Italian bakery, he saw the owner take his old mother's arm and thank the man in the Stetson and fringed jacket. The girl behind the counter watched her boss with an amused smile.

'Do you have any croissants left?' Arthur asked.

She smiled happily when she recognised him.

'Two or four?'

'Two.'

'You got lucky, there'th jutht two left. So you're on your own today?'

'I'm afraid so.'

'I'm like you, I don't like being on my own.'

From the back of the shop came the old woman's piercing cries.

'*Due mascalzoni! Due, mi ascolta, figlio!*'

'*Sì, Mamma, ti sento!*'

The girl smiled.

'I'th not the firtht time. Are you on holiday?'

He paused and then decided not to tell her his life story, pleasant as it was in this gigantically swollen city to feel as if you lived in a village where everyone knew everything.

The working day was ending at Jansen and Brustein. Brustein saw him in his office.

'I don't have much time, I'm afraid. Porter told me. Those things are beyond words. If you come at Christmas, call me. We spend the holidays in New Jersey. Begonia has decorated a little house there very nicely. She'll be thrilled to see you again. You made a terrific impression. Once you pass that difficult exam of yours, the door's always open. Excuse me for being so hurried. I'd given up expecting you. At Christmas we'll tell each other everything.'

He saw him to the office door, then held him back.

'By the way, I must tell you ... do you remember? ... Something funny happened. The Amazonian company we sold to that de Souza … well, of course there was no oil. No. Not a drop. But what there was, was extensive emerald deposits. An absolute fortune. Mr de Souza cashed in. It's what we call a good play. We can't complain. We're looking after his business now. Well, weren't we his inspiration? Funny guy! A head like an eagle. He phoned me yesterday to say he was getting married, in style, in Acapulco. The way movie stars do, or crooks on the run. But how dumb am I! He must have invited you. He owes you, does he not—'

'It must be an oversight.'

'Sure, be patient. He's chartering a plane for his guests, and everyone will have a week in a hotel, he says. He's marrying a Brazilian.'

'It's impossible anyhow. My classes start again in a week's time.'

'Look, let's keep in touch. Take Zava with you on your way out. I have an idea she'll be happy to talk to you. She's an exceptional girl, got a great future. It's a shame she's a bit … awkward physically. Don't bother with the others. They've already forgotten you.'

He was right. In the round room, where they were tidying their workspaces and switching off their phones and telex terminals, his former colleagues hardly recognised him. One said anxiously, 'Are you coming back?'

'No. Don't worry.'

Zava was on her last phone call. She made a sign that he should sit down opposite her. A pink late-afternoon light washed the New Jersey horizon, reflected in the dark waters of the Hudson. Zava hung up.

'Brustein told me you'd be coming by before you went back to Beresford. I heard … I feel so sad for you—'

'How did he know?'

'Allan Porter often calls. Almost every day. You weren't there when it happened?'

'No! I've given myself enough regrets to last me the rest of my life.'

'I'm so sorry. I suppose you'd prefer not to talk about it. Even though, right now, it won't interest you very much, I want to tell you that I'm going to have my operation next month. The surgeon told me I can pay over three years. It's an opportunity I can't turn down. When are you coming back to New York?'

'The end of October, to see a play a friend's putting on.'

'I'm certain we'll see each other again.'

The good news was that Getulio was not at Beresford. Theories circulated. Had he stayed on the beach at Acapulco, roaring drunk, after his sister's wedding? Or had the university authorities got wind of his brief prison visit, which had, after all, been for a reason most of his fellow students would have viewed as harmless? To say he was missed would be an overstatement. Many remembered card games that had been more than dubious. No one had ever caught him out, but there was a generally held conviction that his luck had all the hallmarks of a pact with the queen of spades. His elegance had dazzled them, his wit intimidated them, his pretensions exasperated them, and his professors had shown him considerable indulgence as, with all his youth and gifts, he had squandered his talents and used his expensive studies to support his lazy life. Like all curiosities, however, he faded quickly enough, and within two weeks of the new term no one talked about Getulio Mendosa any more, or his superb 1930 Cord, his Inverness cape, his sister and Elizabeth Murphy, whose appearance at the ball had earned him so much prestige. Arthur was content. After the fortnight at Key Largo and the drama of going back to Paris, he had a blank slate. He buried himself in work with the feeling that, in work at least, he was capable of turning the tables on events. He knew that he had much long and slow reflection ahead of him about the serial sincerities of women. An inexhaustible subject.

At the end of October he got on a train for New York after a short phone call with Elizabeth, who tried again to dissuade him from coming to the play she had been rehearsing for months in such secrecy. He called Zava at Jansen and Brustein with the idea of getting her to share the ordeal with him. Someone told him that her operation had surpassed expectations, that she was recovering at the Brusteins' house in New Jersey, and would be back at work in mid-November.

The show was to be performed in a condemned former customs warehouse on the bank of the Hudson. A team of volunteers had cleared out the sinister-looking building, whose expanse was strewn with rubble, machine tools and rusting crates. Steel girders supported a corrugated-iron roof that screeched at the slightest gust of wind. Inside, garden chairs and benches were arranged in a semicircle around a primitive stage hidden by a curtain made of two sheets crudely sewn together and splashed with paint. Off-Broadway theatre was so fashionable that year that the space was full for the first and – as will be seen – last night. The audience, half café society, half Greenwich Village avant-garde, quickly became impatient, and as they started to stamp their feet they raised a clinging cloud of dust that had an ancient smell of rotting fish and hung in the air as the curtain, not without difficulty, opened on the set of a hospital room – bed, chair, armchair, and, for reasons that never appreared in the script, a candlestick. Elizabeth, who had written and directed the play, had also given herself the leading role, of a psychopath whose doctor was analysing her in hospital. A number of gasps were heard at the crudest parts of the script. After an hour the audience was yawning at the torrent of clichés. Arthur recognised the character of the doctor or analyst: it was the young black man in the pink jacket he had glimpsed in the street outside Elizabeth's apartment. When his wise words appeared to be inadequate to the task of calming his psychopathic patient, Sam – his theatrical name – ordered her to strip off. This was the part the audience had been waiting for. They had hardly stumbled down to the gloomy dockside for an ordinary theatrical performance. They were here for something new, something earth-shattering, shocking, 'sublime', and the level of expectancy was so great and so fixed in their minds that when the doctor, apparently tired of being rebuffed by the wall his patient had set up, pushed her, naked, back onto the camp bed, the expectancy gave way to relief, as if people were at last going to find out why they had come. Their wishes were about to be granted, because this was the point of the play: a scandal in the name of the divine rights of the theatre. Arthur had felt uncomfortable at Elizabeth undressing, and he closed his eyes to keep his memories of her more modest undressing at Rector Street and her apartment intact. He opened them when the audience let out a gasp of shock. The doctor had opened his white coat to provide his patient with a radical cure, in this case a male member of unusual dimensions and a pinkness reminiscent of an elephant's trunk, which he then proceeded to plunge between his patient's thighs, which were openly on view to the audience. Elizabeth apparently had little difficulty in acting out her pleasure. For its part, the audience quickly overcame its embarrassment to start beating time to the accelerating rhythm of the performance until the curtain fell, which it did lopsidedly, so that the right-hand half of the stalls enjoyed the unscripted sight of Elizabeth standing up and wiping herself, pulling her knickers back on, and offering her partner a towel.

The reactions of the Greenwich Village set were as divided as those of café society. There was applause and whistling, and some scattered boos. Arthur kept his composure sufficiently not to react, and he was conscious in any case that his interpretation of what he had seen was too personal. Some of the audience seemed unaware of the derelict customs shed on the brink of collapse, the poverty of the set, the tedium of the psychoanalysis and the clumsiness of the actors, and spoke of genius. Arthritic chairs scraped and benches were overturned at the press of fans hurrying forward to shake hands with Elizabeth and Sam, who had come offstage in dressing gowns to mingle with the audience. Arthur overheard a few remarks that softened his foul mood. 'I haven't seen anything quite as beautiful since I saw Larry Olivier play *Hamlet*.' 'What's tedious about it is that it's really tedious.' 'The moment she takes off her knickers is what you call a "theatrical moment".' 'We never knew Elizabeth had such a pretty p——.' 'Well, that is a lot more effective than a vibrator.' 'A production that cares about its audience ought to distribute Dr Sam's phone number.' 'If I'd known it was so pornographic I'd have brought my grandmother and my fiancée.' When he was finally able to get close to Elizabeth, he asked her if she was responsible for the sets too. He had really found them marvellously bold and simple. She turned her back on him.

The number of audience members who had actually been shocked by the play's outrageousness was fairly minimal. Everyone was afraid of seeming unenlightened. They were now doubtless waiting for some undeniably explicit follow-up, anything at all as long as it was more daring and tomorrow would relegate this evening's show to the level of a chamber piece for emancipated actors. As the audience left, their return journey along the dark dockside, stepping cautiously to avoid the train-track sleepers, tank wagons, bulk containers, and the looming dinosaur-like outlines of cranes and mechanical shovels, must have added considerably to the pleasure of the evening's adventure.

The following day Arthur met Elizabeth for lunch at Sardi's, in the main room where, years later, her caricature would be hung with the other kings and queens of Broadway, but in 1956 she was no more than a fringe player, a stylish student agitator, a poor little rich girl who felt her rebellion was a manifestation of a new kind of art. Their overlapping conversations, a dialogue of the deaf that lasted for the duration of their lunch, were all the more acrimonious because the police and New York City authorities had banned the play that morning and condemned the customs shed where its 'tastelessly provocative' performance had taken place. Elizabeth virtually accused Arthur of having reported her. They parted on bad-tempered terms in Times Square.

'I don't give a damn what you think. I warned you. You

didn't understand anything. Go back to Beresford and your little banker's diploma.'

'You're being unnecessarily nasty.'

'Yes I am. Which is another good reason for you not to see me again.'

They were more cross with themselves than with each other, but they found it impossible to admit it. Arthur watched Elizabeth's slim outline grow smaller as she walked away, then hailed a cab and drove off without looking back.

The subsequent years are of relatively little importance. Zava's operation was a success and she no longer needed a hearing aid. She could finally cut her hair short. Following Begonia Brustein's advice, she began to dress better. Her parents died within a few days of each other, a touching symbiosis of a couple who had never learnt how to set down roots in a new life, nor truly wanted to. Endlessly replayed, their memories eventually wore out and all they had left was a daughter from whom destiny separated them more and more as the years went by. Zava moved to Manhattan, to East 70th Street, and Brustein's intuition was proved right: Miss Gertrude Zavadzinski was an exceptional employee. Following a particularly profitable deal whose details need not concern us, she became a partner and the firm was henceforth known as Jansen, Brustein and Zavadzinski. Zava married a law professor, of Polish origin like her. They had a son they named Arthur, after his godfather. At home the family continued the tradition of speaking French at dinner. Brustein retired as anticipated in 1965 and moved to Seville, bowing to the wish of Begonia who could not bear her life of exile any longer. He sold his shares to Zava, who was not tender-hearted and within two years had moved Jansen aside. The firm was now called Zavadzinski and Co., the 'Co.' standing for Arthur, who, in Paris and Zurich, handled Europe in an apparently most modest way: an office on Place de la Bourse plus two secretaries. Deeply opposed to the bondage imposed by car ownership in Paris, he used a bicycle to reach his office from his apartment on the corner of Rue de Verneuil and Rue Allent. He had risen from a life calculated down to the last cent during his university years in the USA to one it would be appropriate to describe as of considerable material comfort. Perhaps the most interesting thing about this still-young man, so shrewd in matters of business, and widely called on as an adviser, is that he had hardly changed his lifestyle. Of course he dressed better, was no longer afraid of a woman's quick tongue the way he had been with Elizabeth or Augusta, often travelled by private jet, chartered a boat twice a year for a cruise in the Caribbean or Pacific, but most evenings he was home alone, having a tin of sardines or a slice of ham for supper. When a cruise was imminent, he turned to a kindly soul by the name of Madame Claude, whose social circle included a number of mostly very good-looking young women, whose company was enjoyable for a short time and without repercussions. He often visited Brustein in Seville, where they made it a rule to ban all conversation about business. In two rooms of his huge Seville house Brustein had reproduced the little museum dedicated to the memory of his father and the glory of Cézanne, of whom he now owned three pictures, a dozen excellent drawings, and numerous letters. Apart from Cézanne, about whom he was beginning to develop some slight understanding thanks to his friend, Arthur was not terribly interested in painting, but was instead building a fine collection of nineteenth-century first editions. A keen buyer of Stendhal, Balzac, Flaubert and Mérimée, he rarely showed his face at sales, delegating the task of buying to a network of agents. Allan Porter's invisible protection of him had continued until President Eisenhower's departure from the White House in 1961, at which time the former naval officer and special adviser retired to Florida – to Key Biscayne – to a house with a garden that led down to the waterway where he berthed his sixty-foot cruiser, *Cipher*, named after his wartime codebreaking exploits. He had only just settled in when Minerva died, taking the collection at an Adventist church. He sent a short notice to those he knew: 'No condolences, please.' He often slept on board the *Cipher*, preferring its cabin to his bedroom, happy to make do with a narrow room whose only decoration was a glass case that contained his American, British and French decorations. On the night of 2 July 1965, Cyclone Amanda hit Florida, tearing the *Cipher* from its moorings and hurling it into the garden like a ping-pong ball, where it caught fire. All that was recovered from the debris of the cruiser's shell was a blackened skeleton. Farewell, Porter. He had never asked for anything in return from his protégé, except that he should not forget how generous and disinterested the United States had shown itself towards him.

In the early years after his return to France, Augusta had regularly reminded Arthur of her existence by her appearance in photographs in the society pages of glossy magazines he happened to see from time to time, such as *Vogue* and *Tatler*: 'Mr and Mrs de Souza at the ball given by Princess X', or at a charity dinner, or a gallery opening in New York or London or Rome. She was unchanged, although she rarely smiled. With mild *Schadenfreude* Arthur imagined her as sad at the side of the swaggering de Souza. He covered her with jewels, and she was never without a red rose pinned in her décolletage. Sometimes he saw Getulio with them, his hairline receding a little more each year, yet the onset of baldness somehow accentuated his elegance, in contrast to his brother-in-law's flashiness.

*

One evening, at one of those Parisian dinners he much enjoyed, provided they did not happen too often, the attractive woman on his right, in her thirties and wearing a white suit and a red rose on her lapel, suddenly said, after they had been introduced, 'You can't imagine how pleased I am to meet you. Augusta talks about you every time I see her.'

Arthur turned so pale that she said anxiously, 'Are you feeling ill?'

'No.'

'Have a glass of water.'

Water was not enough. For several seconds he felt he was teetering on the edge of an abyss. When his voice came back, he smiled at his neighbour.

'It's nothing serious. I get these turns now and then; they give me the illusion that I'm having an out-of-body experience. Somewhere on the other side of the planet I must have a double who needs me for a minute or two.'

'I don't believe in such things,' the woman said. 'Unlike Augusta.'

'I haven't seen her for at least ten years.'

The woman looked surprised. Who did she suspect of lying? Augusta or him? For the first time – he had been too distracted before – he realised the significance of the red rose and white suit.

'I imagine this isn't a chance meeting. I should have noticed Augusta's favourite colours from the outset.'

'At last! And if you don't remember her, I can guarantee she hasn't forgotten you.'

'Did she give you a message?'

'No, she just suggested that I wear white, and a red rose. I had to beg our hostess to let me sit next to you, which wasn't an easy matter. You're very sought after.'

'That's news to me. How did you get to know her?'

'She was my sister-in-law, although not for long. Yes, I married Getulio. An absolute charmer, but far too high-maintenance. You get tired of that in the end, don't you? Getulio and I were divorced two years ago. I think he's living in Jamaica now. He's a fan … of the sun. Can I tell Augusta that white and red still have an effect on you?'

'You can tell her that I got the message.'

Almost as soon as the dinner was over, he made his excuses, saying he felt light-headed and needed to rest; and left to walk the streets of Paris until daybreak.

Another coincidence persecuted him to the point of obsession. The city's advertising columns were plastered with a red and white poster that showed a coffee-skinned beauty emerging from the waves onto a tropical beach, her soaking-wet dress clinging to her body. She did not look at all like Augusta, but the film was called *Augusta*. Its success kept the posters in place for weeks on end, and Arthur could not open a newspaper or a magazine without the name he wanted to belong to him alone jumping out at him. When the actress playing the title role arrived in Paris, the press and television went wild. She was everywhere, and despite her name being Janet Owen everyone called her Augusta. The image of the 'other' Augusta shimmered over the city before it gradually dispersed into the suburbs, then the provinces, in the film's dubbed version. Insidiously this other Augusta took over Arthur's dreams, and for a while he even considered asking one of the producers he knew – film people who turned to him when their budgets overran – for a favour. It could not be that difficult to meet Janet Owen, who had extended her visit to France, startled by the success of the film (which had not done well in the United States). But to say what? That in a made-up story she had another woman's name, the sound of which still affected him deeply? In any case the resemblance stopped there. Janet Owen walked out of the sea like a dark-amber sculpture. The real Augusta didn't like the sea and never swam.

In Seville, another year – it doesn't matter whether it was before or after the dinner or the film, his arbitrary allocation of lived time having been frozen and there being no longer either present or past in anything that concerned him personally – in Seville then, in the Museo de Bellas Artes, Arthur, with Brustein at his side, stopped dead in front of a little-known work of Zurbarán. Brustein told him that the painting was also not regarded as one of the artist's best and in fact even its authenticity was contested. But St Dorothy, standing in profile like an Egyptian portrait, carrying a porcelain plate with three not very fresh persimmons on it, her waist tightly tied in a billowing dress of violet taffeta, a yellow scarf with black stripes wrapped around her chest – St Dorothy hauntingly resembled Augusta in her youth. The similarity was all the greater because the painter had draped her throat with gauze that, tied in her upswept hair, also floated behind her, lifted by a light breeze from a window that could not be seen but was certainly open to the sun's rays, which were reflected in her dress's taffeta. Augusta liked gauze scarves; she collected white, pink and red ones which she liked to wrap herself in on evenings when she went out with bare shoulders. More than a straightforward resemblance of features, St Dorothy's profile also affected him with its concentrated expression that exactly recalled Augusta's at serious moments in her life, moments whose oppressiveness she could chase away with a tinkling laugh that was as unsettling as her abrupt withdrawal into herself, light years away from those who were talking to her.

Fascinated by the portrait, which he thought both real and premonitory, Arthur returned to see it at the Museo de Bellas Artes every morning that he was staying with the Brusteins. In fact, it was Zurbarán's Dorothy that he spent Semana Santa in Seville with, far more than the Brusteins, so that eventually Brustein – alerted by Begonia, more sensitive than he was to their guest's absences and distractedness – became alarmed.

'Arthur, you're not the same guy. Some idea has gotten hold of you. I don't know what it is, but I'd like to help you.'

And so Arthur, who never told anyone anything, suddenly started to talk about Mendosa and de Souza, and told his friend the whole story. He felt a massive relief afterwards, followed by a short-lived anxiety: that in admitting a torment he had been concealing for years, would he not exorcise it, like the patients who emerge from their analyst's consulting room cured, after confessing that they dreamt of sleeping with their mother or stuck pins into the heart of their little sister's dolls? Fortunately nothing of the kind materialised: the pain remained that made him different from others.

'De Souza went down the tube,' Brustein said, 'in a manner of speaking. He's ruined, the way wheeler-dealers like him tend to be: enough to get by, somewhere in Switzerland, Lugano I believe, but no more. I hear he's planning a comeback, but the banks are catching up with him. As for his brother-in-law, your

Getulio Mendosa, after a failed marriage – you met his ex-wife – he lives from gambling. An unpredictable existence. Begonia met him last year at the Duchess of Alba's during the Romería del Rocío. She described him as a tremendously attractive man, constantly on the lookout for poker partners. By the way, she mentioned you, and he was startled. "I knew him slightly at Beresford," he said. "Some sort of accountant. He wanted to marry my sister. I put a stop to it." You'll appreciate why I said nothing. Anyhow, it's not important now, after what you just told me.'

Despite the omnipotence of illusions, Arthur knew very well that St Dorothy would not step down from her frame but remain Zurbarán's prisoner, painted with such tenderness and care that she might well have been his lover. There was no prospect of her venturing onto the museum's polished parquet floor and making her way out into the street to mix with the crowd, whipped up by the singers of vehement *saetas* and the sight of hooded penitents bent double under the weight of *pasos*. Nor would she breathe the savage smells in which Seville simmered during Semana Santa, the scents of roses, carnations and arum lilies mingled with sweat, incense and mule droppings. Basic common sense told him not to go back to the museum, yet three months later he could not resist. The painting was no longer there. A card informed him that St Dorothy had left Seville as part of an international touring exhibition. He breathed a sigh of relief.

One morning – it must have been about fifteen years after his return from the United States – arriving at the café Les Deux Magots where he regularly had breakfast, Arthur was surprised to see Getulio sitting at a table at the back of the room under a mirror that reflected the sight of his bald crown and the tight curls that spilt over his collar. Hunched into a crumpled, grubby raincoat, he looked as if he was shivering despite the room's overheated atmosphere. Eggshells, sandwich crumbs, the cold remains of a Welsh rarebit and three pots of coffee were scattered over his table, but the most striking thing was his look of distraction, lost in the thoughts conjured up by an empty cup and the leftovers of a lavish breakfast. Arthur was briefly racked with doubt: was this listless-looking man really Getulio, the Getulio who, the moment he set foot in a public place – café, bar, restaurant, theatre foyer, plane, train or boat – would instantly spot a familiar face and hail its owner before overwhelming them with protestations of friendship? If he was to be believed, his circle of friends girdled the globe, and wherever he found himself he was never alone: even in a village in Amazonia, among Indians of whose blood he might well have a drop or two himself, mixed with his African and Portuguese blood, he would soon find a friend.

'You look like a man on the run,' Arthur said, putting a hand on his shoulder. Getulio started as if he had just woken from a nightmare.

'On the run? Me? No, no … not today, but I can't get warm. I was up all night.'

'You're still going to nightclubs!'

'I was on the street, then I slept a bit on a bench in a square and in the first open Métro station I could find, before I took refuge here.'

'Are things as bad as all that?'

'The worst is yet to come. Any minute now the waiters are going to frogmarch me to the door and chuck me out. I've avoided the offence of making off without payment because I didn't order any alcohol, so they won't call the police. But I couldn't stand a scene. So vulgar …'

Arthur called a waiter. Getulio beat him to it.

'A double brandy, please.'

Turning to Arthur, he said, 'You came at just the right time. I'd have been done for if you hadn't turned up. Really done for. I'm supposed to be leaving for Roissy in a few minutes, and I couldn't see how I was going to get there.'

He took an airline ticket out of his pocket.

'I'm getting married tomorrow in Hong Kong.'

'Unshaven? With a week-old beard!'

'The hotel won't let my bags go. I'm two weeks overdue with the bill.'

'So you're leaving, just like that?'

'That's what you do when you start a new life.'

He drank the double brandy down in one. The shock was so violent it brought tears to his eyes.

'I didn't know alcohol could make you cry,' he said, laughing and wiping his eyes with a paper napkin.

The colour flowed back into his grey cheeks. He picked up the airline ticket, folded it, and put it back in his pocket.

'In twenty-four hours' time everything is going to be different. I'm marrying a Murphy.'

'Elizabeth?'

'No, Helen, her aunt. Maybe even her great-aunt. Seventy-two years old, quite delightful, crazy about music, a painter, great friend of Picasso. Her yacht is meeting her in Hong Kong and we're leaving for Malaysia straight after the wedding.'

*

Arthur paid the hotel bill in Rue Castiglione, retrieved Getulio's bags and, to complete the celebration, hired a limousine with a liveried chauffeur. At the airport he helped Getulio check in his bags and paid his excess weight charge.

'Life is a magnificent gift God gave to humanity,' Getulio said as they walked a few steps together before stepping onto a travelator. 'I was wrong to despair. I've been protected ever since I was born. It's the first time I've ever doubted Him. He wanted to test me, the way He tests the best of His sons. I'll pay you back, naturally, as soon as I arrive in Hong Kong. Would you prefer dollars or sterling?'

'I don't want anything from you.'

'No, no, I insist.'

'All I ask is that you tell me whether Augusta is happy or not.'

Getulio stopped, frowning.

'Now you're taking advantage of the situation in which I find myself. Remember that I am, very temporarily, in your debt.'

'And what would you say, my dear debtor, if I were to knock you down and make you miss your flight and your new racket.'

'You wouldn't!'

Arthur admitted the truth of this. It was not his style, even though the desire was there in every cell of his body.

'All right, I wouldn't. But I enjoyed your being scared for a few moments. It more than compensates for the hotel bill, the limousine, and your breakfast at Les Deux Magots.'

'I'll send you a cheque as soon as I arrive. I don't want to owe you anything. And this time … it's goodbye, for ever!'

He took a step onto the travelator that led to the gates. Arthur held him back with such a firm grip that he staggered.

'I've said goodbye!'

'Not yet. Answer my question!'

'In that case: yes, Augusta's perfectly happy, and most of all she doesn't want to know anything about you.'

'Give me her address.'

'Not on your life.'

'Getulio, one day I'm going to crush you. I should have done it plenty of times. This morning especially. I only feel sorry for you because of her.'

'I don't give a fuck about your pity, and you won't crush me as easily as that.'

'We'll see, won't we?'

They parted then, equally resentful of each other. Getulio had already been carried some way by the travelator when he turned round and, cupping his hands to his mouth, shouted back at Arthur, 'You'll never have her!'

A few days later the *Herald Tribune* printed some photos of Getulio's marriage, accompanied by a brief commentary:

> *Mrs Helen Murphy, divorced a month ago from the banker Chen Li, was married on Friday to Mr Getulio Mendosa, a wealthy Brazilian shipowner. Afterwards they left for a cruise to the Sunda Islands on board the* Helen, *a yacht that was a gift from her ex-husband. Mrs Murphy is a board member of Murphy and Murphy's Bank and the aunt of the actress Elizabeth Murphy.*

Getulio a wealthy shipowner? Surely that was an error. A charlatan was what he was, despite possessing an entrepreneurial streak. As for 'wealthy', that was gilding the lily. Used to a life of luxury would be closer to the mark. That as a young man, and Augusta's guardian angel, he had known wealth, Arthur had no doubt, but those assets had been exhausted long ago by the grand gestures that no fortune can ultimately withstand. The aggressive guard he had mounted over Augusta had only been a sordid calculation to make sure she married 'well' and found her place in a world that would make room for her fabulous brother. De Souza's wealth had collapsed for as yet unknown reasons. It was of no importance … marrying into Murphy and Murphy's would relaunch Getulio at a moment when his back was to the wall: nearly forty, balding, menaced by his creditors and his waistline, all resources gone, all he had left was his role as gigolo to an ultra-wealthy woman who was quite possibly not in full possession of her faculties. He would make her laugh the way he had made Arthur laugh when he paid his hotel bill in Rue de Castiglione.

'Why did you choose the most expensive hotel in Paris when you didn't have a cent?'

'My friend, it's perfectly clear that you have no idea how to live. I'd have been just as unable to pay in a third-class hotel, so it was far better not to stint myself.'

Six months later Helen Murphy-Mendosa died in London of a heart attack, and Getulio's affairs took another upward turn.

'In short,' Zava said as they left the meeting, which had lasted all afternoon, 'things worked out much more smoothly than we expected them to. So now I'd love to ask you to come and spend the weekend in the country – Arthur would be so pleased to see you – but you don't much like the countryside, do you?'

'I'll come and see Arthur next month. I'll stay a bit longer and you can lend him to me one afternoon and I'll take him to the zoo. Tomorrow I need to be in Paris.'

'Would you like me to drop you at your hotel? I have a car and a driver. Which is a luxury that's not really a luxury if you need to get to New Jersey. To be honest, those round-table discussions, thrashing out points of detail, bore me horribly, and when I'm bored I feel a terrible weariness pressing down on me. I get to the point of regretting I'm not deaf any more.'

'If you have time, you can drop me at the Copacabana.'

'A meeting?'

'No, just force of habit.'

The bar was heaving, as it was every evening at that hour. Arthur had hardly had time to find a space at the counter and order a Pimm's when Getulio's head popped up from the centre of a cluster of drinkers gathered round him and Arthur heard him shout over the clamour, 'I'll bet you're here to root for Elizabeth in *The Night of the Iguana*. She's divine. Makes everyone else fade away. Tennessee adores her.'

Was he flexing his knees or sitting on a low chair, suddenly appearing like that, a puppet bobbing up out of a stifling circle of friends then vanishing again? Using his elbows and shoulders to jostle his way through the standing crush sipping its martinis and whiskey sours, Arthur inched towards the back of the room in pursuit of details: where was Elizabeth's show, and what lay behind Getulio steering him towards her after so many years? Arriving within reach of the group that had hidden him, he found an empty space. Getulio called to him from the door as he shouldered it open.

'A thousand apologies ... I'm expected elsewhere. See you here tomorrow, same time. Go see Elizabeth, you won't regret it!'

The world on the other side of the swing door carried him away, and as he let it go it swung back and forth several times, leaving staccato images of a man in an elegant Homburg waving an umbrella at a yellow cab, into which he disappeared.

The double magic of lighting and make-up had miraculously preserved Elizabeth's sparkle as it had been at twenty, although she was nearing twice that by now, and the generous fervour of her youth had been rekindled in her face from the moment she stepped onto the stage. Arthur only had eyes for her, heard only the timbre of her voice, hardly roughened at all by her life's excesses. How could he not want to talk to her?

Draped in a polka-dotted black silk kimono, her head bent towards a mirror surrounded with blinding light bulbs, she was cleaning her face, tanned with make-up. He watched her ball of cotton wool, which she held between her slender fingers with their white nails, wipe first the ridge of her nose, then her forehead and her temples. She had said, 'Come in!' without turning round, and now he bent down to the level of her head, his chin brushing her hair, so that his reflection could be seen in her mirror.

'No! Arthur, it's not you!'

'Yes! It's me.'

'How many years?'

'The best part of twenty.'

The cotton wool continued its dance along the arch of her eyebrows, around the corners of her mouth, over the tip of her chin which she thrust forward with a grimace.

'You could have let me know you were coming. Six months ago I was wonderful as Desdemona.'

'You forget.'

'What?'

'We had a falling-out.'

'And we haven't got one today?'

'We're enjoying a general amnesty. A global one.'

'What if I turned down your amnesty?'

'You won't turn it down. Your passion's all spent. You're playing on Broadway and you've given up insulting your audience.'

'Times have changed. You don't need to keep breaking down walls that have already collapsed. Anyhow I have much too much work. I'm on stage every night, and every morning I'm filming from 6 a.m. to midday.'

'When do you sleep?'

'Alone.'

'I didn't ask who you slept with, I asked when.'

She laughed openly.

'I know you did, you big idiot, but I'm allowed to tease you, aren't I? Guess who came to my dressing room last night! It makes it even more bizarre that you should come tonight. Did you spread the word to each other?'

'Who?'

'You and Getulio.'

'I haven't seen him for a hundred years.'

Face to face, he would not have lied to her. It was much easier to lie to her reflection. And weren't they in a theatre, a place tailor-made for the most arch misunderstandings, for cross purposes and barefaced lies, cuckolds magnificent and sad, lovers concealed in wardrobes and providential entries and exits? The auditorium breathed again as the traitor was unmasked … yet here they were on their own, without an audience to call out to them that they had forgotten their lines. There was no logic to the play they were making up as they went along, intent on not hurting one another; there was nothing romantic to be invented in a dressing room that smelt of sweat, worn underwear, cheap rice powder and greasepaint. The explanation which neither she nor he felt any inclination to seek could wait another twenty, thirty, sixty years, until, with one foot in the grave, they finally turned to solving the puzzle and surrendering the missing pieces of a game that had been rigged from the start. Elizabeth untied her kimono and it slid off her bare, freckled shoulders.

'Turn round,' she said.

A wisecrack about her sudden modesty, a reminder of the event that had led to them falling out, would have been in bad taste. Did she remember the pleasure they had shared, and how, sometimes, they had thought those pleasures were love? A youthful mistake, for certain. And did she really remember the production in which she had played a psychopathic woman arousing a black doctor? He felt it was doubtful.

'Are you married?' he asked.

244

'What for?'

'If you'd asked me that question, I'd have given you the same answer.'

'You can turn round now.'

Black jeans and a poppy-red angora sweater made her slim figure look simultaneously bulkier and thinner; she was not tall but she still had a lovely body. A black band held her ash-blond hair off her forehead and ears, whose lobes, distended by the fashionably heavy earrings she had worn in her hippy phase, were the only defect of her classically beautiful face. A capacious carpet bag with an imitation shell clasp swung from her hand. She looked pleased with her middle-American disguise.

'Do you like my sweater?'

'It's revolting. The only thing you've forgotten is a pair of rhinestone-framed spectacles.'

'I knitted it myself.'

'That makes it worse. I can't believe you took up knitting.'

'It's something to do between scenes when I'm filming.'

She laughed, tilting her head sideways, the way she used to when her natural side took over and gave her back her schoolgirlish gaiety.

'I'll take you out to dinner.'

'I'm exhausted, and we have a matinée tomorrow. Come and get me between the shows.'

'I'll be in France.'

'Oh ... All right, let's have a snack together then. Quickly.'

'Sardi's?'

'Good idea. And it's right across the street.'

'We fell out there for good.'

'Are you sure it was there?'

Had she really forgotten? At her most chic, when she slipped back into her Bostonian accent, when she wasn't swearing or yelling a pornographic song as she swept the stage, or covering her dungarees with paint as she slopped it over a set or stinking of fish glue after she had been putting up incendiary posters, at her most chic she had no rival at seeing off an enterprising bore, playing the fool in front of a bluestocking, and coming out with a whopper like her 'Are you sure?' in a tone of such sincerity that it was hard to doubt her.

Sardi's always kept a table for her, and despite her fancy dress and dark glasses, or possibly because of the disguise, a murmur followed her as she walked between the tables. Yes, it was her, and her observers found it delightfully modest that she took herself and her figure so unseriously and was so negligent of the assets the fairies had blessed her with in the cradle: a genuine distinction, a family celebrated among the American elite, delicate features, talent, a captivating voice, honey-brown eyes, and a body that was carefully looked after but concealed with conspicuous self-effacement beneath clothes that were both too big and in hideously bad taste. Few, equally, had forgotten that on her parents' death she had inherited a sizeable fortune that her early extravagance had failed to dent. Arthur remembered magazine profiles that had paid tribute to her as the most intelligent actress of her generation, who had imbibed, from her breakfast coffee onwards, page after page of *Ideas Pertaining to a Pure Phenomenology* or *Being and Nothingness*. When election time came around, of course, she campaigned for the Democrats. But he knew her well enough: the truth was that she only read her own parts and anyhow would not have understood a word of either Husserl or politics. Her talent excused her from educating herself outside the theatre, and she had, apparently, finally wearied of the scandalous and strange that she had once courted in the tumultuous days of her youth. Like many actresses, her real talent lay in having a musical voice and a primitive instinct that led her through the labyrinth of her lines better than a thousand drama classes. In short, she possessed, without knowing it, a gift that she underestimated and that no one could have taught her. As gifts go, it was a fragile thing, at the mercy of the next bad play that, with her touchingly mediocre judgement, she would unsuspectingly throw herself into. An article by Truman Capote in the *New Yorker* had already created something of a legend around her, to which she was beginning to acquiesce. Recognising the transformation, Arthur was burning to poke gentle fun at her, in the hope of regaining something of the tone of their old relations. Sitting down, she removed her dark glasses, took a lorgnette out of her hideous bag and held the menu up to her face.

'You're already long-sighted!'

'No. Not really. The lorgnette was a producer's idea. I'm the only woman in New York – aside from a few great-grandmothers who don't have anything to do with the theatre – to use a lorgnette. Wait a while, and in six months' time, after a few magazine pieces about it, everyone will have one. Then I'll throw mine away.'

'If I were you, I'd get myself a chihuahua and let it eat the foie gras off my tournedos Rossini and leave the rest, while I chewed a piece of raw celery. You'd have the table next to you slack-jawed with admiration and the one on the other side calling the maître d' and demanding he throw you out. There'd be a terrific punch-up and the publicity in the next *Vanity Fair* would be incredible!'

'I insist that you become my press secretary immediately.'

'I'd have liked to, but it's a bit late now.'

'I never understood what it is you do. Things didn't go too well at the beginning, I gather. Getulio helped, didn't he?'

'Yes. Before I became an intern at Jansen and Brustein, he

suggested I work as a bouncer at a nightclub where he and Augusta used to go with their friends. His generosity and willingness to humiliate knew no limits.'

The maître d'hôtel interrupted them. For someone who only wanted a snack Elizabeth was not lacking in appetite. Arthur ordered champagne.

'I see things are going better now,' Elizabeth said.

'Oh, distinctly.'

'I didn't understand what you were studying at Beresford either, or what you wanted to do afterwards.'

'Beresford taught me the theoretical side of the art of business. The practical side turned out to be more tortuous and also less scrupulous. Let me put it this way: for a number of years I've been a financial adviser, which is to say a sort of intermediary who steers a skilful path around the frontiers of legality. But don't worry: I cheat no one, unlike Getulio.'

'He nearly cost me rather a lot. He certainly cost me something. Not too much. No more than a fair price for his charm. He cost Aunt Helen a lot more than that. She ended up snuffing it. He must have screwed her too much, the poor thing.'

She raised her glass.

'Let's drink.'

'Yes, but just to us two.'

'Have you forgotten Augusta?'

'I'll never forget Augusta.'

'I didn't doubt it for a second. What I really liked about you was that you didn't give a damn about the theatre, and that you never made fun of me.'

'Up to a point.'

'Oh, do let's stop talking about it! You're really the only one who remembers.'

'Imagine if your production had been as big a hit as Ionesco's *Bald Prima Donna*. You'd be up to your seven thousand three hundredth theatrical fuck by now. But how could you then do it with the man you loved when you got home from the theatre?'

'All right! It was a mistake,' she laughed. 'But I did it. I went a bit mad. Maybe that'll be something that was missing in your life, to have done something completely mad. But I did it. It's in the past.'

A very young girl in a modest pink velvet dress with a lace collar was standing at Elizabeth's side, a notebook and pen in her hand.

'Excuse me for interrupting you ... I'd so like to have your autograph. I simply adored you in *Cat on a Hot Tin Roof*.'

Elizabeth looked up at her admirer, hesitated for a couple of seconds, generously wrote a few words and signed. The girl gave her a quick timid bow and went back to the neighbouring table.

'How did you sign?' Arthur asked.

'Very simply: Elizabeth. Like the queen. For the rest of her days that delightful child will think she met Elizabeth Taylor. Someone must have told her I was called Elizabeth and was acting in a play by Tennessee Williams.'

'I'm catching a glimpse of your kindness.'

'No, my modesty. Learned by being hit over the head. And you're not entirely blameless in that department either. Do you think it's funny to be attracted to a man who makes no secret of loving another woman?'

Broadway was spilling would-be diners onto the street, and soon the restaurant was full. Elizabeth lifted her hand repeatedly, wiggling her fingers in a comical greeting as actors streamed in in pairs, their faces still shiny with make-up remover.

'We could have chosen a more private restaurant for our

reunion.' Arthur was irritated by the jokey hellos. 'I honestly wonder if a man has ever had you to himself.'

She raised her eyes and sighed.

'My art's not the art of being sincere, except onstage.'

'Excuse me! You're so right. Every night your audience sleeps with you. That must be sexually exhausting. A real person on the side must seem dull.'

'You weren't "on the side".'

'Thank you.'

Arthur closed his eyes, reliving the evening when he had found her waiting on the stairs outside the lift.

He felt Elizabeth's fingers drumming on the back of his hand.

'Hey! Wake up … You're having dinner with me.'

'I can see you now, you and Augusta and Getulio on the promenade deck of the *Queen Mary*, with your reefer jacket and your sailor's cap and long strides, and Augusta turning her head away so she didn't have to look at the ocean, which she hated.'

'I'd forgotten that completely. Who was more beautiful?'

'Augusta.'

'Yes. I get it, you know … We poor North Americans are at a great disadvantage, up against all that charm and Latinness with our doe eyes and flaxen hair. But she didn't screw, did she? Not straight away, anyway. Tomorrow you can tell me the next episode.'

'There won't be a tomorrow. I'm catching the morning flight to Paris.'

'When are you coming back?'

'In a month, or a year. It's not very predictable.'

'We must see each other again. Or perhaps not. We're not going to go round again, are we? I'll be going to France in the spring, to see my Madeleine. She'll be eighty. The day she goes,

I really will be an orphan, and who'll hold me in their arms and let me cry then?'

He saw her back to 78th Street in a cab. A doorman in a red tailcoat, with a bulge under his arm from a pistol holster, hurried to open the cab's door.

'You see, I'm well guarded. I'm not going to ask you up. We'd run the risk of getting sentimental and tomorrow I'd have bags under my eyes.'

She abandoned Arthur with a light kiss on the lips. Pausing at the glass doors, she added, 'Oh, by the way, Getulio told me something about Augusta when he came to see me. I've forgotten exactly what—'

'No, you haven't.'

'Oh yes! He told me – I'm not making any of this up – "Augusta's unhappy, she's getting divorced, and she's started to believe in God."'

'Is that all?'

'That's all.'

Deciding to go back downtown on foot, Arthur paid off the cab driver, and when he turned round the doorman was in front of him.

'Before she closed the lift door, Miss Murphy asked me to tell you that you must come back to New York soon.'

Arthur walked down Madison Avenue, heading for the private club on 37th Street where he stayed on his New York trips. He far preferred it to a hotel; it was a discreet refuge in monochrome colours: grey walls, black carpet, chrome lift, black maids in grey tunics, white valets in black trousers and polo necks, immaculate crockery on grey tablecloths, a breakfast room draped in coarse grey cotton with – the single splash of colour in this symphony – jugs of fruit juice and pots of jam. Only the sound of newspaper pages being turned disturbed the silence. The service was silent and unseen. The guests were mostly men; occasionally a woman sat at a distant table and drank half a cup of coffee, black of course, a briefcase at her feet. At the desk, in her black blazer over a grey silk shirt, stood an unusual South American-looking woman with a luxuriant head of curly hair that went down to her shoulders. Erect behind her counter, she never smiled, a woman-torso who hardly turned to take down a guest's key or tear off a bill spat out by the computer. Because of her severe appearance Arthur called her Medea, to which she responded by pointing to the name badge she wore on the lapel of her blazer.

'My name is Juana!'

He could, equally appropriately, have called her Cerberus, so closely did she attend to the selection of the club's guests and their needs.

'How,' Zava would ask him, 'can you like being in such a dismal place? Every time I come here I think I'm at an undertaker's.'

'Dear Zava, to my lasting regret I've never belonged to a secret society. But here the black and grey give me the illusion of an oratory where you come to give thanks to the All-Powerful – by which I mean the dollar, obviously – for having blessed an infinitely delicate deal.'

'The same old Arthur. Always the same guilty feelings when it comes to money.'

'It wasn't there when I needed it. Now it rains down on me.'

'The day I see you behind the wheel of a Rolls-Royce or a Ferrari and living on Avenue Foch or Park Avenue, I'll start worrying.'

With the exception of a stretch of Broadway and Times Square, and perhaps Greenwich Village where he had hung out with Elizabeth before bourgeois Manhattan reclaimed her, which it always did, New York dies every night. The city is not like Paris, Rome or Madrid, where, as darkness falls, another life awakens. At the heart of this San Gimignano of the future, with its gigantic twinkling towers that rose into a sky daubed with mottles of pink, grey and yellow gas and smoke, Arthur held sway over streets abandoned to their last fevered souls. The walk, which that night took him the best part of an hour, was also an antidote to the memories that Elizabeth and Getulio had stirred up. He would never forget how Elizabeth had extended her hand to him, a young Frenchman adrift in a new, potentially hostile and certainly indifferent world.

Medea handed him his key. When did she sleep?

Next morning, before he caught his flight at Kennedy airport, he called Elizabeth and left her a message on her answering machine.

Paris at midnight was a carnival city in a crown of bright lights.

The apartment in Rue Verneuil smelt as though it had been closed for a long time. He opened the windows wide.

In the narrow Rue Allent below, two women chatted as their dogs pissed on trees made sickly by so much nocturnal urination.

From a drawer Arthur took out the photograph of Augusta, the dried petals of a rose, the sari she had worn at Key Largo, another photograph of Elizabeth outside her apartment, and a programme from the evening at the docks.

A month later Arthur met Getulio again, in Paris this time, and found himself standing on Rue des Saints-Pères in possession of a phone number that he was not sure he wanted.

At Brig he was surprised at me asking him to go via the Simplon Pass and, after Domodossola, to carry on down to Stresa instead of taking the short cut via Santa Maria Maggiore. *'It's much longer!'* But I'm hardly going to explain that, having waited twenty years for this meeting, I have plenty of time and can easily put it off till tomorrow. I must have been over this pass ten times. Patches of grubby snow that the spring sunshine has forgotten still lie here and there. Jean-Émile, that's his name, is a cautious driver; as a Swiss citizen he respects the highway code, never exceeding the speed limit, not even by a kilometre. In New York I remember a day once when I was obsessed by the hairstyles of the cab drivers: there was a Haitian with a frizzy black ball, another skull that was totally bald, a blond man with a perm, and then at the Brasilia restaurant, where they were waiting for me, Luis de Souza's slicked-down waves and Getulio's first signs of baldness. There's nothing remarkable about the back of Jean-Émile's head: recently clipped, not a hair out of place under his cap. The owner of the chauffeur-driven car-hire business must inspect his staff every morning. Jean-Émile's blue suit, white shirt, and black tie are impeccable. He would probably be surprised to hear that in Paris I get around on a bicycle and wear bicycle clips, and sometimes a face mask when the heat makes the air in the traffic jams unbreathable. It's the sort of contrast that makes my life beguiling. When I gave up driving, I discovered the pleasure of being able to talk to myself while I paid someone else to deal with all the boring details: parking, filling up with petrol, changing a tyre. It's practically the only luxury I ask for, and it matters to me. Apart from books, of course, although books aren't a luxury but company. They're conversational partners for a recluse. I deliberately don't count the girls: they're for my health. In the driver's mirror, I catch Jean-Émile yawning again. *'If you're tired, let's stop.' 'No, I'm not tired, but if Monsieur would like a bite to eat there's an auberge just before the tunnel where they serve raclette.'* Not raclette, it furs up your mouth. But I know the place he means; I've often stopped there for a little treat of dried beef and a Fendant wine that copes very well with the altitude. The excellent Jean-Émile becomes embarrassed when I ask him to join me at an outside table under a red parasol with the valley, russet and dark, at our feet. With a toothpick and considerable finesse he cleans his fingernails under the table. To the job description of the ideal chauffeur, his employer will need to add a new section: 'Other skills'. What does Jean-Émile think of his passenger? I wonder. That I'm a multimillionaire? Or an accountant who has fled with the takings, treating himself to a luxury holiday before he's put away for five years? He probably stopped asking himself those kinds of questions a long time ago. In Germany, a chauffeur is an impenetrable robot; in Italy he'll immediately get out his photos of mamma and the children, then look round at you all the time he's driving, taking no notice of the road; in England he'll look down on you, make you feel he's used to driving the crème de la crème, not some wretched commoner; in France he'll stop regularly at country restaurants, 'little places' he knows. Jean-Émile, a Vaudois, is suspicious of everyone including, I think, me. He looks preoccupied, turning to stare at the valley as if something's happening there when the waitress in her Valais costume brings the bill over: an attractive girl who counts out the change from a black cloth purse on a belt around her waist. On the far side of the pass there's an Italian customs post. Only when we're over the border do I start to feel like quoting Jean Giono, his words about his hero Angelo Pardi: 'He was bursting with happiness.' But I can't quite work up the energy, and the detour to Stresa feels more like an excuse to revisit the hotel where I spent a pleasant week with one of the treasured Madame Claude's girls, and to postpone the inevitable moment of truth with Augusta. Or is it because I'm feeling wary? Nothing good can come from Getulio. Why, after so many years of hiding his sister from me, did he suddenly decide, on the corner of Rue des Saints-Pères and Rue Jacob, to let me get closer? I made enquiries: Luis de Souza divorced Augusta for a younger model. He's a very long way from penury, whereas Getulio lives on a pension left him by Helen Murphy, comfortable but decidedly scant for his taste, and cannot draw on the capital. What a curse of Tantalus! Having heard from mutual acquaintances that I went round Paris by bicycle, he must have thought for a long time that I was a down-and-out, till someone set him straight. With perfect synchronicity, Zava, who I confided in last week, said, *Be very careful. You'd be better off going to Kamchatka,'* then ten minutes later Brustein, who also knows exactly how the world works, said, *'Be careful, you'd be better off coming to Seville.'* Elizabeth was next. *'Careful. You can never glue the old bits back together; you'd be better off coming to see me in New York.'* As if, struck by the same premonition, they were all suddenly afraid to see me embark on a dangerous course. Yet the real danger's one I'm already too well aware of: it's the way I accept things, that profound personal weakness of mine; Augusta leaves me and I let her go without a fight; Elizabeth makes an exhibition of herself and I turn my back on her in disgust only to realise afterwards that I reacted like a child. The valley road down to Domodossola is dismal. There's none of the pleasure you expect when you arrive in Italy. The road's so twisting, the traffic so heavy, we creep down it like a tortoise. Jean-Émile's composure starts to slip as the Italian drivers, more devious than he, sneak in front of him and refuse to give way. I look for trees in blossom and see only derelict cars, corrugated-iron sheds, hideous trattorias. What was the name of the girl I took to Stresa? What a telling lapse of memory, when I have no difficulty remembering how perfect her body was and how, the first morning, she got out of bed wearing only a pyjama top, opened the window wide, and leant her elbows on the balcony. Her firm, dimpled bottom was a lovely sight. She called me over to admire another view, looking towards the far bank of Lake Maggiore, invisible in the morning mist. 'I adore the sea!' she exclaimed in her attractive central European accent. I didn't correct her, and for several days she genuinely thought she was at the seaside. She watched for dolphins that failed to appear. During the day she sat on the floor and painted her nails, red, then black, then silver. The smell of acetone and nail polish, a scent of strawberries and boiled sweets, filled our room. Conversation being impossible, I regaled myself with *The Diary of A. O. Barnabooth*, which ever since has gone with me wherever I go. Her name comes back to me: Melusine, which she pronounced Méloussine, a *nom de guerre* that didn't suit her at all. The closer we are to the lake, the prettier the road gets, with big gardens running down to it full of mimosas still in bloom, Judas trees, and the first white and purple lilacs. The style of the houses is remarkably heavy. The mixture of the classic elegance of Tuscan architecture and solid Swiss common sense makes for an unsuccessful marriage. Jean-Émile is driving more and more cautiously and must be cursing my whim of going through Italy instead of over the Furka and St Gotthard passes. He will be even more surprised at my wanting to spend the night at the Grand Hotel on the Borromean Islands. The season has hardly begun. No tourist buses, just Mercedes with German registration plates. The Germans got themselves killed in their millions to conquer Europe when it was so simple, and much more pleasant, to buy it peacefully with nice stable Deutschmarks. There's the hotel, the islands gently floating on the black waters of the lake, the antiquated luxury, the privacy. Here I can escape from the idea people have had of me ever since Elizabeth and Augusta first walked past me without seeing me. At the desk, for almost twenty years now, there's been the same manager, as affable as can be to the guests and odious to his staff. *'Ah, Monsieur Morgan, we were despairing of ever seeing you again. Are you on your own? Your room is waiting for you.'* To be greeted by name in a dozen great hotels around the world is a secret pleasure. His short black beard, trimmed like Marshal Balbo's, has gained some distinguished streaks of silver, and he still wears the same black-edged jacket, striped trousers, starched collar, and gleaming silk tie. Being able to recognise a guest is one of the great imperatives of the hotel business. I remember Flaubert's disappointment when, having enjoyed a bewitching night at Esna with that dancer, Kuchuk Hanem, he hurried back from Aswan, eagerly looking forward to his second meeting with the woman who had shown him so many signs of love, only to discover, absolutely crestfallen, that she had forgotten who he was. Yet I have none of the memorable habits Getulio affects: breakfasts of caviar and champagne, wearing a dinner jacket to dine on a few lettuce leaves and a glass of mineral water. Plus possibly leaving without paying the bill, or settling it with a dud cheque. Another time I came to Stresa, it was with a sweet French girl who had set her heart on dancing. It couldn't be done: the band on the terrace had never played anything but *The Blue Danube* and the barcarole from *The Tales of Hoffmann*. When I got back, Madame Claude was requested not to provide any girl who was an expert at anything in future. The reason I often treat myself to these short-term companions is that without a girl, all the luxury, the windows overlooking Lake Maggiore or the Pincio, the cruises, the San Fermín fiesta at Pamplona, the Fasnacht at Basel and the Setaïs Palace at Sintra, would be unbearable. The few times I've travelled on my own, I find Augusta and the ten radiant days we spent at Key Largo going round and round in my head, to the point where I start to panic. This evening, because I'm going to see her tomorrow, I feel the weight I've been carrying around ever since lifting from my shoulders. It's not important: to have had Key Largo is the most important thing!

Jean-Émile has been on a war footing since eight this morning. From the balcony I can see him patrolling around his car with a chamois leather and a small brush in his hand. He strokes its wings, polishes the radiator cap, rubs a speck of dust off the windscreen with a moistened fingertip, sees off with an energetic (not very Swiss) kick a dog that was about to lift its leg against one of the rear tyres (an Italian dog, of course!). You can hardly see the far bank. The lake is an inky black. Not far from the shore is a pretty boat with a white awning stretched over some hoops. A gold-coloured dog is asleep on its bow. There's a happy man fishing. On the jetty two tourist couples are getting into a Riva, whose varnished hull and chrome are sparkling in the sun. A compulsory tour of the Borromean Islands. The little French girl went on her own. Melusine was no more interested in them than I was. We stayed in our room, her painting her nails, me reading Valery Larbaud.

And you, Italy, one day, on my knees
I piously kissed your warm stone,
You remember ...

The Riva pushes away in a beautiful V out over the velvet waters. A memory of *A Farewell to Arms*: Henry, the American *tenente*, and Catherine leave the Grand Hotel of the Borromean Islands by the service entrance and get away in a dinghy bound for the Swiss border. It's the middle of the night. Thirty-five kilometres to go, but they have the wind behind them, and for a while the parasol the concierge has lent them acts as a spinnaker. Hemingway studied the route carefully. I like these pages for the tender, loving complicity of the two fugitives, their banal exchanges – 'Are you warm enough?' 'Don't you want to eat something?' 'Take a rest and a drink.' 'Tell me when you're tired.' 'Aren't you dead?' 'My hands are sore, is all' – much truer about what passes between two people than passionate bleating and heartbreaking declarations. In the morning – both of them exhausted, he with stiffened hands, she hunched with cold – they arrive at Brissago, on neutral territory, and their first act is to order a royal breakfast: four eggs, coffee, jam, toast, because to Catherine's regret there are no rolls, Switzerland having tightened its belt. But it makes your mouth water. In such small details Hemingway's novels have a reality you rarely find elsewhere. I look for writers for whom sitting down to a meal is a cause for celebration. It's a shame I haven't brought my copy ... I'd have reread that passage on the way, stopping at each stage of that forced row: Pallanza, the lights of Luino on the far bank, the frontier post at Cannobio (too dangerous for Henry and Catherine, half-Italian, half-Swiss), and finally their salvation at Brissago. For heaven's sake ... let's be honest! Shouldn't I be rushing now, putting behind me the last kilometres between me and Lugano instead of daydreaming on my balcony as if this meeting, so longed for since Key Largo, had suddenly left me cold? Am I going to be like that character in a novel whose name and title I forget who travels to England in pursuit of an adolescent love affair, discovers the setting and the object of his love and then, for fear of destroying his dream, makes do with sending her a message and returning to Paris? Imagine me doing the same, for fear of finally coming face to face with the completely unreal image I made of her. It goes this way: I ask Jean-Émile to stop beneath the windows of the Villa Celesta and sound his horn. She appears on the balcony. I say, 'How are you?' She says, 'Very well!' but doesn't ask me to come up. I say, 'Till we meet again, in twenty years' time!' and then, to Jean-Émile, 'Lausanne, please, by the shortest possible route.' He'll need every ounce of his Vaudois impassivity. Come on ... the time has come ... be brave, let's go! The tourists' Riva is tying up at Isola Bella. In a few minutes the caretaker will be showing them the bed Napoleon slept in the night before Marengo. I believe the sheets have been changed.

Once across the border, we're in a different world. At Cannobio Jean-Émile knows the senior customs officer and we pass without showing our passports. Jean-Émile's driving style relaxes. At the lakeside at Brissago I look for the café where Catherine and the *tenente americano* had breakfast. There are four or five. We stop at Ascona, which is unchanged. What year was it? 'Sixty-five, 'sixty-six probably ... After a frantic week I'd telephoned Zava to tell her that the deal was done and that never again in my life would I negotiate such a contract with the Swiss. They had insisted on providing for every eventuality, from the purchase of a vacuum cleaner to the rape of their grandmother.

She listened to me without comment, but I know the silences of that admirable woman. '*I didn't doubt for a second that you would reach an agreement. Why don't you come over here for a few days? Your godson's asking for you. We'll go to the Adirondacks and find some bears. At this time of year they're starting to wake up.*' Me: 'I'm not going anywhere. The Swiss have robbed me of the will to move.' She: '*In that case call Brustein; he told me about a marvellous hotel in the country near Ascona where everything's black and white like your club on 37th Street.*' Shortly afterwards Brustein: '*Go breathe the pure air of innocence at the Hotel Monte Verita. The owner's a friend of mine, a collector of modern art. So nobody's perfect. But you'll see some interesting pictures that his customers walk past without noticing. He even has a Picasso in the lift.*' Like a good boy I do as I'm told. Since going on my own is out of the question I telephone Madame Claude, who gives me the address of a colleague in Zurich. The result: a girl with a figure like a hairpin. (The first one they suggested was a Rubens; I turned her down.) This one was neither blonde nor brunette. Before I spoke she asked, '*Do you speak Cherman?*' Me: 'Twenty words. Won't that be enough for us?' She: '*Nein. So we speak English. I hate French, such a rough language. Not musical. Listen ... in German ...*' She lifted her little finger, as if drinking a cup of tea with the concierge. '*Die Vögel zwitschern in dem Wald ... in French: Les soisseaux kassouillent dans les pois. OK?*' I agreed straight away. The Monte Verita is definitely a hotel after my dear friend Brustein's heart. In the lounge, where no one bothers to go, there are two Leonor Finis, a Magritte, a Balthus, some Kandinskys and a Dalí. The lift bears aloft, from ground floor to second floor and back down again, a Picasso, a simple etching, an artist's proof, hurriedly signed. I have a week of perfect rest, rereading for the nth time André Suarès's *Le Voyage du condottière*, and while the matchstick girl undressed, walking back and forth across the room, looking for coat hangers and opening drawers to put away her underwear, I realised he was talking about her, as if she was a Botticelli: '*That long body, so elegant, so flimsy, so supple and so wiry, that reed of tender passion, stronger than an oak at resisting the tempests of love, that grace of a whole being, that womanly shape with the breasts of a young girl and the delicate hips of a cypress or a Ganymede, that deceptively skinny frame, as we say in Paris ...*' She stuffed herself as I have never seen a woman stuff herself. And yet there wasn't a fold of fat on her tummy or her thighs, her body was well muscled and she was full of life. Unfortunately she mangled her words in English as badly as in French and spent too long sitting on the toilet with the door open. I kept having to get up to close it. She tried to talk to me about her fiancé, who was able to finish his degree in medicine thanks to the little extras his bride-to-be was providing. She told me her name was Greta. Why not? They nearly all discard their real names, which they feel are too low-class, and bestow magical new names on themselves, borrowed from movie stars and princesses. After three days, tired of her conversation and of seeing her enthroned, I sent her back to Zurich with a generous present. As she left she said to me crossly, '*You don't like vimmen!*' Oh yes, I do. But only certain ones. '*Pardon, Monsieur?*' Jean-Émile says. Now I'm talking out loud ... 'I said: I don't intend to get out of the car. I just wanted to see the hotel from the outside. Let's head for Lugano.' What would be the point of going in? Everything is in our memory, and we need to let it tell us its lies. I shan't confuse it by accusing it of misleading me. It has every right to do so. The better part of wisdom isn't to go digging to find out whether your memories are illusions or not. This was Augusta on the phone a month ago, saying in a dying voice, '*I've* got flu; wait till I'm back on my feet again. Today you'd only see a ghost.' Me: 'I love ghosts.' Her: 'Ghosts hate living people. You wouldn't recognise me.' Me: 'Yes I would, by your voice …' Her: 'I'm just a shadow of Augusta Mendosa.' Me: 'If you saw me, you'd hesitate: getting a paunch, ageing, bald, false teeth, doubled up with sciatica.' Her: 'Liar. Elizabeth saw you in New York a month ago. You're younger than you were at twenty. Listen to me … I want to see you, but in a week or two. My head's in a mess. Come on the train.' Me: 'Absolutely not. I'll hire a car and driver and I'll be there.' Her: 'You have a chauffeur! Things must be going well. Getulio claims he often saw you riding round Paris on an old bicycle. Are you still broke these days?' Me: 'Did I look like such a big loser when you knew me?' Her: 'That's what Getulio said.' Me: 'Why do you have a brother?' Her: 'Listen, this isn't a good moment. I've got no voice left, I'm just a poor thing buried under my sheets.' Me: 'I love your voice so much, I could spend hours listening to you. You'll see that when we meet face to face, we won't have anything left to say to each other: I'll read the paper and you'll knit by the fireside.' Her: 'I don't know how to knit.' She hung up. The lovely mountains are still here, with their forests of firs all in perfectly straight lines, neat and tidy; there's still snow on the summit of Monte Tamaro. The year I set up the Zurich office I used to go hiking at the weekend in the Engadin and Ticino and the Bernese Alps: cleated boots, knee-length breeches, a stick and a haversack with a snack. My mountaineering period. The need to suffer. It was all too easy for me. I met families dressed the way I was, we exchanged our *Grüss Gott!*s, them in single file: father, mother, pink-cheeked children. They offered me their water bottles. Everywhere there were freshly painted benches, taps of drinking water tightly turned off so as not to waste a drop, litter bins at every view that invited meditation. Sanitised mountains, like something from a Walt Disney movie. In Paris I'll read Augusta what Chateaubriand writes about Ticino. He crossed it in haste, but he took it all in. He even believed the guide who told him that when the weather was fine you could see the Duomo in Milan from the top of Monte Salvatore. The last words of his lament come back to me: '... to die here? To make my end here? Is that not what I want, what I'm looking for? I have not the faintest idea.' No one has the faintest idea, even those who aren't particularly clever. Chateaubriand hasn't the slightest desire to die. All he wants to do is bring a tear to his reader's eye, a 'No, no, maestro, you mustn't let yourself die here!' It's impossible not to like the old thespian, with his dramatic flourishes and those choked-back sobs that take such advantage of sensitive souls! Of course no one knows, no one chooses. Concannon's reasoning was correct when he insisted that the sequence of historical events was down to chance. Why, in the last twenty years, have I met Getulio three times and Augusta never? She and I must have missed each other a hundred times. A matter of minutes, seconds even. Without a second thought I've delegated every decision about my personal life to fate, while my public life has been entirely bent to my will. Brustein calls me 'the bulldozer'. Having two faces – one for business, the other for myself – is exhilarating, my most secret possession. I'll say to Augusta, 'You don't know me. I have two faces. Which one would you like? Me, or my double?' The girls I hire watch me, dumbstruck, leading a life in their company they did not expect: I read, I daydream, I listen to music, I take them to the theatre, to a concert, on boat trips. They get bored with me. I'm afraid that if they complain I become rather charmless, remind them I'm paying them. I have no scruples. They're with me for the siesta, for the night. There have been perhaps two at the most who have been offended. It's unimportant. There was the one I took to Cannes, who I booked a separate room for and only saw at mealtimes. I wanted to test my resistance to the most easily satisfied temptations. As we went our separate ways – she called herself Griseldis! – she said how sad she had been to find out I was 'impotent'. I didn't disabuse her. What a face she'd have made if another girl of Madame's had told her what we got up to. So that's my secret! How could I have borne Augusta's disappearance if my remorse at not having seen Maman had not obliterated it, a remorse I cauterise every day by realising her wish: that I'm moving in the world of 'the great and the good'. The moment of truth is approaching. To say I know Lugano well is an exaggeration. All lakeside towns look alike. Riva Caccia. Griseldis – or was it Greta? – bought herself some costume jewellery in a hideous Italian jeweller's here. The promise of a fine weekend has brought the tourists out. They're eating outside on the terraces by the lake shore, surrounded by plastic bags, haversacks, children who won't keep still. 'Let's stay away from the crowds, Jean-Émile. Take the road for Gandria.' I have good memories of the village at the foot of Monte Brè, just below the place where we've arranged to meet. I've always liked it, a neat, clean perch between the road and the lake. They serve an excellent risotto at Il Giardino. Waiting time: twenty minutes. Not to worry: we'll have a Campari. Better still, I'll order a carafe of that light red wine they serve, Bardolino, that has an aftertaste of strawberries. 'Not in glasses, please, *signorina*. We'll drink it in your pretty blue-and-white earthenware cups.' '*You mean a* boccalino, signore?' Yes, a *boccalino*; I'd forgotten the name. She's not in her folk costume, thank God. She speaks French, German, Italian, English. Jean-Émile has left his cap in the car. He looks as uncomfortable as a rooster in a pond. Perhaps I should have let him have lunch on his own. He feels so awkward he's cutting his bread with a knife. I haven't asked him if he thinks the risotto and wine are a good choice, but still, it's hardly a punishment, is it? '*Coffee?*' 'Yes, no milk, thank you.' I know the cows with their cowbells would be condemned to death from hypertrophy of the udders if the Swiss diet forbade cream, but too much of it makes you feel sick. '*The telephone's at the far end, on the left.*' Shall I call? Or shall I turn up without warning? If I tell her I'm quietly having my coffee on the terrace at Il Giardino twenty minutes away from her, she'll be furious. I can hear her already. '*Who are you with?*' Me: 'With Jean-Émile.' Her: '*How can you travel with someone with a name like that?*' Me: 'He's the chauffeur.' Her: '*Too complicated, you can explain to me later. Come!*' In the end I don't call her. The element of surprise. No time to touch up her make-up, to look her calmest. The biggest difficulty is finding a florist in a place where the gardens are bursting with flowers. The waitress asks the manageress and comes back with a red rose still in bud. Let's take the thorns off. Silver paper from a chocolate vending machine. All that's left for me to do is paint my face white and put on a squashed top hat like Marcel Marceau. 'We'll take the little road to Brè, Jean-Émile. The house we're going to is called the Villa Celesta. Do you know it?' The Bardolino has put some colour in his cheeks. He doesn't dare say no and drives with one hand. It wouldn't take much for him to start whistling. A pretty zigzag road. On the hairpin bends you stare almost vertically down at the green-bronze lake. What persuaded her to live here? As if she feared a tidal wave. A traffic jam. Inevitably! We hardly have room to squeeze past the badly parked cars. I'm sorry: it's the cemetery; there's a funeral. I have a horror of funerals. It's enough knowing that I'll have to go to mine. Jean-Émile is a driver of genius. Without him I'd have gone round in circles, not daring to ask for directions, but he finds the house at the first attempt. The gate wide open onto the uncared-for garden, a semi-wilderness that makes me wonder whether the frost-damaged palm tree, the puny lilac, the ampelopsis timidly climbing the front wall, the chronically wasted geraniums, aren't all intentional, the expression of a sense of ruin and decadence that has always tempted her. We're from another world, she used to say, and she wasn't talking about class but about another era when she and her brother were clinging together like two castaways on a desert island after a storm. Jean-Émile brings his car to a gentle stop in front of the villa's steps and, in grand style, doffs his cap to open my door, his heels together. Two blue sphinxes, their paint flaking, a discreet smile on their identical faces, with broken noses, guard the ten steps up to the villa. Must not take the steps two at a time, red rose in hand, calling out, 'You see, I haven't forgotten a thing,' but calmly and unhurriedly, like a man whom nothing ruffles. The door is open, the shutters on the first floor closed, apart from one. If she's at home, she must have heard the tyres crunch on the gravel in the garden. A dingy hall, painted chocolate-brown. On the coat hooks on the wall hang Getulio's old Inverness cape and the cloche hat and coypu coat she wore on the *Queen Mary*'s promenade deck. Like a stage set. All it needs now is for her to appear in a sari. A door to the dining room, one to the sitting room, a small study. A glance is enough to know that Augusta hasn't furnished this house: its rustic mountain style, combined with an excessive reliance on ebony veneer, speaks volumes. The staircase has a chocolate-coloured carpet: it's obvious that this house, already gloomy in its design, has not gone out of its way to be cheerful. There are china nameplates on the door panels, Johanna, Margret, Leonor, Wilhelm, and at the far end, 'Facilities'! The coyness of it! No sign of life in Johanna's or Margret's room. They're empty, curtains drawn, beds made, but visibly no one lives there. Wilhelm's door is locked. There's only Leonor's to go: my last chance. Or have I got the wrong house? Villa Celesta, Brè, Ticino, and we talked on the telephone. The silence is the worst part of it. The stairs didn't even creak as I came upstairs; the doors open noiselessly. I would, just now, give anything to hear a phone ring or a shutter bang or the wind howl over the roof. If I don't open the door named 'Leonor', if I leave now, I won't have lost anything. But she's there, I can hear her. Augusta, I'm opening the door …

He was leaning his bicycle against the wall of the little garden when the front door opened.

'Why don't you bring it in and close the gate? I'm not saying people steal things around here, but don't tempt fate.'

She was exactly the way he had imagined her from Elizabeth's descriptions: a stout, tall woman with a face that was astonishingly unlined for her age, her white hair parted in the middle and wound in plaits at the side of her head, pink cheeks, a deep voice with a touch of authoritative severity, dressed in grey and black with a white cotton openwork shawl around her shoulders. Arthur put his bicycle inside the garden, which was blooming with anemones and sweet peas. Above the door the clustered flowers of two wisterias intertwined. The single-storey house, in pale Touraine stone with a roof of Angers slate, its two front windows framed by climbing roses, had little to distinguish it from the other houses of Saint-Laurent-sur-Loire. As he had pedalled from Les Aubrais, where the train from Paris had stopped, he had glimpsed dozens of a similar modest charm, grouped protectively around their churches, all along the banks of a broad river that flows through the memory of France.

'Have you eaten?'

'Only a glass of beer and a sandwich at Cléry.'

'I thought so. I've made you a snack. Elizabeth's at Blois. She's educating herself. Yesterday it was Chenonceaux.'

The snack was waiting under a glass dome in the kitchen. She laid a place with a blue plate, silver cutlery, and a carafe of golden white wine.

'It's a Roche-aux-Moines,' she said. 'Whenever my father had something on his mind he would open a bottle and sing softly to himself,

> *'When Madame Joséphine*
> *Is despairing*
> *She drinks a little glass of it …*
> *After all, it's her right*
> *To be tight …'*

The light voice was a little reedy for her height and obvious strength. She poured herself a glass and swirled the wine before tasting it and showing her pleasure with a clicking of her tongue.

'Madame Joséphine was the empress, obviously. She was easily consoled. I made the pâté myself. The bread's from the village. We don't ask the rest of the world for anything here.'

'You're very wise.'

She took a bowl of strawberries and a pot of cream out of the refrigerator.

'Strawberries from your labour / Cream from your neighbour … Everybody talks in verse here, ever since Ronsard.'

'I can't remember the last time I enjoyed being French so much,' Arthur said.

They went through to the sitting room, a grand description for a room cluttered with a large sofa and two deep armchairs. There was a loom with a piece of tapestry in progress, and photos covered one wall, photos of Elizabeth at every age and in many different roles (except, as may be imagined, that of the psychopath cured by her psychiatrist. Did Madeleine know about that episode in the life of 'her' child?).

'Do you want to rest? Your legs must be tired after those thirty kilometres from Orléans.'

'I've never felt better.'

She sat in front of her loom, disentangled a ball of wool, and put her glasses on.

'It seems I'm starting to get cataracts. Elizabeth wants me to have an operation in America. Honestly … as if we didn't have just as good doctors in France. Are you looking at the photos? That's her whole life … well, what she wants me to know of it. I've got albums too, if you're interested. As she hardly ever comes more than once or twice a year, at least I have them to look at.'

There was Elizabeth in a short smocked dress riding a sheep on wheels between her father and mother, on a lawn in front of a grandly colonnaded house. The following year the parents had disappeared and the child held Madeleine's hand, then a chubby girl who was clearly dressed in hand-me-downs from Madame's wardrobe, with a feathered felt hat pulled down over one eye.

'If it was up to me, you'd never have seen me got up like that. But the trustees insisted I shouldn't look like a maid. On the other hand, they let me do what I liked with Elizabeth. If only they'd known …'

They inched towards each other, step by step. Arthur found it comical how she was scrutinising him with such circumspection that it stuck out a mile. She was worse than a domineering mother. Arthur too was watching her closely: she had a part to play in the affair at hand. He did not think she was Machiavellian, more preoccupied with protecting the overgrown child she had been given to look after. An old habit made him look for the books the former nanny might have kept by her. He did not see any. Everything was based on her good sense and her certainty of belonging to a nation endowed with an innate intelligence about life. She was a rock. The photos told him almost nothing he did not already know: the elegant, outrageously handsome parents; the little girl with a doll's round cheeks, terribly serious expression, and a ribbon in her hair; the angular adolescent whose face radiated irony, followed by the girl (or young woman) posing like a model, half naked on a leopard-skin sofa, and finally the actress and, most recently, her performance in *The Night of the Iguana*. Always on her own, without a man to hold her tightly during her long years of struggle against platitudes and mediocrity.

'Do you recognise her?' Madeleine asked.

'There isn't one "her". There are at least ten, and I didn't like all of them.'

The Elizabeth who would be his for ever was the young woman sitting on the top step at Rector Street, smoking cigarette after cigarette in total darkness. Or the one biting into a croissant on the pavement outside his building, next to the cab that was waiting to take her away. Madeleine was still bent over her tapestry, as detached, it seemed, as if they were discussing tomorrow's weather.

'Help yourself,' she said; 'it's easier than me getting up every five minutes to fill your glass.'

'I mustn't overdo it. I need my legs to get back to Orléans this evening to catch the train to Paris.'

'Oh, so that's what you have in mind! I'm quite sure Elizabeth won't let you get away as easily as that!'

If, having been warned that he would arrive in the early afternoon, Elizabeth was not there to meet him and was instead feigning an irresistible passion for the chateaux of the Loire, it was as much because she was trying to deceive herself as Madeleine, or possibly because she was leaving to the said Madeleine — which was unusually reasonable of her — the job of judging the man who had come into her life without ever truly seeing her. The thought that, as in Baronne Staffe's guide to good manners, this stout, outspoken woman would soon be grilling him on his origins, qualifications, family, and financial situation made him smile.

'A penny for your thoughts, young man.'

Arthur admitted what he had been thinking.

'Now that's a good idea! But I've already known you for twenty years. You didn't need to cycle all the way here on your bicycle. I know perfectly well that one shouldn't trust appearances.'

'Did you know that we fell out for a long time?'

'I think I even know why. You'd have to find more than that to set me against you. I'm not so stupid. And nor is my little Elizabeth all peaches and cream.'

Bent over her tapestry, she was unpicking a thread of wool from the canvas.

'I'm getting old, my mind wanders off more and more. Red ... when it should be yellow. So you went to Lugano?'

'You really don't miss a thing, do you?'

Madeleine laughed. Her bosom wobbled in her tight blouse.

'No, no ... far from it. For instance, I shall never understand why two people who loved each other the way Elizabeth and you did are scared stiff at the thought of admitting it to yourselves and wait twenty years to discover that the feeling is mutual. As for this Brazilian—'

She could not even bring herself to say her name.

'— I should certainly have liked to see her to understand what was so attractive about her. In the sideboard, on the right, you'll find some *marc de Champagne* and little glasses, or even some big ones if you're feeling honest. Yes, there, on the right ...'

The window framed a gentle curve of the Loire and, just below the road, a path along which a man and a woman were cycling with haversacks on their backs.

'Cycling along the towpaths is such a good idea. If only I'd known—'

'Don't worry, you didn't miss much. There's only about five kilometres where you can do it. Yes, a tiny bit for me; just wet the bottom of the glass otherwise I'll be seeing double threads. This Brazilian—'

'Augusta Mendosa.'

'— I expect this Brazilian had many charms, but charms are short-lived. If you're still acting like a hummingbird when you won't see forty again, there's a strong chance you'll end up looking like a goose.'

'You're very hard.'

'I promise you I'm not at all. For example, it pains me to see you sitting so awkwardly. Throw those things off that armchair and flop down in it. It's perfect. It was a present from Elizabeth, like almost everything I own. Pull that little table towards you for your glass.'

'No,' Arthur said, 'a person's charms don't really die. They just lose their element of surprise and so we're no longer the same. We've lost our virginity about what love is.'

The feeling of regret that he felt as he said it was still there, and would always be there when he thought about her. Trembling a little, he stretched his hand out to his glass and knocked it over.

'It's nothing. Get a cloth from the kitchen and pour yourself another glass.'

When he had cleaned up the mess Madeleine, who had not moved from her sofa, put down her needle and took off her glasses.

'The more I look at you, the more I tell myself that women are really too stupid. Always the old fear, that if they throw themselves at men they'll be taken advantage of. Your hand was shaking for a few moments then. Do you still feel vulnerable, after so many years have gone by?'

'I'd worry if I couldn't feel vulnerable any more.'

'I share your view.'

This woman was a rock of certainties.

'I escaped the worst of it,' he said.

'Don't say that. It's yourself you'd be wiping from your memory if you believed it. Elizabeth loved her, despite all her reasons for not loving her.'

All her reasons? He excluded all the mean feminine rivalries, unworthy of Elizabeth, and could only see one reason, whose shadow had passed without his paying it much attention. Men can be a slow lot, and in a not entirely innocent way.

'As soon as I walked through the door,' he said, taking the plunge, 'I was on my guard: the Inverness cape, the cloche hat and coypu coat hanging up in the hall. The remains of a glorious past, sending me back twenty years. Getulio, not believing I would come, had left for Campione, leaving her in the care of a nurse in a white tunic who, as I walked in, shut a drawer sharply and hid something in her pocket. Augusta was sitting in a tall armchair facing the open window, a rug on her knees. She must have seen the car arrive, but didn't even turn her head. I could only see her shoulder, her bare arm on the armrest, a leg hidden by a sari like the ones she had worn at Key Largo. We were about to shoot the same scene all over again: a remake, the Americans call it. I wasn't ready for it. I'd arrived with a rose in my hand like Marcel Marceau's poor Bip, the only difference being that I'd lost my much-vaunted innocence.'

'So you think! Would you be very kind and pass me my basket of wools, on your left on the table by the wall?'

Arthur walked over to the window. The Loire, murky green, slipped between the sandbanks. On the other bank, to the north, were the first houses of Beaugency. His lips murmured the soft litany his mother had used to croon: '"Orléans, Beaugency, Notre-Dame de Cléry, Vendôme, Vendôme——"'

'I taught Elizabeth to sing that. When she came to France for the first time – she was five years old – she wanted to hear the cathedral bells. We waited till evensong, sitting on a bench and licking caramel sweets till the bells began: "Vendôme, Vendôme …" Was Madame Mendosa on her own with the nurse?'

'That woman stuffed her with tranquillisers and plundered the drawers with impunity. Apart from our two weeks in Key Largo, I think Augusta lived on antidepressants: they helped her erase the terrible visions of Ipanema, of her father's head blown to pieces. And she ended up in that gloomy villa at Brè, shut up in a cold bedroom and stuck in front of a window overlooking an abandoned garden, just so that Getulio could carry on gambling across the lake at Campione, at the only casino that hadn't banned him. The only recognisable part of Augusta that was left was her eyes. They'd sunk into two deep recesses under the arches of her eyebrows, and from there, from the cavity they made, they looked out as if at something vague or inexpressible, then suddenly jerked out of their contemplation to sparkle in a way that I found unbearable. They pierced your soul … if such a thing exists. Maintaining eye contact with her was unbearable.'

'Did she recognise you?'

'In the heat of the moment she thought I was Seamus Concannon. She was afraid of me touching her. I couldn't even stroke her hand. She started to let fly a stream of obscenities, she who was so shy ... I asked the nurse, who was watching us triumphantly, to leave the room. I had taken a dislike to her the second I walked into the room. As soon as she wasn't there any more, Augusta became calmer. She carried on speaking for a moment as though I was Seamus, and when I said, "Seamus has been dead for twenty years," she sighed, "I know. And who are you? ... Arturo, oh yes ... kiss me." She spoke like someone who has woken up with immense relief from some appalling nightmare, and is back on solid ground. She took my arm to walk around the room, showing me the furniture and the bad engravings on the walls. We went into the garden where Jean-Émile was discreetly smoking a cigarette, which he immediately dropped and stubbed out with his shoe. She went towards him and kissed him. "I'm so happy to see you again. Why don't you ever phone me?" Jean-Émile behaved perfectly. Getulio arrived, behind the wheel of a knocked-about little Fiat. He wanted to know where the nurse had gone. Augusta could catch cold or fall and hurt herself. She could; she frequently fell over because of her medication, which made her lose her balance. Women fall over so often, don't they? To make men feel sorry for them. In that area Augusta was about as experienced as they come. They were about to leave for Marrakesh. The Ticino climate was no good for Augusta's convalescence. She listened, clinging to my arm, and nodded. She smiled for the first time, maybe because she remembered all the fabulous projects that had soothed their passage through life. Getulio envisaged me coming to visit them as soon as they were settled. A wealthy Moroccan friend was lending them a small palace for as long as they needed it, a jewel at the edge of the medina, an absolute gem, with servants as handsome as gods to look after them. In short, everything was normal, and when I arrived I'd simply fallen victim to an illusion, which Getulio had waved away in a few words with his charmer's eloquence. We walked in circles round the garden, under the astonished gaze of Jean-Émile, and gradually, despite her lightness, despite her being less than a shadow of herself, I felt the weight of her on my arm as though she herself were rediscovering her own mass, which she had forgotten for so long as a result of the tranquillisers. Her nails dug into the skin of my wrist. With unexpected violence, through clenched teeth, she said, "I wasn't expecting you. You could have warned me. And why didn't you come with your wife?" Getulio made light of it. Augusta had been marrying off all her friends for some time. She looked at him pityingly. "You're trying to make out that I'm mad. Arturo knows perfectly well it's not true. Arturo, you must come back and bring Elizabeth. She loves you so much … We hurt her at Key Largo …" Getulio raised his arms heavenward. "Key Largo again! In the past few days she's started talking non-stop about Key Largo, where she's never set foot in her life. The doctor has no idea what she means. Do you?" I had none whatsoever, as you can imagine. Augusta asked again, "How is your relationship?" That word, Madeleine, "relationship", a word that'll make the most ardent of men run a mile, a word no one dares utter any longer, full of intrusion and stupid compromises … I told her, "We're very well, perfectly happy." She looked as though she was thinking for a moment, then said in a whisper, "So I suppose I must be forgiven." There was nothing to forgive her for. We said goodbye at the car, whose door Jean-Émile had opened. "You have a chauffeur?" She offered me her cheeks to kiss. I could see Getulio was desperate to know what was going on. He wanted to have dinner with me. I suggested a hotel at Lugano. She tried to run after the car. The nurse caught her arm and stopped her. I waited till midnight for Getulio. There was no answer when I phoned the Villa Celesta. In Paris a telegram had been pushed under my door. I had to be in New York that evening. Elizabeth was waiting for me at Kennedy airport. We cried a lot. Apparently it wasn't the first time; the nurse had stepped out of the bedroom, leaving the window wide open. I didn't get any news from Getulio, but friends told me that the day after the funeral he sold the jewels that were left and went straight to Campione to put it on the tables. The gods that had always looked on him so kindly saved him yet again. He broke the bank, left a wealthy man, for a few months anyway, despite his aching soul … oh, I'm sure it was aching, he never had anyone besides her, but he'll recover; I don't have any worries on that score.'

Madeleine put down her needles and her wool.

'I'm getting stiff sitting here. Would you like tea? Elizabeth will be back soon.'

He followed her into the kitchen, where she plugged in a kettle.

'I usually find it so difficult to talk about myself,' he said. 'I'm surprised how easy it is with you.'

'You're not talking about yourself, you're much too introvert to do any such thing! You're talking about other people, and through them I understand you better. I've always been like that, ever since Elizabeth found herself alone in the world and I devoted myself to being her confidante. People don't know me for five minutes and they start telling me their life story. I'd have had to say no from day one, when my little girl decided she wanted to tell me some little bad thing she'd done. But I let her, and ever since then I've had no life of my own, only the lives of other people.'

She was about to pour the boiling water into the teapot when Elizabeth's voice stopped her.

'Madeleine … didn't he come?'

'Do you want tea?' Madeleine called.

'Shit! What's wrong with him? Why didn't he come?'

'I think you should dump him. He's obviously a philanderer.' Elizabeth materialised in the kitchen doorway.

'You're so naughty. I was going to say some horrible things about you. How did you get here?'

'By bicycle.'

'And do you intend to go back to Paris by bicycle?'

'With you sitting on the luggage rack. Unless we buy a tandem and some bobble hats.'

'Madeleine, do you realise? For twenty years I've fancied this guy who cycles all over deepest darkest France on his bicycle, as if it was still the Middle Ages!'

'Are you staying tonight?'

'What is there to eat?'

'Is love making you hungry?'

'That's nothing to do with you!'

'You won't be disappointed. I think you'll be staying with us tonight, Monsieur Morgan—'

'Arthur. Call him Arthur.'

'He can put his beloved bicycle in the boot of your car. We're having salmon with a *beurre blanc* sauce for dinner.'

From his window the view swooped down the narrow tunnel of Rue de Verneuil and between the concrete wall and mute buildings of the mysterious Rue Allent where on weekdays, at the little school opposite, you could hear the shouts and laughter and tears of the children for whom, lunchtime and evening, their mothers waited on the pavement, eyeing each other distrustfully. The night fell as it does in Paris, taking the city by surprise, cloaking the provincial-looking block in a light silence.

'You're not going to be sad, are you?' she said, leaning on her elbows next to him.

He shook his head. But she had to agree that it was a moment to be thoughtful. Who doesn't feel lost for those minutes when the night robs us of what's left of a day? In a moment they would go their separate ways, and the decision he had been incapable of making would be thrust on him by Augusta's fall like some blinding truth. There was plenty to wonder about.

'Did you say worry about?'

'No, wonder about.'

'When are you going to stop wondering? Time is passing, right under your nose. One day you'll discover that the play's over and the set's collapsed. You're like Augusta. She took for ever to realise she was just dancing and singing among the ruins and that no one was watching any longer, not even you, because you were so relaxed about seeing her show that you hung on endlessly in Paris, then dawdled all the way there.'

'Unlike you she didn't need a large audience. One was enough.'

'One at a time. Several a day.'

'She liked to charm.'

'And the day she was locked up in Lugano in that dreary house, with no audience to charm, deserted by her husband and with Getulio more unpredictable than ever, and realised that in those twenty years you'd finally grown up, she panicked. Unfortunately this time it worked.'

'Were there other times?'

'Two or three, not really serious.'

'You're being hard on her.'

'The more I liked her, the more angry I was with her for having stolen the man who interested me.'

Arthur enjoyed 'the man who interested me', though he found it hard to believe her.

'I can still hear all of you saying, "She's unique!"'

'Who said it?'

'Getulio, Concannon, Porter, you, everyone who watched her as she went by, like a star: Mrs Paley, Mandy, Cliff. On the *Queen Mary* no one had eyes for anyone else. At Beresford, the night of the Thanksgiving Ball, she wasn't allowed to sit down for a second.'

'Yes, but it was in your arms, in the back of Getulio's car, that she went back to the hotel.'

'At Key Largo Mandy and Cliff looked at her as if she was from another planet.'

'But you were the one who slept with her. Pretty enviable, don't you think?'

'Why did you lend us Key Largo?'

'An irresistible urge to self-sacrifice.'

'You mean—'

285

Elizabeth shrugged.

'What I mean, and you heard what I said.'

'You talk in too many riddles. I can understand your invitation to Saint-Laurent better. I passed the test, apparently. What if I'd failed?'

'There wasn't much chance of you failing, but I wanted to be sure. Anyway it was fun, wasn't it? And you couldn't know me properly if you didn't know Madeleine. I must admit that arriving by bicycle was a stroke of genius. You'd passed before you opened your mouth. If you'd come in a Rolls you wouldn't have stood a chance.'

A car stopped at the door of his building.

'That's your taxi. I'll see you to Roissy.'

'Absolutely not. We're starting the first day of a long-distance life together. Very long-distance. It needs careful thought, tact, and a long learning process. But I'm not afraid any more, not of anything.'

He went to pick up her overnight bag.

'Leave it, it doesn't weigh a thing. I travel light. You'll be light with me too, won't you? I'll give you, and you'll give me, the lightest and happiest of what we both have to give.'

'By which you mean that we're both promising to be perfect …'

She stroked his cheek affectionately.

'Of course there'll be the occasional row, but we're not children any more, and as you saw in New York I've lost my taste for revolution. I loved these two days with you. Oh, not just for the pleasure, which isn't new, and which was very nice, just the way it always was.'

'Your productions are always excellent.'

She laughed with a laugh full of sweetness, her head on one

side, as though he had caught her out.

'Thank you for not overdoing the praise. I was furious with you and so I decided our falling-out had to be spectacular. And you went along with it, so much that you exceeded all my expectations. For far too long!'

She lowered her head, refusing to look at him. With his finger he lifted up her chin and bent forward to kiss the lids of her eyes, which were clouded with tears.

'Get some chalk, mark the position of your feet,' she said. 'Make a note that you're wearing tan-coloured corduroy trousers, a brown sweater and a pink shirt. When we see each other again, we'll take exactly the same marks again. Next time you come to New York, we'll do the same with me. So there'll be parallel lives: one when we'll live together, and another when we'll be apart and supposed to be asleep, with nothing happening at all. You'll see: life is a fairy tale, and lovers live for ever. Now, don't move till you hear the cab drive away.'

Later she phoned from the airport.

'I'm boarding an hour late. Just when I most wanted to stay. I'm the last one. I just rang to blow you a kiss.'

'Wait.'

'Hurry, they're going to leave without me.'

'I found a quote by Stendhal in a collection of his sayings, which you can think about during those six hours in the air that are going to steal you away from me so cruelly. Listen. "Love is a delicious flower, but you have to have the courage to go and pick it on the edge of a precipice."'

*

He wasn't certain she had heard the end. The public address system at Roissy was repeating with desperation, 'Miss Murphy! Miss Elizabeth Murphy!' Poor Stendhal. He had rarely been happy himself, but he could teach others how to be.